AIMING BLIND

AIMING BLIND

JUSTICE BEGINS™ BOOK TWO

MICHAEL ANDERLE

DISRUPTIVE IMAGINATION®

LMBPN Publishing
PMB 196, 2540 South Maryland Pkwy
Las Vegas, NV 89109

Version 1.00, November 2021
ebook ISBN: 978-1-68500-577-1
Print ISBN: 978-1-68500-578-8

THE AIMING BLIND TEAM

Thanks to the Beta Readers
Larry Omans, Kelly O'Donnell, Rachel Beckford, Allen Collins, Kit Mitchell

Thanks to the JIT Readers

Dorothy Lloyd
Daryl McDaniel
Dave Hicks
Wendy L Bonell
Rachel Beckford
Zacc Pelter
Peter Manis
Deb Mader

If I've missed anyone, please let me know!

Editor
The Skyhunter Editing Team

DEDICATION

To Family, Friends and
Those Who Love
to Read.
May We All Enjoy Grace
to Live the Life We Are
Called.

— Michael

CHAPTER ONE

"Watch it!" she snapped as the straps of her armor chafed against her hips and armpits. The men absorbed with tying her down to the truck—aside from the one holding a gun on her—ignored the complaint.

Daria Barruk sighed and grimaced. There was nothing she could do for the moment, but she still had a trick or two up her proverbial sleeve. It would merely be a long, uncomfortable ride until she had the chance to play her hand.

Three men had captured her in the city, crudely tied her up, tossed her in the back of the truck, and brought her here, to an obscure crossroads of two dirt trails in the foothills that loomed behind the town. Their employer had requested a rendezvous.

Upon arrival, they found a car—better suited to the city but less well suited to the highlands—waiting for them. A man had seated himself in a folding chair under an umbrella, and two of his employees stood nearby. One of them, called Javier, now helped with the business of re-securing Daria to the truck's bed and leaving her immobile.

Supposedly immobile.

The man sitting in the chair under the umbrella watched and

laughed. He wore a turquoise shirt, half-open at the top, and a gold medallion hung from his neck to rest against his chest hair. The hair on his head was dark and slicked back, and he had a heavy mustache and knobby hands along with a deep tan. He'd probably been handsome in his youth. Now, in his fifties, he was letting himself go to fat and developing deep bags under his eyes.

A gold-plated Colt 1911 pistol was in his right hand, and though he at least kept his finger off the trigger, he nonetheless swept the gun haphazardly about in grand gestures as he moved and spoke.

Daria knew his name before he introduced himself. He was her target, after all.

"*Hola.*" He spread his hands and waved his gun carelessly across the chest region of the man standing beside him, who looked faintly uncomfortable but said nothing. "You are one of the Executioners, yes? The Polish woman. I am Mateo Pastor, one of the leading citizens of this great island. You have heard of me?"

His veneer of friendly, boisterous charm was astoundingly thin. The core of smarmy arrogance and cruelty was visible through it at all times. The other men standing around also had smug looks. Although Daria happened to know *why* the one who'd helped strap her in seemed so confident.

Daria couldn't nod in her current position, so she simply spoke. "Why, yes, Mateo, I've heard all about you. I understand that you were a supremely important individual in Caracas and its surrounding environs, supplying all manner of narcotics and amphetamines to many, many satisfied customers. Now you've retired to Atlantica, where your fortune can purchase you *anything* you want."

Pastor chortled as he waved at the man on his right with his golden gun. The henchman spoke to the thugs who'd driven the truck this far, instructing them to return to the city using the car and leave their vehicle for Pastor to take over. He added that all would be well.

"Yes." Pastor sneered. "I've earned it. No other man in Caracas was my equal. I am, as they say in English, the top of the heap."

Daria stared at him, her gaze cool, steady, and even. The report from the Executives had explained how Pastor intended to reward himself for his past business acumen. His pet project on Atlantica was assembling a harem at his remote villa, composed of women abducted from every corner of the world. A veritable menagerie from which he might sample many different versions of the same base pleasures, regardless of how the women might've felt about it.

He could afford it. In his mind, and that of some others on the island, it was all that mattered.

The drug lord took a step closer to the bound Daria and waved his pistol in a circle so it crossed her waist before looping back up toward her face. "You're so helpless," he observed. "I might've added you to the ranks of my companions ten or fifteen years ago. A pity you're growing old, no? I'm also disappointed at how easily we captured you. The Executioners have such a... *scary* reputation. I expected more."

"Of course you did. It seems you set *very* high standards for yourself." Daria smiled.

Pastor chuckled, turned away, and went back to his chair. He folded it and holstered the pistol in his waistband. "It was foolish of them to send a woman. I've heard that you're wily, but your sex lacks strength and determination. So, this outcome was inevitable. If they'd sent that other man, the Oriental one, maybe he would've put up more of a fight. It would've ended the same way, though. He would've been the one tied to the back of a truck instead."

Daria's nostrils flared. "You mean Tyler Katakura, the first Executioner. Saying that he would 'put up a fight' is... shall we say, one way of putting it." She'd never seen anyone fight the way he did. In battle, he was nearly terrifying to witness.

Laughing, Pastor walked over and tossed his folded chair in the bed of the truck. It landed about half a meter from Daria's head and clattered to the right against the spare tire. She didn't flinch.

He gestured at the cab. "*Vamos*. Javier, you stay in back with the *puta*. Nicolas, you drive."

Javier was the man who'd been standing to Pastor's left a moment ago. The one who looked especially smug. Daria caught his eye and smiled at him as he added the umbrella to their load, clambered into the truck's bed, and crouched beside her. He secured himself with a bungee cord as a makeshift seatbelt.

Nicolas started the engine, and the truck began its rumbling ascent up the dirt track into the hills north of Atlantica City. As Daria recalled, the highlands continued for quite some time, growing high enough in places to be called mountains before they began to drop off closer to the island's central basin, which human hands had barely touched. It was overgrown with a vast and impenetrable forest—a jungle, as some people called it— shrouded in mist and incredible in its lushness and verdancy. Although Atlantica lay far north of the tropics, not far from Nova Scotia and Newfoundland, its climate was oddly mild all year round.

Daria said and did nothing while the truck *clanked* over the rises and falls. Its wheels occasionally bottomed out in ruts or bumped up after hitting stones or mounds of dirt. The straps of her armor rubbed her raw in places, and her head kept bumping into the metal surface of the truck's bed.

Javier noticed and slid a folded-up tarp under her head with his foot.

"Thank you." She said it although he might not have heard her over the truck's racket.

The air grew cooler as they came to a high pass, then grew

warmer and thicker again as they descended into the foothills on the other side. Pastor's villa was allegedly in the low hills, not far from the rainforest.

As Daria had expected, the truck ran out of gas about two kilometers beyond the pass. Pastor and Nicolas cursed up a storm. The driver whacked the gas gauge, which had been tampered with to make the tank look half-full when it was anything but. There was a can of gasoline in the truck's bed, though.

Nicolas brought them to a halt on a broad ledge next to the winding hillside road. He and his boss got out, grumbling in Spanish. Daria was glad that despite Pastor's wealth, he still employed vehicles that used petroleum-based fuel rather than making the expensive switch to ones powered by Atlanticore crystals.

Daria moved her hands and arms. Then she returned her wrists to their previous position, keeping them out of sight. Her bonds *looked* tight and had sufficed to keep her attached to the truck during the bumpy ride. As far as truly keeping her restrained, though...

Javier handed the gas can to Nicolas, who dutifully set to work refilling the tank. While that occupied him, Mateo Pastor came around to the vehicle's rear and opened the back hatch. He gazed at Daria with a gloating expression. He must've grown bored during the drive and wanted to posture in front of her again.

"Enjoying yourself, *señora?*" He'd left his golden Colt in his waistband, and for the moment was content to gesture with his empty hands.

Daria put on her best expression of disinterest. "Your suspension needs work. You've been neglecting your vehicles. Please hire better mechanics."

Pastor snorted. "Such bravado from a woman in your predicament. Ahh, I still cannot believe your overconfidence.

Sniffing around my townhouse in the city and thinking I wouldn't notice. It was so easy to catch you. Do you know how? Maybe you've guessed. You underestimated the loyalty of my men."

Daria raised an eyebrow. "Oh, really?"

Javier had climbed down to stand beside his boss. Nicolas finished pouring gas into the tank and came over to join his compatriots, waiting for his boss's go-ahead before they resumed their journey. The empty gas can dangled from his right hand.

Pastor seemed in no hurry to get back to his villa. "Javier and Nicolas are my best men. They spotted you with no difficulty. I know that you tried to turn Javier against me. Ha! He came to me at once and told me everything. After that, your life was over.

"You're a dead woman as we speak. We're only being merciful in giving you time to repent of your useless acts. When the moment comes, we shall see how well you beg. If your remorse is sincere, your death will be...quicker."

Daria jerked her arms sharply outward. The bonds, which Javier hadn't tied properly, came loose. She rolled forward with one fluid motion, free and mobile, and reached under the truck's rear bumper. Her hand closed around the grip of a large pistol, and in a flash, she'd raised it at the three men.

Pastor abruptly stopped talking, stumbled backward, and awkwardly reached for his gun. Nicolas attempted to draw his sidearm, but he'd forgotten that he still held the gas can. He wasted a precious half a second dropping it before he could draw.

He was too slow. Daria fired twice, striking Nicolas in the chest and forehead. The crackle of gunfire drowned out his short, sharp cry. He fell to the ground like a sack of stones dropped off a balcony, his gun only halfway out of its holster as his body rolled toward the edge of the ridge and came to rest against a mossy rock.

Daria pivoted the handgun toward Pastor at the same instant

that the drug lord slipped his 1911 free of his pants. For a fraction of an instant, it looked as though he and the woman would get a bead on one another at the same time.

Then Javier held his gun, a snub nose .38 revolver, to the side of his boss's head.

Pastor froze, his mouth going slack as the truth of what had happened dawned upon him. Javier snatched away the gold-plated Colt and stuffed it down the front of his pants while snickering.

Daria's smile was faint but readily apparent to the man who *thought* he'd captured her. She kept the pistol, a Browning Hi-Power, aimed at his chest.

"Well," she remarked, "it would seem that Javier didn't tell you *everything*, did he? For example, he might've let slip that you always keep a gun stashed under the bumper of this truck. And he admitted to me that he's *terrible* at tying good knots."

From her kneeling position at the edge of the truck's bed, she swung her legs around and hopped down to stand in front of Pastor, who had turned his head sideways toward his bodyguard as his face flushed red with fury.

Javier had taken a step or two back, but his gun was still close enough that Pastor didn't dare to try anything.

Mateo snarled, "How is this? You dare to betray me, Javier? For some withered bitch like this?"

The henchman shrugged. "She understands me, *jefe*. She understands what I want." He fished in his pocket and produced a pair of frilly, lacy underwear far too small to belong to an adult woman.

Daria shook her head and addressed Pastor. "That's the problem, Mateo, with cultivating perversions all around you and seeking to dominate everyone you know. Then suddenly trying to claim the moral high ground when someone close to you happens to enjoy the company of younger girls."

Javier's unpleasant, curdled grin made her skin crawl, but she pretended it didn't bother her for the time being.

Pastor turned away from his crony to stare at Daria. His eyes were wide with shock, and his jaw hung open in abject horror.

"You hate me so much," he spat, becoming unhinged with disgust, "that you would give little girls to this sick bastard to turn him against me? You people are far worse than I am!"

Javier let out a sudden sharp, donkey-like laugh. "She promised me a lot more than that." He waggled the panties around on his fingertip, and his eyes went vacant as he fantasized about what was to come. "A slice of the *pice*, as they say. My fair share of—"

Daria cut him off with a gunshot. A red hole appeared where his eye had been and the back of his head scattered across the dirt and gravel beside the road as he toppled. The undergarment fell from his hand and wafted off the edge of the cliff.

The barrel of the Browning smoked as Daria aimed it at Pastor. "Promises, promises." Again, she shook her head, slower this time. "You might've held yourself to *some* standard, Mateo. Not high enough for me."

Her limbs and back hurt from a combination of pretending to remain bound for so long and the truck's constant jostling along the mountain trails. She decided to stretch and sit on the truck's bumper. It would be far more comfortable, but it would entail turning her back on her target for a second or two.

She craned her neck, raised her arms high to extend her spine and back muscles, and looked away from Pastor as she stretched her legs and trotted a couple of steps back to the vehicle before plopping down.

At the same time, Pastor dropped to his knees in her peripheral vision, ostensibly to beg for his life. She noticed something else, though. In the same motion, his hand swept briefly over Javier's body. Something flashed gold in the afternoon sunlight.

When she looked at the drug lord, he knelt before her with his hands clasped in front of himself. His forearms seemed too close to his body—as though he were concealing something behind his elbow and bicep.

"Please," he began. "I'm responsible for many people. The men who work for me need my money to support themselves and their families, yes? The women who are my companions, too. They are well cared for. Many come from poverty, and now they live in luxury, you see? Without me, my organization will fall apart. Everyone will suffer. There will be fighting between my men for who claims my—"

"Get to the point," Daria snapped. His desire to be spared was undoubtedly sincere enough, but it seemed safe to assume that he was simply stalling her, trying to lull her into overconfidence until the time was right to make his move.

She had every intention of allowing him to do so.

He kept pleading, saying whatever came to his head to move her or distract her. Daria looked away from the absurd spectacle at the sun, which was past its zenith and moving westward toward the ocean. "So you think all of this blubbering will save you?" she mused.

"I think," Pastor snarled, his voice and demeanor switching instantly back to a ferocious arrogance, "that it will give me the chance to end you, bitch!" The gold-plated 1911 was in his hands, aimed at Daria's face. He pulled the trigger, then again twice more.

The gun *cracked* and flamed. The shots didn't seem as loud as they ought, nor did the pistol recoil as much as the drug lord expected. As he blinked in amazement, Daria sat unharmed, looking as though nothing had happened.

He fired again, emptying the magazine of its full seven rounds, probably cursing himself for his lapse in marksmanship under pressure. He *knew* his aim was better with the subsequent shots. There was no way he could've missed the woman at such short range.

Still, she remained unscathed. She brushed a gray-streaked lock of her dark, wavy hair behind one ear. Then with a fast catlike movement, she pounced and had the barrel of her pistol pressed against his nostrils, aimed slightly upward. His face froze in despair.

"Blanks," Daria pointed out. "Javier was as bad at preparing your weapons as he was at tying up your captives. As I made sure."

Her finger squeezed the trigger. "What can I say? I'm *thorough.*"

The single shot echoed down the mountainside. Silence fell. Then, a few minutes later, a truck's engine started.

CHAPTER TWO

Beneath the higher reaches of the hills, the landscape settled into a gently rolling mass of scrubland covered with thorny vines and ferns. It almost looked like a subtropical semi-desert zone or savanna with its thin sporadic trees, despite Atlantica's northerly latitude and moist climate. The vegetation would grow thicker if she kept driving deeper into the jungle-swathed interior lowlands.

There was no need to. She was almost at the villa.

The dirt tracks were difficult to follow since Pastor and his people were the only ones who ever used them, and they were too recent to have made more than a cursory impression upon the ancient landscape. Still, they'd driven over the most obvious route through the labyrinthine wilderness. Plus, she had good intel on what to expect thanks to how cooperative the late Javier had been.

The truck made a lot of noise. Not only because its bulk *clanked* over the rough landscape but also because the body she'd tied to the rear bumper by a length of heavy rope continuously bumped and scraped along the ground.

She finally came to a broad valley where an unusually dense

stand of trees grew beside a small blue pond. Not far from the water's edge was a Spanish colonial-style mansion. It was rather new and hadn't been completed, with one whole wing still under construction. However, Pastor had been living here for close to a year.

There was no true fence or gate; the drug lord had relaxed his security somewhat since coming to the island. He relied upon bribes, the loyalty of his henchmen, and the remoteness of the location to protect him. Two white marble pillars marked the entrance to the property.

As Daria drove toward them, two men ran out. It was getting dark by now, and she had her headlights on, interfering with their vision. They couldn't see who was driving the vehicle, but she could see them well.

The one out in front, a tall and muscular fellow, held a double-barreled shotgun. Behind him was an older, pudgier man who wasn't visibly armed. He probably had a handgun concealed somewhere.

"Boss!" the guy in front shouted in a thick American accent. Unlike some of Mateo's other men, he'd clearly been hired on Atlantica rather than brought over from Venezuela. "The women are going crazy inside. We had to lock them all up. We didn't, uh, put any markings on them, though, don't worry."

The truck stopped. The corpse dragging behind it was out of the men's line of sight, and they waited patiently for their master to emerge and tell them what to do.

Daria opened the door and hopped down. The man with the shotgun leaned forward, squinting at her slimmer silhouette. Then the air thundered with the report of her pistol as a 9mm round slammed into the man's head.

The other guy stammered and reached frantically into his jacket as his partner toppled, but he wasn't fast enough. Daria shot him twice in the chest, then once more to be sure. He staggered sidelong, groaning and gasping before he slumped against one of the marble columns and lay still.

Daria waited, hugging the side of the truck for cover in case anyone else came out of the mansion. According to Javier, these two should've been the only others of Pastor's minions on duty. Still, she believed in being thorough.

No one came. She shrugged and walked forward. The pistol had no spare magazines, but she had a respectable five rounds left. To be safe, she went to the second man and retrieved the gun he'd tried to pull from his coat, which turned out to be a surprisingly tiny .32 ACP pistol. It was far better than nothing if the Browning ran dry. She slipped it into her pocket and headed for the other man, who had a ring of keys on his belt.

So equipped, Daria passed between the pillars and let herself in through the front door.

At first, it was quiet, but then she heard jostling and banging somewhere deeper within, along with a chorus of shouting female voices. She headed toward them without pausing to appreciate the fine decor of the place beyond an initial glance. Pastor did have good enough taste for decorating, but only because he took no chances. His palace was identical to that of any other rich Atlantican with pretensions to high society.

The door she sought lay at the end of a long hallway on the first floor, probably leading either to a lounge of sorts or perhaps to the basement. It shuddered as the women beyond banged against it.

Daria stood an arm's length away. She was here to help, but since the members of Pastor's unwilling harem were agitated, it seemed wise to be cautious before she assumed they would greet her as a friend.

She waited for a lull in the frenzy of noise. Then she spoke in a loud, clear voice, hoping that at least one or two of them understood English and that her Polish accent wouldn't impede their understanding.

"Hello there," she began. "I'm Executioner Barruk, and you are free. Please calm yourselves."

There was a moment of silence, followed by a bit of whispering that Daria couldn't make out. When no one responded, she began trying keys from the ring, eventually slipping one into the door and turning it.

The Browning was still in her right hand but aimed at the floor.

The door *creaked* open, disclosing a huddled mass of beautiful young women. Most were in their early to middle twenties by the look of them. Pastor hadn't been idle. There were six, and each girl came from a much different part of the world. Daria couldn't identify specific nationalities, but they formed an impressive selection of global womanhood.

There was a dark-skinned girl with long braids, perhaps from Jamaica or the West Indies. A copper-hued young lady whom Daria guessed came from Pastor's native environs in Latin America. A pale and freckled girl with strawberry blonde hair, a Hindu with long brown locks and a bindi dot on her forehead, a woman from the Mediterranean with astoundingly large breasts, and a frail-looking East Asian, probably Chinese or Vietnamese.

They all stared blankly, hovering on the borderline between human reason and the animal urge to attack and flee.

Daria nodded at them. "They're dead. You're free. Come along." She beckoned and turned, walked back down the hall, and heard the women's footsteps following her.

They didn't try to attack but only followed without speaking. Daria led them out of the house and into the savanna, where twilight was dwindling, and the truck still idled with its headlights shining brightly ahead.

Daria didn't go to the vehicle's cab but around to the back. The women behind her gasped when they saw the two dead guards, but all of them froze in silence when they saw the body of Mateo Pastor.

The man who'd abducted them from their homes or jobs and used their bodies for his amusement lay lifeless and ravaged in the dirt. The trip had torn his fine clothes, he was scraped and dusty, and there was a burn mark across his face, centered on the nose. A large portion of the back of his head was missing.

Daria wasn't sure how they would react. It was up to them. Still, she felt that this was something they ought to see. She leaned against the side of the truck and lit a clove cigarette, enjoying two long draws while the women thought things over and grasped their situation.

The Jamaican girl asked, "What do we do with him?" She might never have seen a dead person before, except perhaps a funeral for a relative who'd died peacefully.

Daria waved vaguely. "Whatever you want. You're free, after all."

There was a moment of hesitation. Then four young women —the Latina, the blonde, the Mediterranean, and the East Asian —sprang at the corpse, kicking it and spitting on it or seizing rocks and handfuls of dirt to throw in the dead face.

The Jamaican and the Indian lingered behind. The Hindu girl glanced back at the estate, then looked at Daria. "What do we do? Ourselves?"

"Whatever you want," Daria repeated. She blew out a cloud of fragrant smoke and watched it waft away on the gentle evening breeze. "That's what it means to be free. No obligations. Only responsibility."

She stood there, giving herself a break from the day's long labors, as the young women came to grips with their situation. The quartet who'd abused their tormentor's corpse calmed down and rejoined the others, and they all talked. Not all of them spoke English, but there were enough common languages that one or two could translate for the rest when necessary.

Daria caught most of it. They were debating whether to return home or to stay on Atlantica and how to go about each possibility if so. Only two seemed to have much interest in leaving. The others came either from poor backgrounds with no opportunity or in some cases from years of hustling the streets and fleeing from place to place. Such people had no home to go back to.

It sounded familiar. Daria's parents had died shortly after the Nazis had rolled into Poland when she was only in her teens. After that, there'd been a long period when "home" wasn't a concept she could conceive of.

The conversation drifted instead to taking over the now-vacated estate of the late Señor Pastor and living there as a group.

"We have weapons," the strawberry blonde pointed out. She spoke with what sounded like a Latvian accent, but it was difficult to be sure. "We can learn to shoot."

The Jamaican added, "And make this place defensible. It can be our stronghold. There are food supplies. We can last a while until we can figure out how to make money."

It didn't take long for them to glance at Daria. Then they approached her as a group.

The Hindu asked, "Miss. Will you teach us? Can you stay and help us? We could use someone who understands these things. It would help so much. We can have a good place to live here, helping each other, safe from everyone else."

The other nodded or voiced their agreement. They waited, tense and pleading.

Daria shook her head. She'd nearly finished her cigarette, and she flicked it into the dirt. "I'm an Executioner, my dears. I cannot stay with you. I live in the present, to make right what others have done in the past. What you're talking about is living for the future. I'm afraid I don't *do* that."

The faces—so young, it seemed, all of them at least twelve or fifteen years her junior—fell with disappointment, or in some cases alarm and indignation. They fretted while glancing into the surrounding wilderness.

"What?" the Indian cried. She stepped forward and grabbed the hem of Daria's armored vest. "How can you leave us like this? That man, terrible though he was, took care of us! Now we have no one who can help us to live. You *must* do something! We cannot—"

The Executioner slapped her across the face, cutting short her pleas. The others gasped.

Daria took the girl by the shoulders and looked into her eyes. She was trying to look away in her hurt and shame but relented when she saw that Daria's gaze was less unkind than she'd feared.

"Free," Daria stated. "You're all free—like me. Freedom is what you make of it. It's not easy. It's harder than servitude, in many ways. If you wish to make it, to prevail, *you* must do it, yourselves. You must take responsibility for everything that happens from this day, this *minute*, forward. That responsibility belongs to no one else."

Her only response, as she'd expected, was a deep silence full of unspoken brooding. Not wishing to leave the girls with nothing, she took the little .32 pistol from her pocket and handed it to the Hindu girl, then released her. She drifted back among the others.

Daria nodded at them. "I will perhaps send someone to check on you in another two days, we'll say. Otherwise, you must decide for yourselves. I wish you luck."

She turned away, took out the palm-sized knife she kept concealed beneath her armor, and used it to cut Pastor's dead body free of the truck. Then she climbed into the still-growling vehicle, shifted into drive, and rumbled away from the mansion, leaving it behind her in the night's growing shadows.

CHAPTER THREE

Daria sat at one of the small round tables outside the cantina with a half-drained glass of vodka and tonic before her. She'd been here before. It was where she and Tyler Katakura had met for a drink the day he'd asked her to join him as Atlantica's second Executioner.

That had been about three months ago. In all honesty, she'd lost track of the exact dates. The lack of seasonal variation on the island had thrown off her ability to judge the passage of time as easily as she had back in Europe.

The labor town, originally a borderline wretched shantytown, had begun to grow and flourish into a proper village. The streets were on the verge of having rudimentary paving, the residents had painted half of the houses, and gardens had grown.

Once again, Ty sat across from her, sipping a whiskey and cola.

"So," he asked, "does it all sit well with you? Do you have any regrets? You seem more thoughtful than usual. Like something is bothering you."

She let out a dry chuckle. Usually, he was the one who talked more, who revealed his feelings without recognizing them himself, and it was Daria who guided him toward whatever conclusion he needed to reach.

She confessed, "I'm not sure. I've been thinking it over these past four days. When my friend went to check on them, they decided to remain at the villa. They're far away from everyone else there. That means they'll be safe—for now—but they'll have a difficult time procuring supplies and so forth. We shall see."

Ty nodded, and a black forelock fell across his face. He was in his early thirties, a few years younger than she, and of average height, lean but strong. His hair had been growing long when they'd first met, but he'd cut it short right after he'd recruited her. Now, it was getting shaggy again. He'd been too busy, too preoccupied with work to pay much attention to grooming.

He swigged from his drink as people from the town milled by. A few of them waved to the pair as they walked to their jobs, errands, or social engagements.

"Sounds like you lied, in a manner of speaking. No offense." He shrugged.

Daria flashed him a sharp glare but waited for him to explain himself.

He did. "You told them that they had to take care of themselves and that it wasn't anyone else's responsibility. What you're saying to me today means that you *are* taking responsibility for them, at least in your head. If not, you wouldn't worry about it, would you?"

She scowled, looked aside, and muttered, "Perhaps you're right. It would be different if their circumstances weren't so strange. And if," she sighed. "If I'd been speaking only to them. I was speaking to myself as well, you understand? If I lied to them, I also lied to myself. Am I truly free?"

Ty glanced around. Ostensibly, he was checking to see if Eleanor Cervantes, their contact with the Executives, had arrived yet. Daria suspected he also wanted to give himself an extra moment to decide how to respond.

He drew a deep breath. "No more or less free than most other people. I don't know. I'm not sure how to answer that. Sounds like something you have to answer yourself."

Daria guzzled the remainder of her drink. The bartender noticed and caught her eye. She shook her head and held up a hand. Although she could hold her liquor, she didn't want to get drunk, only to unwind a little. She would probably have work to do later today.

"These few months—three, isn't it?—that I've worked with you, Tyler," she began, "haven't been spent in regret. I enjoy working with you. You're so certain, so determined all the time, that it...how do I put this...*inspires* me. I don't feel as hollow and weary as I used to. Your sense of purpose is contagious."

He laughed. "Well, thanks. Some people think I'm too obsessive. The 'all work and no play' type. I guess when I'm not fighting, I feel like I should still be *doing something*, no matter what it is."

Daria swiped a slim hand through the air. "Yes, yes. That is admirable. But we're not identical. I begin to fear that I've walked into a trap. It's an old fear of mine, the wish never to be held in one place against my will."

Ty glanced at her forearm. Her sleeve covered it, but he knew what was there—a serial number tattooed into her flesh.

She went on. "I worry that I'm allowing myself to become tied to the job. I've had little time or energy for anything but my duties. It's never been like this before. In smuggling, I had much to do, of course. But it wasn't like this."

Her partner frowned. "Do you think you can handle being an Executioner long-term? Maybe it's not for everyone." His tone implied that he had no real doubts about it being right for himself.

Daria had revealed much, yet her thoughts expanded far beyond what her words had articulated. Trying to talk about all of it would likely be pointless. Ty was a good man, but he was also a *man*, and men tended to have simpler, more direct minds that sought to eliminate anything but the "main point." It was difficult to discuss one's feelings with them.

Plus, Daria generally didn't discuss her feelings with *anyone.*

"I'm fine." That was usually enough to keep men from prying too much.

Ty fidgeted and sipped his whiskey again as though he were debating whether to press her on the matter.

To head him off, Daria inquired, "Are we going to bring more Executioners into the fold? We might need them. The two of us have handled things so far. But as Ms. Cervantes once said, the population is growing, and it's a big island."

"Not sure." Ty motioned for the bartender to refill his drink, although he held his finger at the halfway point of the glass. The older man strolled over and poured a roughly half-and-half mixture of cola and bourbon, then smiled, nodded, and went back to the counter.

Daria raised her eyebrows. "Is there a plan?" Although her partner could be quite intelligent at times, he tended to deal with things as they came rather than plotting them out in advance.

Ty shrugged. "Not really. If the Executives ask us to hire someone else, we will. Otherwise, I figured we would wait and see if anyone fits the bill. If so, we'll bring them in."

Daria leaned forward and rested her face on her hand. "Who 'fits the bill,' as you say? How will we know what sort of person is suited to the job?" She had ideas but wanted to hear his input. Not that she entirely expected to hear much from him.

"I don't know." He shrugged again.

She sighed, her emotions a tangled mess of irritation and affection. Tyler Katakura was frustratingly obtuse at times. Yet she knew, perhaps better than most, that he was entirely capable of "winging it," as the Americans said. His faults in planning were forgivable when he possessed the ability to brute-force his way through almost any situation, no matter how dire.

They sat unspeaking for a minute or two, having come to a temporary impasse, but comfortable with one another regardless. Both considered saying more.

Before the conversation could continue, Eleanor finally showed up.

"Good day," she greeted them, emerging quietly from the passing crowd.

Both Executioners looked up and waved. Eleanor Cervantes was a lovely woman of about twenty-five, prim and businesslike, although she didn't mind riding in trucks or stomping through the mud when she had to. She came from a wealthy family in Jalisco, Mexico, and sought to make her fortune in service to the Executives—who, it seemed, found her indispensable as a middlewoman.

Ty pulled out a chair for her. "So, what was it you wanted to talk to us about? Let me guess—the Executives have a concern."

Eleanor smiled and seated herself. She held a manila folder against her chest that was undoubtedly full of documents pertinent to their mission. "Yes. *Two* concerns, in fact."

Daria perked up as her interest spiked. Somehow, the job was more tolerable when there was an element of choice involved since it was likely that she and Tyler would be able to decide between them who would handle which job. Or, perhaps, they would work together on one and tackle the other next. She waited to hear more.

Ty flexed both hands. "I see. Tell us about them, then."

"Briefly, one matter we need to deal with is an arms dealer who is causing some problems." Eleanor laid her folder on the table. There was another beneath it, which she placed beside the first. "The other is an archaeological dig. The archaeologist overseeing it has raised some unusual complaints and has problems with the local labor groups."

Before Daria could say anything, Ty snatched the first folder, the one about the arms dealer. "That one sounds more up my alley."

Daria looked squarely at him, her gaze even but her mouth twisted with skepticism.

He looked at her. "You're the people person, after all." His face cracked into a smile.

The two women exchanged a glance, full of the shared aggravation of being patient with certain people. Both had worked with Ty for some time now. Daria polished off her vodka with a fast swig, upending the glass before setting it firmly on the table before her.

Eleanor blinked twice. She'd composed herself once more as her eyes opened the second time. The younger woman folded her hands in her lap and looked ahead at a space between Ty's and Daria's heads rather than at either of them directly.

"The archaeologist who is supervising the dig, your contact, is known for being somewhat, ah, *eccentric*, I believe is the word. You might find that speaking to her is difficult at first. Please, have patience. This woman is also a genius and has done many great things for Atlantica."

Ty was half-listening, but he'd begun to flip through his folder at the same time. He nodded vaguely.

Daria focused her full attention on Cervantes. Presumably, her dossier held the information required, but she would rather hear what Eleanor had to say. There might be things that the Executives had neglected to print or collect on paper, but which Eleanor could tell her in person.

Not to mention, Ms. Cervantes's reactions and emotional attitudes were instructive in themselves.

"Go on." Daria rested her chin atop her folded hands.

"Dr. Limbu," Eleanor continued, "has consistently been able to find samples and fragments of ancient Atlantican artifacts. A great many people have expressed interest in this island's history, particularly with regard to whether humans have inhabited it before its modern discovery. Or rediscovery. She's received substantial funding from various wealthy donors on this basis. And…"

Daria suspected she knew what was coming next.

"Atlanticore is also involved," Eleanor added, confirming the suspicion. "It's not the main thrust of her excavations, but Dr. Limbu has turned up several large crystal deposits. I hardly need to emphasize how important this is to the Executives and the island in general."

Flashing a brief, wry smile, Daria quipped, "Oh, no, not at all."

Atlanticore crystals were of incredible value, although still not fully understood. They acted as a power source, seemingly more efficient than any of those involved with modern combustion engines. People were willing to pay vast sums of money for them. People were willing to kill for them.

Eleanor concluded with, "So, you see how a woman of her skills could easily go anywhere and find eager patrons. She's an important asset."

Daria nodded. Everything that Eleanor *hadn't* said outright was clear—their mutual benefactors, the Executives, currently retained the archaeologist and were scared of losing her to another backer. Thus Ms. Cervantes had been instructed to practically *beg* the Executioners not to offend Dr. Limbu or otherwise drive her away from completing her current contract.

"I will handle it," Daria promised and took the second file, opening it at once. She didn't bother to read anything yet but simply flipped through to get a feel for how much info there was. Not as much as she would've liked. Still, it would do.

Eleanor smiled. "Good. I'll be available if you need to call me on your radio. Please do so if you have any questions or concerns. Again, you have the full support of the Executives, and your expense accounts will not run out of funds any time soon."

Ty chuckled at that. "As long as the price of ammo doesn't go up too much, yeah, I don't think we'll have a problem."

While the Executioners perused their dossiers, Eleanor stood and excused herself, said her goodbyes, and vanished into the streets. The labor town lay in a small valley in the foothills not too far from the city. Only one crude road led out, and Eleanor presumably had a ride waiting for her.

It reminded Daria that she needed to gas up her truck.

"Ty." She closed the folder and caught his eye. "I'm going to deal with this directly. Based on what I see so far, I don't think it will require much preparation. I might only need to moderate an argument, perhaps hold a gun to a head or two, and if more is required, maybe you can help." Her smile had a distinctively evil edge to it.

He shut his dossier and leaned back in his chair. "I would be willing, although I have to prioritize my assignment. I'll need extra gear for it, so I don't plan on moving until later this evening. Let me know if you need me to roll in."

Daria nodded, rose, left a crumpled banknote on the table for her drink, and strolled down the crude lanes toward the corner of the surrounding ridge where she'd parked her vehicle two hours earlier.

The Executives had gifted Tyler with a huge, armored truck, the kind that militaries would use to transport troops or prisoners. It was fun to drive, but it also lacked subtlety, which was perfectly commensurate with Ty's way of dealing with problems.

For her ride, though, Daria had requested something slightly different. It was a smaller truck, still armored and with enough room for extra supplies or unwilling passengers, but not as conspicuous.

There was a certain irony involved. It was *less* fuel-efficient compared to Ty's truck because prototype Atlanticore technology powered his. The Executives did not—yet—have access to a smaller truck that could boast the same.

Daria sighed as she approached the truck. "All right, you pile of steel, it's feeding time. When will they make an engine powered by Polish vodka? It would make things easier, only needing to bring one container on a long drive."

Then she shook her head, reminding herself of what had happened the last time she'd driven a vehicle while severely drunk. She was lucky to be alive.

She got the gas can out of the back compartment, where it was carefully secured in a corner and draped with an old jacket. Fuel theft was relatively common. Then she opened the small hatch before the tank and lifted the can, leaning against the side of the truck and watching the town bustle while the gas gurgled down the fill pipe.

The village wasn't much different from any other place. It reminded her of the dockside community near her home, close to the ocean south of the city.

"I wonder," she mumbled, "if my life is different forever now. Can I go back? Or did taking Mr. Katakura up on his offer change it all for good?"

She hadn't been home much. Her duties as an Executioner kept her busy. The last time she'd spoken to her contacts in the smuggling community, they'd been standoffish and had largely avoided speaking to her—most probably because the rumors had suggested that she was a "cop" now.

In a way, she was. However, Atlantica *had no laws*. It had no "government" in the traditional sense. She often wondered if the Executives were planning to create one and what that might mean for the role she would play in the future.

So far, the mere act of smuggling wasn't a "crime." Especially given that the leaders of the rest of the world stuck unwaveringly to their moronic policy of TINA—"There Is No Atlantica." Their refusal to even acknowledge the island's existence meant that normal trade couldn't proceed. What would've qualified as "smuggling" in other lands was simply the usual way people got what they needed here.

The gas can ran dry. Daria pulled it free, capped it, and closed the hatch. She wanted another cigarette as she clambered into the driver's seat but decided against it. Smoking too much made her short of breath.

Plus, she had work to do. If her assessment was incorrect and the archaeological dig was more than a mere "personal dispute" between the scientist and her employees, she might have to do plenty of running.

Before she left, Daria checked to ensure her pistol was still in its holster under her jacket. She could feel it, but visual confirmation never hurt. She also reached under the seat and felt her Uzi and her spare magazines in their usual place.

"Off we go, then," she whispered and turned the key in the ignition.

CHAPTER FOUR

Unsurprisingly, the excavation site where the dispute had taken place was in an obnoxiously difficult and out-of-the-way portion of the island, albeit not too far from the city or the little labor town in the valley. Much of Atlantica was still uninhabited, yet even many areas close to the main centers of development were largely still wilderness.

"Dammit," Daria grunted and added a few other, more creative curses in Polish and Yiddish as her truck bumped and rumbled along. The road leading to the dig was much like other roads leading to remote areas. It consisted of two barely identifiable tracks through land that was marginally flatter than the surrounding terrain.

Based on her quick review of a map of southern Atlantica, the site was only a short distance from Ty's labor town. Yet getting there required a substantial detour due to the extreme ruggedness of the terrain between them. The road looped around to the west before veering back northeast.

Most of the island was hilly or mountainous, and even the lower hills often had a jagged or labyrinthine quality that made them hard, if not impossible, to drive through. Vehicles had to make do with what nature provided.

On her dashboard was a two-way radio provided by the Execs for communication with their representatives—which usually meant Eleanor. It buzzed and hummed. Daria flipped the necessary switch.

"Hello, this is Barruk. Over."

The static faded and Eleanor's voice told her, "Hello, Executioner. Have you arrived at the dig site yet? Someone there radioed us and asked that you please hurry since the dispute is growing more heated. There hasn't been any violence yet, but the individual sounded most concerned. There was an accident there recently, and the aftereffects of it have created a climate of stress and anger. Over."

Daria nodded. "From what the map tells me, I'm almost there. I'll assess the situation before I do anything. Running straight into a fight is often a good way to fail at ending it. Over."

"Use your judgment, but please don't waste time. Remember, the Executives consider this excavation to be of...*significant* importance. Thank you. Out."

Daria left the radio on to be safe but didn't try to continue the conversation. She picked up her speed. Due to the poor quality of the road, she could only go so fast without the risk of crashing or damaging the vehicle's undercarriage.

It was frustrating. Driving Ty's massive truck through the city on the first day they had met had been so much *fun*. It might not have been her finest or most mature moment. It had been worth it.

She glanced at the map. The valley where the archaeologist had set up shop was right around the coming bend.

Daria saw a flattish area beside the road off to the left. She pulled over there, parking the truck out of sight, and inhaled. It would be better to approach on foot. It would cost her a minute or two but would make it easier to scope things out before she charged blindly in.

As she hopped down from the truck, she heard people talking or yelling. It was still too faint to make anything out.

"This is probably nothing." She adjusted her armored vest and clipped her hair back from her face with a barrette. "Some *glupeks* want more money after a toilet stall collapsed, and the bookworms don't know how to handle it."

The afternoon was on the warmer side and humid, but not to the point of discomfort. The sky was a patchwork of sun-brightened blue and dim wafting clouds. Westward, closer to the sea, it was raining. The wind might blow it toward her. The weather on Atlantica was strange and unpredictable. Some said it was *unnatural*.

The sounds of voices going back and forth and sometimes trying to interrupt or talk over one another grew louder. Not only because Daria was getting closer. It seemed that whichever persons were speaking were raising their volume as the discussion grew more heated.

There were other noises, too. People shuffled around, dropped equipment, packed or unpacked things. Most of it was audible despite the soft hissing sound of nearby rain and the natural ambient sounds of the encompassing wilderness.

Daria compulsively laid a hand against her hip, feeling the comforting weight of her pistol. She began to wonder if she ought to have brought her submachine gun as well but dismissed the notion of turning back. She would approach with care, and if things looked dangerous, she would retrieve the bigger gun. First, she ought to assess things as they were.

As she came around a bend in the road, the foliage parted enough to reveal a small valley nestled within the forested hills, with most of the greenery cut down in a broad area next to a cliff face. That, Daria guessed, was where the digging operation had taken place.

She stopped upon sighting a crowd of people within the clearing. A couple of quick steps to the side took her within arm's length of a small outcropping of dirt and stone attached to the nearest hill. It mostly blocked her from view of the persons down below. She could still see them with ease, though.

Two distinct groups had separated and now stood facing one another. Their membership in their respective camps—and their opposition to one another—was as clear as if they were rival teams on a football field preparing for an aggressive championship game. Most of the shouting came from the obvious leaders or representatives of each faction.

To the left was a much smaller group consisting of individuals who looked mild-mannered and unathletic. Some of them wore safari clothes. The others were in what essentially amounted to business attire, totally inappropriate for the conditions in which they found themselves. There were perhaps half a dozen of them total.

At their head was a tall, willowy, dark-complected woman with black hair piled atop her head. Daria suspected that she was none other than Dr. Limbu, but it was hard to be sure yet.

To the right was a bigger group, composed mostly of burly, tough-looking men in dirty clothes that were well-suited to the environment. Miners, roughnecks, and general workers of all sorts, undoubtedly. The "labor" half of what Eleanor Cervantes had specifically described as a labor dispute. Representing them was a man with a square chin, thick arms, and broad shoulders.

Daria leaned forward. The big man was the one currently speaking his piece.

"...not going back down until we get some reassurances here. I don't care about fuckin' 'labor laws' on Atlantica. We're still able to negotiate for our contract, get it? We ain't gonna be pushed around and deal with this kind of risk. A lot of these here men got families. They don't get *paid* enough for that shit."

The tall woman had been holding herself still, but Daria realized that she'd merely placed a brief hold on virtual hysteria and had probably been agitated for a long time. She blew up.

"You stupid fools!" she screamed. "Do you not realize what's at stake? We're doing *incredible* research, and the people funding it are *important!* Stop wasting time, imbecile! We'll be more careful. That's all that is necessary!"

She threw her arms in the air as she ranted. Daria frowned. She didn't know enough about the situation yet to be certain of how to react, but the woman's demeanor and choice of words certainly didn't appear to be helping calm things down.

The foreman chewed on a lip and readjusted the cap he held between a thick finger and a clublike thumb. "Listen, lady. I already told you what's up. I ain't sending any more of my men down into that damn hole until things get sorted out. We need to know why the hell three of my guys are dead. *Dead,* get it? Two of your people ain't returned, either. Maybe they ended up the same way."

He glanced past the woman toward the other people in her small entourage. "You pencil necks want to go down there and never be seen again? Huh?"

A few of the other workers chimed in with vaguely worded shouts of approval or simply by nodding. The academic types looked sheepish. They seemingly didn't want to be there and hoped the argument would end as soon as possible. Two appeared angry but not necessarily willing to do much about it.

The willowy lady rolled her head and clenched her fists as she stomped back and forth. Obsessed with whatever her goal was, she almost totally ignored the foreman's concerns. "You have a contract! A signed *contract.* You cannot break it. You *must* keep excavating, or your entire payment is forfeit! That is the *deal.* How difficult can it be to understand this? Can you even read?"

Daria's frown deepened into a scowl. The situation wasn't promising. Unless one of the principals adopted a different approach to their disagreement, or someone else intervened, things could turn ugly.

She eased out from behind the outcropping and walked the rest of the way down to the valley. So far, no one noticed her, but they would soon enough. In the meantime, she continued to observe and read the two leaders.

They verbally blasted one another again. Neither had anything new or constructive to say. They kept repeating the same basic things, trying to win the emerging power struggle through a mixture of brute force, persistence, and attrition.

Daria first gauged the woman, who resembled the photograph of Dr. Akshara Limbu enough that it was highly unlikely *not* to be her. Limbu was brave; that much was certain. Without any significant support from her crowd, she was standing up to a large group of large men and refusing to back down.

However, she was doing nothing to ease the tensions. Her words had an arrogant edge, and she refused to negotiate or acknowledge the men's point. So far, all she'd done was focus on her concerns while dismissing anything else. Daria had encountered such people before. Scientists were sometimes like that— fixated on their studies and discoveries. They forgot that other people had to live in the real world.

As for the foreman, he, too, had legitimate worries but wasn't handling things well. His concern for the workers' safety for whom he was responsible seemed honest and valid. However, he lacked any ability to communicate what he wanted. He could, Daria surmised, have tried to negotiate a compromise whereby his men could return partially to work while they investigated the others' disappearance.

Instead, like Dr. Limbu, he refused to disengage from the headbutting that had ensued. Both group leaders were proud and stubborn types. Plus, the scientist's shrill ranting was stoking the fires of his temper.

Daria read his body language. He had pulled his pants up, and he was growing more still, more focused. They were classic indicators of potential incoming violence. He might lash out soon if things didn't calm down.

If he did, the argument might turn into a brawl. It would be ludicrously one-sided, given that the academics were a reedy-looking bunch in addition to being outnumbered at least five to one.

A brawl, let alone a massacre, would make Daria's life and job far more complicated than they needed to be.

She was suddenly glad that she, rather than Ty, had taken this particular job. Mr. Katakura might deal with it by simply barging in with his sword drawn and threatening to decapitate anyone who didn't shut up. Of course, if things *did* go south, having him around as backup might be helpful.

Daria hastened her pace toward the encampment. One of the scientist types noticed her, as did four or five of the laborers. They squinted but neglected to speak up. They all seemed wary of interrupting the verbal sparring between their respective spokespersons.

Then Daria's eyes bulged in sudden horror as Dr. Limbu made her stupidest error yet. Daria had figured that the woman would continue shrieking indefinitely. Instead, she pressed forward, pointing at the foreman's chest and shouting directly into his face from half a meter away.

"No, no!" Daria grunted. She broke into a run, trying to reach the group before the inevitable occurred. They were still a good hundred meters away. It was doubtful she would make it.

Dr. Limbu shouted, "...and you will never again work on this island so long as—"

The foreman roared and shoved her hard. She flew backward, landed hard on her rump, and rolled to the side. Everyone else on both sides roiled and readied themselves for action—fight or flight, or both.

Daria called, "Hey! Stop it. We can talk about this." A few

heads turned toward her, but the scientist and the foreman paid her no heed.

The foreman hadn't finished yet, either. He stomped closer to his fallen opponent and loomed over her. His big hands balled into thick, bony fists. Daria's stomach and spirits sank as she ran. Her hand went to her gun. She didn't want to have to shoot anyone, but she couldn't allow a woman to be beaten to death, either.

Then, to her shock, one of the onlookers sprang forward. It wasn't one of the workers. It was one of the archaeologist's entourage, a short, stocky man with graying hair. Like Dr. Limbu, he looked more or less South Asian.

His speed was incredible, and he held two objects—a Webley revolver in one hand and a kukri in another. Daria's heart leaped into her throat. Bloodshed was imminent. She drew her pistol.

Then everything stopped. The entire scene, rife with tension that was boiling over, froze. The small dark man stood paused in mid-stroke, the edge of the thick recurved blade held against the larger foreman's throat.

At the same time, he aimed the revolver around the foreman's side to wave it at the crowd of laborers, some of whom had begun to advance. They froze, too.

"I think," the small man commented in thickly accented, partially broken English, "that is quite enough."

The foreman had stopped moving the instant the steel had touched his neck, but his violent intent had remained. He didn't act. He only stared at the man who'd interceded. Then he relaxed. His urge to pound the shit out of Dr. Limbu melted away as he grasped the nature of what had happened.

Daria realized it, too. The small man both looked and sounded calm. He was in complete possession of himself and was ready to do anything he had to in response to the slightest provocation. In a way, he reminded Daria of Ty.

The foreman saw it too. "Okay," he rumbled, still perturbed

but no longer dangerous. "But I'm not sending anyone else down there. If she wants our help with her special project, we need to figure out what the hell happened to my workers."

The other man nodded. "Yes, good. That is understood." Slowly and cautiously, he drew the hefty knife away from the foreman's throat and lowered it.

Daria had slowed her approach to a trot again. She didn't want to burst onto the scene and startle anyone who hadn't already noticed her coming. Still, the sooner she could intervene and stop the tensions from flaring again, the better.

The two men in the center of the clearing stood staring at each other a moment longer. Then the foreman took a step backward before turning and gruffly telling his men to disperse and return to their camp. A low chorus of voices rose from the group as they trudged off, away from the excavation site proper and toward a cluster of tents and lean-to shacks at the far end of the small valley amid the trees.

Dr. Limbu had remained sitting on the ground during the brief standoff. Several locks of hair had fallen around her face, patches of mud showed on her clothes, and dirt smudged her face as she stared in amazement. Perhaps alone of everyone present, she didn't seem much calmer.

The small man put away his kukri and pistol before turning and helping the archaeologist up.

"Gaje, what were you doing?" she scolded him. She'd lowered her volume a little but hadn't softened her tone much. "There was no need for that. I had things under control! He was about to do as I said, as he is supposed to. Now look! He's gone off, and none of them are returning to work. I might've convinced them with another minute or two of persuasion. We're going to lose *hours* over this. Days, even!"

The man called Gaje was unaffected by her tirade. It slid off his cool bearing as easily as rain off the back of a duck. He clasped Limbu's hand and brought her to her feet, his face relaxed and neutral.

"I am sorry, Ak. Are you hurt?"

Akshara Limbu waved a hand with a tense, jittery motion. "Yes, yes, I'm fine. Who is that?" Her head turned toward Daria, noticing her for the first time. "You there. Who are you? What are you doing here?"

Daria had finally reached the clearing's edge. She'd also reholstered her pistol but kept her jacket swept aside for easier access...just in case.

"Good afternoon," she said in a flat voice. "I'm Executioner Barruk. I received word that you have a labor dispute that needed mediating. It would appear the dispute is ongoing."

The tall woman rolled her eyes skyward and scoffed. "Oh, well, you're late. If you'd arrived two minutes earlier, this all might've gone the way it should. I'm Dr. Akshara Limbu or Ak for short. It doesn't matter. I'm running a most important operation here.

"We intended that you would arrive to hold that stupid foreman to his contract. I have come here from Madras in India, you know, and I'm renowned the world over for my work. Now I'm impeded by common ruffians such as that man."

Daria gently bit her tongue. She didn't doubt that Dr. Limbu had worthwhile things to accomplish with the dig, but it was functionally impossible for her to *like* the woman. She hoped that Ak would grow more pleasant as she calmed down.

"Doctor," Daria began, "I came here today to negotiate a compromise while also enforcing justice. I agree with you that people should keep their word and abide by their agreements. However, forcing compliance at gunpoint isn't exactly my purpose. If several people have died or gone missing, it would seem *that* is a matter of more pressing and significant concern."

She kept her eyes on the archaeologist but also observed the other academic types as she spoke. One of them, a skinny man who stood with a hunched posture, visibly winced.

Again, Ak scoffed. "It's easy for you to say that from where you stand. If you knew what we were doing here, you wouldn't say such foolish and shortsighted things. This isn't a matter which normal concerns should interfere with. I wouldn't have come here otherwise."

It suddenly occurred to Daria that she could probably resolve all the problems at the excavation site instantly if she were to pull her gun and shoot Dr. Limbu in the face. However, that might cause certain other problems.

Instead, annoyed that she would have to calm herself as well as everyone else, Daria drew a long, slow, deep breath in through her nose and out through her mouth. Then she put on her best smile. The pleasant, open one she used when trying to charm one of her smuggling contacts into entering a risky deal.

"Dr. Limbu, or Ak," she began, "allow me to suggest, then, that you explain the situation in more detail. What about your work is so important? I didn't have time for a full briefing since I rushed here to help."

It was true. She hadn't thoroughly read the dossier. If she had, she would have a better grasp on things, but she also would've arrived even later to the scene of the argument.

The scientist blinked as though the Executioner's words had confused her.

Daria added, "If you tell me more about what's going on and show me the evidence, I can make judgments more accurately. Science is all about evidence, is it not?"

"Oh," Ak mused, her face abruptly going distant. She tilted her head, and her mouth took a pensive twist, as though having to *prove* how important her work was had never occurred to her before.

She must've been used to saving the scientific method for her professional activities while, in the personal domain, expecting her Ph.D. to cow other people. "Very well. Please follow me, Executioner Barruk. You might find this interesting."

She turned and walked toward the end of the clearing opposite where the workers had gone. Her gait was uneven, the noticeable limp probably thanks to a bruised tailbone. The other scientists parted to let her pass.

Daria coughed. "Yes, I'm sure I will."

CHAPTER FIVE

As Daria followed the lead scientist away from the scene of her embarrassing spat with the foreman, she took a moment to examine her surroundings in more detail. The urgency of intervening in the argument had prevented her from looking things over earlier.

Ahead of her and to the right lay the rocky face where the excavation proper took place. Foliage, distance, and a light mist blocked clear sight of it, but she could see the broad outlines well enough.

A multi-peaked mound of dirt, dust, and gravel, like a miniature mountain range, sat out front and to the sides. It was the debris from digging into the earth. Daria would've thought they'd dump it somewhere farther away, but she wasn't sure exactly what equipment they had. Besides, Dr. Limbu had probably been pushing them to do everything with maximum haste.

The cliff was a strangely marbled layer cake of what looked like limestone and granite. The island's geography and geology were still poorly understood. Based on the construction Daria had seen in the city's vicinity, it appeared that the rock here was about the same as what predominated on the south-central coastal plain. The cliff's face wasn't perfectly vertical but angled backward like a steep slope.

In the center of the wall was a roughly square, black, yawning opening. No light emerged from it, nor was anyone bothering to shine one into it for the time being. It looked like a long-abandoned mine shaft or an ancient cave more than the product of a recent dig.

Once Ak, Daria, and Gaje had passed, the other four academics fell into line behind them. Daria wondered if they had work to do elsewhere—and if so, whether they were simply following the lead doctor for the sake of keeping her appeased.

The valley's floor sloped gently up beyond the central portion where the standoff had occurred. Beyond a thin screen of tree branches, ferns, and tall grass lay another open area, this one on a tiny plateau or natural terrace of sorts that nestled in the corner of two high mossy ridges.

Daria saw a trickle of silvery water flowing down from a natural spring within the rock about five meters overhead and noted with approval that the crew had set up jugs to catch the runoff. Plumbing was rare outside the city. The humid climate meant that freshwater wasn't exactly hard to come by, but in the wilderness, it never hurt to have extra to drink.

Upon the terrace, the scientists had set up a combination domicile and cataloging station for the artifacts that the roughnecks had helped discover. Presumably, the research team was studying them.

Dr. Limbu waved. "Here we are. This is where the most important work takes place. Consider yourself privileged to witness it."

"Of course," Daria responded in a polite tone, while her gut nonetheless clenched in aggravation. She'd done a lot of different types of work over the years, and it had always seemed "important" enough to her when it helped her survive, no matter what it was.

It appeared that each of the researchers had a tent in which to sleep. Additionally, at the center of the little plateau was a communal study area consisting of tables with chairs, stools, and stacks of equipment nearby. They'd erected a canopy above it on a set of poles. Daria recalled the rain she'd seen blowing inland from the coast and gave silent thanks that the scientists had the foresight to be prepared for Atlantican weather.

Dr. Limbu stood off to the side and folded her hands behind her back with a smug expression as Daria came close enough to observe what lay upon the tables.

The Executioner moved slowly. Her eyesight wasn't as good as it used to be so she went to the edge of the nearest table to examine the objects in detail. "What are these?"

She already knew the general answer. People found similar things all over Atlantica. Odd fragments of metal sticking up from the ground. Whether in the form of shards, or bars, or half-cylinders, or rough cubes, they turned up from time to time. Often they were in poor shape, resembling naturally occurring mineral deposits as much as artifacts.

In other cases, they looked like manufactured implements of some sort. Most people didn't give them much thought. Daria generally had other things to worry about, yet the ubiquity of the metallic fragments had piqued her curiosity from time to time.

The instance that stood out most strongly in her mind was the old, worn, rusted tower she'd seen at the edge of the scrubland before the interior jungle. It had revealed itself on a scouting trip that had preceded Mateo Pastor's execution.

The huge column of iron—or so it appeared—sat in a small hollow amid the craggy, weed-covered badlands, far too big and too symmetrical to be a naturally occurring formation. It had been much smaller than the tall buildings going up in the city but certainly large enough to qualify as a human structure.

At the time, she hadn't paid much attention to it. She half-assumed it was an abandoned watchtower built not by some ancient people but by the American or German military during the fighting over the island that had taken place in the 1940s. That little episode was one of many Atlantican truths that the rest of the world liked to pretend had never happened.

Now, seeing similar objects on the tables as part of an *archaeological* expedition...

Dr. Limbu chuckled. "Look more closely, Executioner."

Daria did. Nothing stood out in her mind, save for one detail. The scraps of metal were clean and intact, not rusted or corroded in any noticeable way. Aside from that, though, they were simply random fragments. None of them formed anything she could identify.

Ak took a step toward her with an imperious flourish. "You see?"

Clearly, she expected that her collection of scrap would cow her guest into awestruck compliance.

"No," Daria shot back, "I'm afraid I don't. All I see are old pieces of metal. They aren't much different from anything I could find at any dump or junkyard in Europe or America. As far as I'm concerned, these things, whatever their significance, aren't worth the sacrifice of people's lives."

Dr. Limbu's mouth fell open, and she looked sharply off to the side as though she had no idea how to respond to such a statement. She put her hands on her hips and tapped her foot with blatant impatience.

"Executioner Barruk," she pronounced, "don't be dense. Do you not understand it? These 'pieces of metal,' as you call them, are far more than junk. They suggest that there was an advanced civilization on this island at one time.

"People lived here long ago, people with knowledge of metallurgy, architecture, and engineering. They used Atlanticore crystals as their source of power! It's the only explanation we have that begins to tie everything together. There is no other logical way to address all of the mysteries of this strange place."

Behind her, Daria heard a couple of the other scientists murmuring their assent.

"Well, that's interesting. I understand that the Executives, and many others, are curious about the history of our island. Plus, anything that has to do with Atlanticore is always…" She sighed. "*Lucrative*. I still don't see anything worth dying for."

As the archaeologist continued to balk, Daria held her gaze and went on, not allowing her to squeeze another pompous comment in edgewise.

"They've already learned how to use the crystals as a kind of energy or electricity. This is well known whether the elites admit it openly or not."

She thought back to Ty's truck, powered by a matrix of refined Atlanticore stones, but chose not to mention it aloud. People might overhear and assume that *all* Executioners used similar power sources. In their curiosity and greed, they might not believe her when she told them that the Executives had saddled her with a traditional gas-powered engine until further notice.

"So," Daria concluded, "unless there's more that you aren't showing or telling me, I see nothing to justify the deaths of up to five innocent people. Let alone still more if the excavation is as dangerous as the foreman says."

To her total lack of surprise, Ak had become more and more agitated as Daria spoke. Ripples of anger and disbelief went through the scientist as though she were prepared to launch herself at the rock wall in frustration.

Now, as Daria seemingly took the foreman's side in the earlier argument, the woman was practically apoplectic.

"You—what—how—*how?*" Limbu choked out. Indignation was strangling her ability to speak with any basic coherence. She was breathing in as though preparing for another screaming fit.

The short graying man, Gaje, stepped in and raised a single finger. "Ah, if I may! A recommendation. Ms. Barruk hasn't seen what we've seen. A demonstration! She cannot know everything we know without one."

Daria looked at him, then nodded and looked back at Ak.

Dr. Limbu's eyes had turned away from the Executioner and toward her subordinate. "Gaje! Stop interfering in other people's conversations. The importance of what we have here is plain to see, and this woman is only pretending to be thick. She's trying to annoy us to prove a point.

"But, fine! So be it! Maybe she truly is that ignorant. Go ahead and show the jackboot what people of normal intelligence have already come to understand."

Before anyone could respond to her latest outburst, the scientist twirled on her heel and marched off beyond the encampment's edge.

Daria watched her go. The rational part of her mind was glad the woman had left. Hopefully she'd cool down and come to her senses.

Another part of her seethed with wrath. Based on her past experiences, being called a *jackboot* didn't sit well with her. At all.

She wondered if, in a way, there was some minimal truth to it. Was she only a thug in a uniform to these people? Did they have a reason to see her as anything else?

Before Daria could ponder such things, Gaje took a step closer to her and gently motioned her to follow him over to another table. "Come here. Let us show you. This is most interesting."

She ambled to the edge of the next display. Another of the scientists, a thin blond man of average height, came along beside her to assist if necessary.

On the table that Gaje had indicated were a pair of metallic disks that differed from the others in readily apparent ways. They were smooth, unblemished, and perfectly round, for one thing. They also had been wrapped with something that looked almost like braids of what Daria at first thought was wood but was copper. It ran between the two, connecting them.

She pointed at it. "What's that? Did you find them like that, or did you add that?"

"No," said Gaje. "I mean, we did it. Ah, Johnson, can you explain? My English is not always good."

The blond man nodded and said, in a Received Pronunciation English accent, "The copper is soldered like that to link the two disks, while the protruding copper tail simultaneously acts as a conductor. An interface with sources of power, you might say. Knowing that, you can probably guess the general nature of the experiments we've been carrying out."

Daria smiled. After dealing with Limbu, these two were a relief. Both seemed friendly and unassuming and didn't treat her like an imbecile. "Yes, it's beginning to make some sense."

Gaje knelt and reached under the table, grabbing something out of Daria's sight. Once he had it, he stood with a small, hand-crank-operated electromagnetic battery. She'd seen ones like it before. Turning the crank would produce an electric charge, but generally not a strong one.

As the Executioner watched, the scientists worked together on the demonstration. Johnson attached a wired probe to the battery's terminal while Gaje worked the crank enough times to build up a charge.

"Now," Gaje announced, and a faintly childlike excitement grew in him, "watch and listen. This is what happens when we use electricity." He took the probe and touched it to the end of the braided copper tail connecting the disks.

The two round pieces of metal trembled as though they rested on rumbling ground. At first, there was no other reaction. As the trio observed, Daria noticed a noise, initially faint but growing louder. It was a thin, squeaking, scratchy sound that rose in strength and volume until it was nearly a shriek.

Daria cringed. It was fascinating to see the Atlantican metal produce a weird effect, but the noise was unpleasant. It sounded as though the disks were in pain.

Then the screeching faded as the battery lost its charge and the power from the wire probe ran down. After a minute, the disks fell silent and ceased their vibrations.

Daria was no expert in mechanical matters, but she'd picked up a respectable smattering of knowledge over the years. "That's strange. I've never known metal to do that."

"Indeed," Johnson confirmed. "There's more though. Here's where it becomes truly intriguing."

Gaje put away the crank battery and went back under the table. When he emerged again, he held a small box containing a glowing blue crystal sitting within an elaborate wire harness. Daria recognized it immediately. She couldn't mistake it for anything else.

He'd also detached the wire probe from the battery, and now he affixed it to a terminal on the crystal box's frame.

The small man grinned with anticipation. "This is what happens with Atlanticore energy."

He touched the probe to the braided tail of copper wire again. Once more, there was no immediate reaction, but they didn't have to wait for long. The disks let out a low hum, pleasantly harmonized, almost musical. The contrast with the electrical battery was obvious.

Then the disks rose in the air. Daria's breath caught in her throat, and she stared, transfixed by the bizarre spectacle. Their movement was graceful, natural-seeming for something that rarely if ever happened in nature. They hovered a hand's breadth above the table's surface, taking the wire tail with them and stopping.

Daria peered at them closer. They had floated up as far as they could go while allowing the probe to remain in contact with the conductor-tail. It was as though they knew not to part from their energy source.

The Executioner shook her head. "I'm impressed," she admitted. "Dr. Limbu should've shown me this to begin with if that's the effect she wanted. This is quite incredible. I can see why the Executives, along with the scientific community, are so keen to conduct this type of research."

Gaje disconnected the probe, and the disks fell the short distance back to the table, landing with a dull *clank*. He left the box with the Atlanticore matrix where it was.

"Yes, yes," he said. "We have found much. There is more to be done."

Behind them and off to the side, air rushed, and Daria's sixth sense alerted her to sudden movement. She tensed, turned her head, and saw Ak Limbu sweeping toward them, having reappeared suddenly from whatever place she'd gone off to stew.

Between the lead archaeologist's expression and the general vibe she gave off, Daria decided that her mood had improved. She wondered if that was a *good* thing.

"See?" Ak asserted in a sharp whisper, her eyes gleaming and her face stretched with a look of rapturous triumph. She suddenly reminded Daria of a mad scientist she'd seen in an old horror film, years and years ago. "Do you not see? This is the evidence. Evidence for how we could use Atlanticore in ways that we never could've dreamed of before."

Johnson nodded politely at Daria and excused himself. Gaje stayed where he was.

Daria said, "Perhaps. I've never seen metal...float in the air before. It's quite incredible."

"Absolute, undeniable evidence," Ak went on, as though Daria hadn't spoken at all, "of the existence of an ancient, advanced civilization, such as one purported in fables and legends. Kumari Kandam! The lost continent. Beneath our very feet, it is waiting to be discovered and empowered. There could be forgotten devices here, the likes of which, once properly activated, could change the fate of humanity forever."

The scientist's hands were trembling. She seemed happy, at least, now that she could focus on something that interested her.

Daria held herself aloof. After witnessing the doctor's earlier behavior, her current madcap zeal was more than a little off-putting. She drew out a clove cigarette.

"You could argue that Atlantica has already done that." She kept her tone cool, trying to sound bored, and didn't look at Dr. Limbu as she lit the cigarette.

Instantly, the archaeologist roiled again with indignant annoyance, and Daria had to admit that she enjoyed nettling her. "What?"

Daria shrugged. "How many times can you supposedly 'change the fate of humanity' before humanity realizes that there is no fate?"

Ak scoffed and folded her arms over her narrow chest. "Hah. A poetic flourish. Something that would sound good with artists and philosophers and such people. Others of us are focused on real results that will improve our world. What we're studying here, *today,* suggests wonders that could improve the lives of everyone on this planet."

Daria puffed out a wafting jet of clove-scented smoke. "Or *end* a great many lives if all does not go exactly as you plan. Speaking of which, what's the story behind these dead and missing people? Three confirmed dead, and two missing, if I recall. That seems like something I should investigate further."

Dr. Limbu threw up her hands in disgust and spun toward the small dark man beside her. "Gaje! You handle the jackboot. I'm finished with her!" She stormed off in a cloud of anger, the type generated by wounded self-importance.

Daria looked at the woman's assistant and waited to be "handled."

Gaje reacted with a gentle, half-ashamed, yet oddly reassuring smile. "Do not worry," he offered. "She treats everyone like this."

Taking another draw on her cigarette, Daria quipped, "That fails to surprise me."

CHAPTER SIX

Daria's work at the dig site was far from done, and Dr. Akshara Limbu was of no meaningful help. Fortunately, the pleasant man with the kukri was more than willing to accommodate her.

"Please." He offered a short bow. "Allow me to introduce myself properly. I should have before. But we were busy with things which Ak wanted to show us."

They'd strolled away from the cataloging station on the small natural terrace and back down into the valley proper, which at present seemed almost eerily empty and quiet despite the laborers' camp nearby giving off a noticeable rumbling of voices and activity.

Daria had finished her cigarette. She crushed the tip between her fingers and tossed the butt onto a damp-looking patch of soil. "That's fine. I'm pleased to meet you. My name is Daria Barruk, Executioner of Atlantica, but I believe you knew most of that."

He gave a short chuckle. "Yes, yes. My name is Gaje Gurung. Many people cannot pronounce 'Gaje,' so you may call me 'Gage.' It is close enough."

"Ha. That will do, then. Gage. May I ask where you're from?"

He undoubtedly hailed from somewhere in or near the Indian

subcontinent, but she was hesitant to leap to any conclusions beyond that. She walked at a casual pace, moving toward the excavation shaft, but in no hurry for the time being. The threat of violence here seemed to have abated.

Gage wasn't offended by the question. "Of course. I am from Nepal. If you have not heard of this country, it is north of India, in the mountains."

"I've heard of it," Daria pointed out. Nepal would've been her first guess. Given the man's weapon of choice, she speculated further as to his background. She didn't press the issue. "I'm from Poland, in Eastern Europe. Although I lived in the United States for a short time before I came to Atlantica."

Her guide nodded and uttered a couple of half-comprehensible pleasantries. They were treading through a stretch of tall grass that grew from soft, muddy ground, so the swishing and squelching noises made by their passage rendered his response difficult to hear.

Beyond the grassy patch lay the flatter, firmer land before the cliff where the team had dug the shaft. No one else was present. The other scientists had returned to work, and Ak had returned to bossing them around. The large group of roughnecks was taking an extended break at their encampment nearby, ignoring the researchers and the Executioner.

Up close, Daria instantly noticed several details she hadn't been able to perceive earlier. The workers had dug a broad, shallow basin in front of the rock wall first and dumped the dirt elsewhere, probably beyond the edge of the woods. Doing so had given them extra space where they could pile the debris from the cliff without having to make time-consuming trips to get rid of it.

Furthermore, from the position at which she stood, she could see farther into the tunnel's mouth. The rain clouds had drifted elsewhere, leaving them with clear skies and a more advantageous angle of sunlight.

The shaft was roughly square, but since the crew had no intention of transforming it into anything other than a hole in the ground to pass valuable items through, they hadn't bothered to smooth it out or keep the sides perfectly even.

It also began by going straight forward into the cliff, staying parallel with the ground, for perhaps two meters before veering downward at a relatively sharp angle, at least thirty degrees. Daria wondered how safe that was. They probably had specialized equipment for dealing with the descent. The Executives were rarely stingy when it came to funding projects they wanted done right.

The sunlight penetrated about ten to fifteen meters deep, showing Daria that the layer cake of granite and limestone gave way to an even more variable mixture of stone and packed dirt and clay as the tunnel passed below the earth's surface. She imagined it would be possible to see much farther with proper lighting.

Gage led her right up to the mouth. His face was earnest, but there was a subdued kind of awe in his expression, as though he were showing off a treasured heirloom passed down through multiple generations of his family.

"Look," he urged while pointing into the tunnel.

Closer than she'd been a moment ago, Daria found that her sight extended farther into the shaft than previously estimated. There was something else, which piqued her attention at once.

The darkness deepened as the tunnel descended into the earth, only to recede near the end as it curved to the left out of sight. A faint blue glow, barely visible, shone against a wall of mottled stone.

Daria's nostrils flared. Anytime someone found a deposit of Atlanticore, bad things tended to happen. Some time ago, she'd had the misfortune to be aboard a ship where some idiot tried to smuggle a crystal off the island.

For reasons unknown, Atlanticore became unstable and ultimately exploded when it got too far from its homeland. The ship had sunk, and she'd been lucky to survive, courtesy of a smaller boat following them.

Her first informal case, accompanying Katakura, had involved one of the Executives trying to kill a great many witnesses after he'd discovered a vein of crystal on land he'd claimed. Useful though it was, the mysterious blue mineral brought out the worst in most people.

She turned to Gage. "Dr. Gurung, please tell me the full account of your dig here. How you began, when you found those samples, when you found that deposit, everything. The more I know, the better I can help you."

"I understand," he responded. "When we first came here, the excavation was very slow. Careful. Doing everything, how do you say, by the book. We determined that there would be artifacts near the surface. Those pieces of metal, which you saw. There was a layer of them in the topsoil. Slow and careful. We dug, examined everything carefully, took the pieces, and allowed the unearthing to resume."

Daria focused most of her attention on the man's words, but she kept peering into the dark hole at the same time. Some of the tunnel, particularly the deeper portions, looked smoother than they had at first, as though the crew *had* been trying to turn them into something fit for long-term human usage, after all.

Dr. Gurung went on. For the most part, his English was good enough. Occasionally he struggled with certain words or more abstract expressions. Daria had to either suggest ways to communicate what he meant or patiently wait for him to find a way to work around his difficulties. English wasn't her first language by any means, but she'd become fluent years ago, which gave her a better perspective than some on how hard it could be at times.

By working with him, she got the whole story. It grew both darker and more interesting as it went on. The faint distaste for the job she'd felt earlier, which had given her pause before she left the labor town, faded away. She grew more and more fascinated by the possibilities Gage suggested and how they related to Dr. Limbu's madcap statements.

It seemed that the digging had been fairly easy once they got through the initial rock of the cliff and into the layer of dirt beneath it. It didn't last. As the shaft grew deeper, the crew hit stone.

Then it had collapsed, filling the space they'd won with rubble. The dig hit a snag. So all the workers had pitched in, pausing in the act of actual excavation to clear out the detritus and haul it away. Once they'd succeeded at that, they proceeded, drilling and chipping hundreds of feet farther into the earth.

Oddly enough, they increasingly broke into open areas that, at first, they'd assumed were natural caves. Those began right at the point where the tunnel curved out of sight from the surface—the place where Daria could faintly discern the telltale blue glow.

"Then, *then*," Gage went on, raising a finger, his eyes growing wider and his voice falling to a hushed whisper. "We realized that it was a...room, a chamber, artificial. No cave. It too was filled with dirt and loose rubble, which we again had to haul out. Very difficult, it took us a long time. But we were all excited. Ak was becoming crazy to find out more. Even the workers were most curious."

Daria had a good idea of what would come next. The discovery of a rich vein of Atlanticore, perhaps stashed there by whoever had built the mysterious chamber.

She was half-right. There turned out to be far more to it than that.

Gage went on to explain that once the chamber was clear, everyone had been stunned to find it adorned with extensive carvings along the walls, in some cases inlaid with Atlanticore crystals—hence, the azure light.

For a week or so after that, the crew had settled into a pattern. The researchers focused on observing the crystals and recording information about the carvings. In the meantime, the roughnecks worked to clear out the caverns, halls, rooms, and tunnels that lay beyond. Many were similarly clogged with refuse but also seemed to be part of a human-constructed underground complex.

A few nights ago, things had gone terribly wrong.

Most of the teams worked during the day, but two archaeologists and six laborers had the nocturnal shift assignment. Both scientists and half of the workers were down in the carven chamber when a brilliant flash of light emerged from the tunnel's mouth, along with sharp cries of pain and fear.

The other three workers underground were impeded from checking on the five by the rubble they were trying to clear. The sleeping personnel on the surface took five or ten minutes to get down there and investigate. By the time anyone reached the chamber, all they could find were the empty clothes of the three laborers smoldering among piles of ash. There was no sign of the two scholars.

Gage sighed, his face heavy with sadness. "The workers are assumed to have been incinerated. A surge of power from the crystals, much like when a battery is, ah, overcharged? It is the best explanation we have so far. Some of us think the same happened to the research men. They would've been closer to the crystals, so perhaps every part of them burned up, even their clothes. Not everyone is so sure."

Daria rubbed her chin. "Are there any theories as to how it happened? Who thinks they might not be dead?"

"Yes. The workers believe that our two researchers 'set off' the crystals from poking them, or something like that. No one else knows. Akshara is the strongest believer that they're missing. She refuses to hear of them being dead."

That was odd, Daria reflected. There were far too many questions about the entire incident and nothing that resembled a solid answer. So far.

"Since then," Gage concluded with another heavy exhalation, and his brow lowered over his tired eyes, "the dig has been shut down. For more than two days. The workers have argued with Dr. Limbu and have made no progress. Nothing.

"Ak insists on digging. She says, over and over again, that the excavation must go on. It is true, that is what the Executives hired us for. But never does she say anything about finding our missing scholars."

Daria scowled. "The one good thing I'll say for her is that she's highly motivated to accomplish her main job. But her style of leadership doesn't seem to inspire much confidence or loyalty. Then again, the foreman hardly seems to be much better."

"Oh, no, he hasn't helped much either," Gage agreed. "His name is Mr. Boucher. He is a man with a good heart but not as good at talking things over."

Given that he'd nearly assaulted Ak, Daria wasn't so sure about the "good heart" thing, but at least his concern for his men had seemed sincere. She had to admit that she already understood how someone could respond to Dr. Limbu's shenanigans in...unconstructive ways.

Gage elaborated that Boucher, the foreman, had continuously refused to do anything until he knew it was safe to send his men back down. The problem was that verifying the safety of the tunnel was impossible *unless* someone *did* go back down. He seemed not to grasp as much, having forbidden even the archaeologists from entering the chamber.

His lack of cooperation and unwillingness to compromise had been as much of a sticking point as Limbu's monomania and callousness. Neither would budge or even attempt to see the other's point of view. Both saw their rival as basically an obstruction to be removed or bypassed.

"So," Gage wrapped up, "that is why they called you." He grinned. "The one thing on which everyone could agree was that no one would ever agree unless another person made them."

Daria chuckled at that. "I believe it. Who made the call to the Executives?"

"I did. Ak told me to. She, of course, wants you to tell the workers to work, and that is all. I tried to, ah, be more understanding. I think that if the foreman had made the call, he would've demanded that someone spend a month digging into the chamber from the other side to study it for safety. That would not have worked well, either."

Daria glanced around and saw no one else nearby. She lowered her voice anyway. "No, I don't think it would've. I'm here now, and as you say, they all expect me to resolve this situation. It might be best if I investigated by myself. Can I go down there?" She gestured toward the shaft.

At first, Gage's expression showed alarm, his eyebrows rising, and she thought he was about to protest. However, he stopped and thought before he spoke, his mouth wrinkling. After half a minute, he nodded.

"Maybe? We could try. We would have to rig something up to let you, ah, rappel down there. That would be difficult. Very dangerous. It might be far easier with help from the workers."

Daria didn't doubt it, but involving either of the two hostile camps might create the impression that she was taking sides. She wanted to maintain the appearance of a neutral arbiter, if possible.

"What could they do to help?"

Gage glanced into the tunnel, then back at her. "They can set up a winch that will lower us. Then bring us back up."

She didn't miss his choice of words. "Us? What is this *us* you speak of?" She cocked an eyebrow.

As though it were too obvious to need explaining, Gage declared, "I would like to go down with you. I want to know what is happening, too. Plus, I can be helpful to you. It is better not to be alone."

It was difficult to argue with his logic. Still, there was something that bothered her. She looked back toward the miniature plateau where the scientists had their base camp. Dr. Limbu was nowhere in sight.

"Well, Gage," Daria countered, "I see no reason why you *shouldn't* come with me. But I must be clear on one thing. I will not let anyone use my investigation into these matters simply to restart the project on Ak's behalf. I'm not here to do her dirty work and force everyone into total compliance with her arbitrary whims."

So much for remaining neutral. Then again, she had no intention of allowing the foreman to continue his endless obstruction, either.

Gage let out a low, dry chuckle that seemed nearly cynical. It was an attitude that was foreign to him. He didn't impress her as being the cynical type.

"No, no, I understand." He raised his hands, palms outward. "I will only go down to help you find out more. Also, I must say, I am the one who discovered how Atlanticore energy interacts with the artifacts. The demonstration. That was my doing. So I am probably the best one to aid you in understanding the strange things down there."

Something in his tone of voice sent a brief chill down the back of Daria's neck. The impressive yet bizarre display with the metal disks has been weird enough when viewed in broad daylight on the surface. The idea of encountering even more obscure phenomena deep below the earth came to her married with a subtle feeling of dread.

Plus, there was still the camp's politics to contend with.

"Fine," she conceded. "You may come with me. To keep another fight from breaking out, I want you to stay in Ak's camp and keep her busy while I go and talk to the workers." She coughed. "That way, we can avoid complications."

Gage smiled. "I completely agree."

CHAPTER SEVEN

Daria waited until Gage had covered half the distance between the shaft and the scientists' terrace before she started toward the other camp at the opposite end of the clearing. Dr. Limbu needed to be distracted before she made any major moves.

Confident that they'd timed everything correctly, Daria set off around the side of the cliff face toward the temporary home of the laborers. At six or seven times the size of the academics' encampment, it wasn't difficult to find despite being located at the edge of the forest amid the trees, ferns, and shrubs.

Daria saw the mass of tents and the men lounging or strolling among them and heard the general din and buzz of their voices before she could identify any individual conversations. The overall "feel" she got of the place, so far, was that the men were trying to relax, but that tensions were still high.

A mixture of boredom and anger could be dangerous. Most of them, except the foreman, were probably at least more reasonable than Ak, but they were also far more numerous. Caution would be mandatory.

Everyone seemed to ignore Daria until she came too close for them to deny her presence. Nearest to her were two men sitting opposite one another, the first on a folding chair and the second on a tree stump, pouring drinks from a clear glass bottle. They muttered back and forth, alternating between complaints about their situation and random speculation about the weather, their pay, and what the various sports teams back in the U.S. and Canada were getting up to.

"Excuse me." She smiled and stood where she was until they looked up at her. "I would like to speak to your foreman. Boucher, I believe his name is. Can you tell me where to find him?" She couldn't see him amid the general crowd.

The one on the stump was rangy with dark skin and tired eyes. He shook his head, looked away, sipped his drink, and didn't speak.

The other guy, who was pudgy, white, and sported sideburns, snorted. "I dunno, lady. Look around. He's here somewhere." He tilted the bottle and refilled his glass, carelessly splashing a bit of it onto the ground.

Daria allowed her smile to dim to a more neutral expression. "Very well." It was likely that the two drinkers didn't know where Boucher was. It was also clear that they had no interest in helping her and wanted her to go away and leave them alone.

Walking past them, she looked around for someone who seemed more accommodating. A short, thin, olive-skinned man ambled in her direction. His face was friendly and open.

She waved at him. "Excuse me. Can you tell me where I can find Boucher, the foreman?"

The guy glanced at her without stopping. "He's taking a shit." He laughed, then trotted off and disappeared between two tents before she could ask him anything further.

Daria turned toward a group of men sitting around a small grill and cooking canned meat and potatoes. Two of them looked up at her with malevolent glares, then turned their gazes back down to their culinary duties.

The message was clear. They'd overheard Daria questioning

the others and weren't interested in wasting time on having to tell her not to bother them.

The more time she spent among them, the less welcome she felt, and the thicker and more suffocating became the miasma of hostility and repressed rage. She wasn't the cause of it, but she might end up the *recipient* of it, nonetheless.

One more attempt at questioning a mellower-looking older man failed. He simply shrugged in response to her question.

"So be it." She sighed, more to herself than to anyone else. A different strategy was in order—one which was more assertive and therefore would require a more aggressive Plan B.

It was time to fetch something from her truck.

She strolled away from the camp, making sure to move at a nice, casual, sauntering pace until she came to the mouth of the valley where the dirt track led off into the hills. Once she was out of sight of the workers, she broke into a jog.

There wasn't too much time to waste. Getting back up the few hundred meters of the track and around the curve in the road to where her truck was parked felt like it took far too long. She blamed the intensity of focus that had set in when she'd first arrived on the scene and tried to approach the camp while the argument was ongoing. It had distorted her perception of time and distance.

Reaching the vehicle at last, Daria whipped out her keys, unlocked the door, and plunged headfirst across the seat, reaching for her Uzi. Her hands closed around it, and she retracted her upper body. Halfway across the seat, the radio on her dashboard buzzed and beeped.

Cursing, she thought about ignoring it, but her employers might simply want to check on her. Daria set the gun down, snatched the microphone, and flipped the switch.

"Hello, this is Barruk. I'm somewhat busy."

Eleanor's voice responded, "Hello, this is Cervantes. I'll leave you to your work. I only want to ask one or two things. Are you all right? Is the situation under control? Over."

"Yes, for the time being. No deaths or anything like that. I must persuade the workers of something with haste. The archaeologist is making things excessively difficult. In all fairness, the workers and their foreman aren't helping. I'll check back in later. Out."

Eleanor briefly thanked her and signed off with a reminder to call her if she needed any additional aid. Daria shut the radio off, hopping down to the ground with her submachine gun in both hands. She'd attached a sling to it some time ago and hung it from her shoulder while locking up the truck. Then she thought of something.

Daria took off her jacket, only to tie it around her shoulders via the sleeves like a low cape to cover the Uzi. Astute observers would still recognize that she had something on her back. Still, going into a situation that called for negotiation first and force only as a last resort would be easier if everyone didn't see that she was heavily armed.

She trotted back to the clearing within the valley, noting that the day was growing warmer. Not exactly hot, but close enough that an hour of exertion would be sweaty and unpleasant work under the sun.

She suspected, though, that any work she might have to do would take place far underground. That was the goal, anyway.

Once back in the clearing proper, she slowed her pace again to something more casual so the men would perceive her as being coolly self-possessed and not given to hustling around on their account. Few of them paid her any attention as she returned to their camp.

Once over the threshold, a few workers glowered at her, but most were trying not to notice her presence.

It was time for a different approach. She drew a deep breath. Then...

"Excuse me!" she shouted, loud enough that her voice carried across the whole of the miniature tent city and probably across the valley to the scientists' base. "Where is your foreman, Boucher? Point me in his direction."

Most of the men, at least two-thirds or so, snapped their heads toward her, wearing dumbfounded or aggravated expressions. No one spoke or directly acknowledged her at first. She stood her ground, scanning them with a cool gaze and waiting.

After a moment, a man stood and advanced toward her, taking five steps and stopping. He wobbled a little. She could immediately tell that he'd been drinking. He wasn't utterly smashed—the foreman probably wouldn't have allowed it—but he'd probably downed a few shots of strong spirits. Enough to go to his head and addle what brains he had.

"Leave us alone, lady," he barked. "We're not helping you. Why the hell would we? Get lost."

He was a fairly young man in his middle or late twenties with deeply tanned skin and sandy blond hair, in good physical condition. He was all but bursting with energy. It occurred to Daria that the total halt in activity these last several days had probably made him antsy and aggressive, and the alcohol was undoubtedly making it worse.

She addressed him in a firm tone without being combative. "That's for your foreman to decide. Allow me to speak to him, and we can get your problems sorted out."

A handful of the workmen nearby made vague moaning or muttering sounds, and she caught a couple of curse words and half-comprehensible sarcastic comments. Before she could try a different tack, the young drunk took another heavy step forward and flung out his hands as he railed away.

"We know exactly why you're here. You," he went on, "are another one of those rich folks that come here to get fat off the work of people like us. Up in your skyscrapers back in the city, you don't give a shit what happens to us. We're only worker ants who make the money you get to spend.

"You don't care if it means sending us into a goddamn death-trap. 'Cause that's what that place is. It'll kill more people before this is over, I guarantee you that."

Daria felt as though a pipe had burst somewhere within her and was gradually filling her with scalding water. It was anger, combined with a trace of shame.

"No," she insisted, "I'm not one of those callous rich people you speak of. I came from a humble background and was only moderately successful before I became an Executioner. The reason I'm here now is to help you. We want to investigate the shaft before anyone else has to go back down there. You see?"

He didn't seem *too* drunk. He might still listen to reason and allow for the possibility that she would rather see him and his coworkers able to complete their contract in safety, collect their pay, and go home to their families.

It was futile. Full of piss and vinegar, as the English or Americans or Canadians might say, the young man wanted a fight. He would keep looking until he found one.

"Bullshit. *Bullshit!*" he cried and shoved her.

Daria had been about to take action until she realized what he was doing. If he'd tried to strike her in the face, or grab and hold her, or throw her to the ground, she would've hurt him badly. For now, he was using only the minimal amount of force it would take to make her angry. He wanted her to be the first to overreact.

He hadn't used his full strength, but it was enough to drive her back a step. She allowed it to happen and kept her balance as soon as it was over. Otherwise, she barely reacted. By now, practically the entire camp was watching.

Daria didn't look at the blond guy. Instead, she glanced at the others. "You boys all seem to enjoy pushing ladies around." The dry, cutting tone ought to shame those not addled by drink and exasperation.

If it worked on the observers, though, it only made the young man confronting her more furious. His eyes bulged and his lips contorted around his mouth. "I'll do more than give you a little push, bitch," he snarled and cocked his arm back while his hand clenched into a fist.

He was slow and made no effort to disguise what he was doing. Daria stepped toward him, allowing him to begin his clumsy and brutish swing. Then she drove her elbow upward into his jaw. His mouth was still hanging open, and he jerked back, wincing and sputtering not only from the blow itself, but because he'd bit his tongue. Blood glistened on his lips.

The man paused, froze, and stared at her in disbelief. Daria stood, waiting for his next move.

During her time in America, a man called Herschel had shown her a thing or two. He'd studied martial arts with Imi Lichtenfeld, the hand-to-hand combat instructor of the fledgling Israeli Defense Forces. The three or four months Daria had spent under his tutelage had been almost as useful as the years of street fighting experience she'd accumulated beforehand.

It didn't surprise her when the young man's disbelief gave way to rage, and he tried to tackle her head-on, overwhelming her with his greater size and upper-body strength. She stayed loose and low, yielding to his charge so easily that, with a slight shift of her body after she struck the ground, he rolled right over the top of her.

A couple of men in the impromptu audience laughed or said, "Whoa!" They hadn't expected things to play out this way. Others stood, looking incensed that she would dare to fight back.

As the man spun over himself, flopping awkwardly on the ground, Daria stood. A half-second assessment showed her two other guys, probably the blond man's friends, coming to his side to help him up. Others narrowed their eyes and moved closer to the woman who'd invaded their break so rudely.

She wasn't humoring them anymore, especially if they planned to gang up on her.

While the man who'd started the fight sputtered insults and curses, Daria whipped the jacket off her shoulders, exposed her slung Uzi, and shrugged the submachine gun into her right hand as she drew her pistol with her left.

Even the drunkest workers paused. They were smart enough to grasp that the whole game had changed.

"Hey!" someone exclaimed. "She has *two* guns!"

Daria nodded, glad he could count. She waited.

Stomping footsteps approached and another, familiar voice bellowed, "All right, enough of this crap! You hear me? Back off! That's *enough*."

Men parted as Boucher stormed through their ranks, pausing at the edge of the loose circle that had formed around Daria. He took in the situation with a glance, tensing noticeably at the sight of the firearms but hardly terrified. For all his obtuseness, he grasped that she was giving them a final chance to cooperate.

Still, Daria had no illusions about how ugly things might get. There was no guarantee that the laborers would obey their foreman's order to stand down. If they all decided to rush her...

There were three dozen or more, and possibly others still lingering in their tents. Between the two guns, she had enough 9mm rounds for each of them to get one, perhaps with a couple left over. Nice and fair. As good a shot as she was, her prospects of dropping each of them with one bullet before they swarmed her weren't encouraging.

Plus, it often took more than one bullet. Angry men lived longer than fearful ones.

So far, nothing was happening. The confrontation lay poised on the brink, ready to topple one way or another at the slightest nudge.

Daria opted for a calculated risk. She slid her handgun back into its holster. Then, gripping the Uzi with both hands, she pointed it downward, keeping it held close to her midsection—ready to bring up if needed, but no longer in a position of direct threat.

"Ah," she piped up, "just the man I was looking for." Thanks to years of practice, she *sounded* perfectly at ease. The look on half of the men's faces told her that they bought the act, too. "I would've found you much sooner, Mr. Boucher, if someone would've simply told me where you were."

The foreman jutted his chin and ambled toward her. He kept his eyes on the gun without being too obvious about it. Cowering before her would've diminished his authority in the eyes of his men, but he had enough sense to appreciate how easily she could kill him with a weapon like that.

"Yeah." He glared at several random men. "I agree. Next time, you assholes need to come get me when a lady asks to talk to me, got it?"

Sheepish nods or sarcastic comments of "Sure, boss, whatever" were his answer.

The worst of the tensions eased. The drunk young man had been carted off by his friends, probably to splash some water in his face or encourage him to lie down in a tent and take a nap. At last, Daria was able to discuss things with Boucher.

"So," she requested, "I ask you to aid me in exploring the excavation shaft. I understand that there were some highly unusual disturbances down there. If I have a look, perhaps I can solve this mystery."

The rest of the men continued to watch. Boucher was simmering but half-cooperative as he explained what had occurred. Virtually everything he said corroborated what Dr. Gurung had told Daria half an hour earlier. That was a good sign. It meant that neither was trying to deceive her.

The differences were in their attitude toward the bizarre accident. And their employer, of course.

Boucher opined, "She's been nothing but a nightmare to work with. Ain't she?" He looked around, and most of the workmen nodded. "Always pushing, pushing, and pushing some more, like she doesn't realize we're only human. Work faster, dig deeper, and ignore any of the usual safety precautions if you can. She's that way with her chump scientists, even, not only us."

Daria nodded. She didn't doubt anything the man was saying, based on her experience with Dr. Limbu.

"I'll tell you what," the foreman continued in a lower voice. "If anyone told you, 'Oh, Mr. Boucher thinks Limbu and her eggheads are to blame for those guys getting turned to smoke down there,' they're lying. I don't *think* that. I *know* it. I'm pretty sure everyone else does too."

That was roughly what Daria had assumed. Their anger, fear, and resentment were all understandable, but allowing it to flower into mindless hatred of Ak wouldn't be constructive.

She opted to shift course. "Did anyone see anything in the shaft, or the chamber, that might shed light on what happened? Whatever you saw, I would like to hear about it."

Not only Boucher but a handful of other men gave their two cents. In terms of raw information, they didn't have much; no more than Daria had already gleaned from Gage. But their attitude and choice of words were revealing.

The tension among them wasn't only due to their loathing of Dr. Limbu. It was also a fear beyond the merely physical, a kind of superstitious or quasi-religious dread.

The foreman retook his role as spokesman for the rest. "So yeah. Something ain't right down there. It's like the place buried beyond the shaft, whatever it is, is cursed or haunted. Bad stuff. Really bad."

Daria had tried to remain placid, the neutral observer hearing the men out, assessing them and their positions while never giving away her thoughts or feelings. With a case as bizarre as the present one, there was only so much she could do.

When she realized that she'd cocked an eyebrow and her face was stretching into an increasingly skeptical expression as her eyes narrowed, there was no longer any point in pretending to be objective. She might as well needle the man a little. Just enough to get a reaction out of him. Responses could be informative, after all.

"Haunted?" she offered. "I'm sure it's strange and eerie down there. We're well past the point at which people still believe in ghosts, aren't we? Doesn't the real world provide enough horrors of its own?"

Saying that might force the man to speak more openly instead of dancing around the subject and expecting her to understand his grunted insinuations.

It was also an honest expression of her feelings. After her experiences in the Third Reich's system of special camps, she had little patience for people's superstitious beliefs in dybbuks and sprites and gremlins.

Boucher curled his lips in under his teeth as though biting them to keep himself from blurting whatever his preferred reaction would've been. He looked off to the side at nothing particular, and his nostrils flared as he breathed in and out.

A second later, he turned his head back toward her. "If you were down there, ma'am, believe me. You would know what it was we've been talking about. Then you wouldn't be so high and mighty about all this, acting like we're kids scared of the boogeyman in the closet. It's fuckin' *weird* down there."

"Ohh." Daria saw her opportunity and pounced on it without hesitation. "So you're saying that I should have a look myself. That's exactly why I came to talk to you, as you would know if you'd listened a little more carefully. I'm here to resolve the conflict between your men and the good doctor's team. If people have died in an accident, it's my job to make sense of things."

The foreman blinked as though it were only now occurring to him that the situation wasn't black and white, and it might behoove him to step outside his narrow focus on his ego battle with Akshara Limbu.

Before he could change his mind and reassert his litany of complaints and refusals to budge, Daria moved in for the proverbial kill.

"If those deaths happened wrongfully, maybe someone needs to be held accountable." She allowed one of her hands to rest on her Uzi's grip. The gesture wasn't threatening, exactly, but she was quite sure that everyone noticed it.

She concluded, "Or maybe that strange chamber needs to be filled with concrete and never disturbed again, for the good of everyone. There are many possibilities. Still, I cannot figure that out, or anything else, unless I go down there and investigate things for myself."

The men's agitation was palpable. Everyone watched the pair and their argument, hanging on every word and trying to keep their emotions in check. They seemed to grasp that things would be coming to a head.

Their faces, a motley variety of men from all over the island and the world, bespoke deep exhaustion combined with an urgent need to see action taken, to have things resolved even if it made their hard lives more difficult.

Boucher again chewed on his lips as his mind churned in its efforts to arrive at the correct answer.

Instead, he asked a question. "So, who's it going to be? Will it be only you down there?"

Daria hadn't expected this. Her mind raced. Lying would be a poor idea since the valley was too small for anyone to keep a secret for long. She considered telling Gage to stay behind for the sake of appeasing the workmen—their suspicion of the scientists ran deep enough that they might object to the presence of a single researcher.

Plus, Gage had held a knife to Boucher's throat only a little earlier.

He would be too valuable. Daria had little knowledge of archaeology and might have no hope of appreciating what she was looking at without help.

She cleared her throat. "For the sake of having some assistance and getting the necessary background information, I wish to take one member of the research team with me."

Instantly, the men around her groaned or shouted in protest, and Boucher clenched his jaw while tightening the cap on his head. His bushy eyebrows appeared to bristle at her. "The men don't like that idea much, ma'am."

Daria allowed some of the exasperation to show. She sighed, closed her eyes, and held up her hand. She didn't want to look weak, but it might help to indicate as clearly as possible that their suspicions were unfounded.

"No, please understand what I mean. It will not be Dr. Limbu, but one of her better people. I'll instruct them that they're only to help me discover what happened to your people. All they'll do is explain to me what they'd learned so far about the carvings. Those might be our key to understanding all of this. I'm no archaeologist, so I'll need someone to help me."

The foreman glanced to both sides as another round of grumbling rose from the crowd, though they seemed weaker and less vehement this time. Then he focused his eyes on the Executioner.

With a sharp motion of his beefy hand, he demanded, "How do we know that this isn't some excuse to make us start digging again? You spend ten minutes standing there, then decide that it's safe and force my guys back down without really knowing what you're talking about? They won't react well to that."

Daria gave the man a slightly evil little smile. "I would be happy to allow one of your workers to accompany us. To observe, and—what's the American expression?—to keep us honest. If anyone wishes to volunteer, please speak."

Silence reigned as frowning faces looked away, or at their feet, or up at the sky. A few men coughed or sniffled. No one spoke.

Boucher's expression turned sour as it sank in that she'd outmaneuvered him. He was probably so used to Ak's one-dimensional harangues that he was out of practice when it came to negotiating with someone capable of layered subtlety.

"Fine," he declared. "We'll do it your way. We'll get everything set up to lower you and one of the dust-scratchers down that hole. But hear this, and let's everybody be clear on one thing, okay?"

Daria lifted her eyebrows a notch while staring at the man, indicating that she was listening.

He pointed a thick finger at her. "We ain't coming down there. If something happens, you're on your own, so don't expect the cavalry to ride to the rescue. You got it?"

She responded with a single slow nod. "Yes, of course. I'm sure everything will be fine."

"Good." Boucher turned to his men and shouted at them to get off their asses and set up a crane with a winch system and to fetch a couple of harnesses while they were at it.

Daria watched as about half the men hopped to it. Some of them were blatantly annoyed, whereas the others had shed their mantles of tension, as though relieved that there would finally be progress on their dilemma. The workers who didn't participate were probably the ones who weren't qualified to operate the necessary equipment. They drifted back to their tents or their food and drink.

She was about to head back to meet with Gage when Boucher took a couple of quick steps up to her side.

She stopped and looked the man full in the face. His demeanor wasn't threatening, but there was still an edge to it. He wanted to tell her something.

The foreman took a few furtive glances around. No one was within ten meters of them now that the crowd had dispersed.

"Okay, one more thing." His voice was low, a growling whisper. "I want you to swear something to me since I'm goin' out on a limb here by helping you. Promise me that if you find evidence Limbu and her team are responsible for this shit—that it's on them why those guys died down there—that I get to be there when you..." he paused. "When you do your Executioner thing."

If Daria had suspected that the man's only motive was petty vengeance on Ak for embarrassing him, she would've been disgusted. His grim, calm demeanor suggested otherwise. He simply wanted justice for the men under his care.

"Agreed, Mr. Boucher. It is, as you say, an *if*. I'll have no biases one way or another in inspecting the evidence. But *if* things are as you say, then you have a deal."

CHAPTER EIGHT

The truck rumbled down the short length of road that separated its hiding spot from the excavation site. Now that Daria was reasonably sure she had the situation under control, it would make life easier to have her vehicle close at hand.

Bustle and hubbub had arisen near the rear-center of the valley, next to the shaft. Workers shouted instructions or muttered among themselves as they set up an industrial-grade winch machine and prepared harnesses. They would only be able to lower one person at a time. With a total of two individuals heading into the caves, that wouldn't be much of an issue.

She piloted the truck off to the left of the road's mouth, coming to rest on a mostly bare patch of earth near a fern-covered slope. Here, she was about equidistant from both tent villages while also being marginally closer to the excavation shaft within the opposite cliff.

Daria shifted into "Park." A glance convinced her that it would be a few minutes yet before the workmen were ready to send her and Gage into the depths. She flipped the switch on her radio and took the microphone in hand, bringing it closer to her face as the speaker crackled. She could faintly hear the buzz of someone else talking from what sounded like a considerable distance.

Then Eleanor spoke in a rushed and harried tone. "Ms. Barruk, excuse me a moment, please."

Daria was about to make a polite remark and excuse her, but Ms. Cervantes launched straight into a rapid series of instructions and cajoling—but they were quieter and less clear. She was speaking into a different microphone, on the line with someone else.

"No, no. Try to avoid confrontation with them until we can get the rest of our security people there as backup. What we want, ideally, is for the sale to go through first so we have proof of what they're doing, *then*, if necessary, you can take them into —*mierda!*"

Gunshots *crackled*. The speaker clipped off their volume, but it was still clear what they were.

Daria started, suddenly fearful that Eleanor had come under attack, but then she blinked and shook her head. The gunshots had been secondhand—they'd come through the other radio, through Eleanor's receiver.

Eleanor's voice returned. "Mr. Katakura! Are you all right? You didn't take that shot, did you? If they shoot first, it'll be easier to justify. Please keep that in mind. Over."

"Yeah," a familiar male voice responded, though it was faint. "That was me, but only because the son of a bitch was aiming a gun at me. I might be able to talk the rest of them down, but not counting on it. Don't worry, though. I can handle this. Out."

The speaker *crackled*, and Eleanor audibly sighed. After a short pause, while Daria envisioned the elegant woman rubbing her eyes and forehead, she spoke directly to Daria.

"Ms. Barruk, are you there? Over." Her crisp, professional tone was back.

Daria almost wanted to laugh, but her gut clenched. There was no guarantee that Ty's skills, considerable as they were, would get him through *every* possible situation. Or that his luck would hold out forever.

"Yes, I'm here. It sounds as though Tyler will be too busy to offer me any aid soon. I hope he's well. Over."

It sounded as though Eleanor were lighting a cigarette. "Yes, I hope so as well. I will have to stay on the line to take his calls if he radios me again. He was in the process of infiltrating a major distribution center for the gun runners when he was discovered or ran into opposition. Now, he's in yet another firefight. You have other problems to deal with. How is the situation developing? Over."

Daria told her, briefly explaining everything that had happened so far and reassuring her that there had been no violence yet aside from the necessity of roughing up a single drunken fool who'd attacked her. Nothing serious.

Ms. Cervantes replied in a long-suffering voice, making no effort to hide her relief. "Yes, that is good. We—the Executives and I—appreciate your willingness to pursue diplomatic solutions where possible instead of simply shooting everyone who causes you any trouble. Over."

It took a moment's effort not to laugh. It almost sounded as though Eleanor were contrasting Daria with someone else, strangely enough.

"Of course." Daria heard another of the faint breathy sounds on the other end that suggested smoking. She wanted to have a cigarette too but decided against it. Shortly, she would be rappelling down into a cave, and other physical challenges might present themselves as well. "Now, my report as to what happens next and what the plan is. Over."

"Yes, go on. Over."

Daria filled Eleanor in. She'd considered withholding some of the more bizarre details of the case since she wasn't sure how her contact would react to so much strangeness and all the superstitious nonsense that went with it. It might be wiser to keep things vague, to wait until she knew more for sure before she inspired worry or doubt by repeating the workers' ill-thought-out rumors.

Then again, Daria had an odd, intuitive feeling that this case was different. Plus, Eleanor might know something she didn't.

So, she revealed everything she'd seen and heard.

Ms. Cervantes listened with patient attentiveness, not speaking in response until after Daria was finished and turned the line over to her. Then she began talking in a rapid, animated manner, stumbling over words here and there as she tried to speak English too fast in her obvious excitement.

"Executioner Barruk, that's incredible. You might not realize it, but things like this are a significant part of what the Executives wish to find out more about to begin with. A major goal is to uncover more of Atlantica's history, learn how Atlanticore came into being, and what sorts of civilizations might've existed here before modern humans arrived.

"I've personally been curious about it, as well. There *is* a history here, one which runs back many centuries, I believe, and has been buried beneath the earth for all this time."

Daria wasn't sure how to respond. She'd heard that people from Latin America placed a great deal of faith in magic, but Eleanor seemed too well-educated for such things. It was as though Daria was the only person in a room who hadn't laughed at a joke, failing to get it.

Was everyone on the island a believer in curses and dybbuks? That, in itself, was beginning to pique her curiosity.

Eleanor added, "We must not lose sight of the dangers. The situation you describe is volatile, and lives lost. Since we speak of Atlantica's history, there is another episode of it we need to remember. Over."

Daria glanced around, suddenly uncomfortable. No one had shown up to bother her so far. All seemed well. "What episode is that, Eleanor? You mean when the Americans and the Germans fought here twenty years ago? Over."

"Yes. How much do you know about that? Over."

Daria scanned her brain. She'd heard all the rumors and done some reading in the limited available material, but not much. The U.S. government had locked away the finer details. "I know some. But not everything."

She briefly summarized the information she had. A German U-boat had discovered Atlantica in 1939 and had sent a message back to Berlin, which the British intercepted. Then, the Americans claimed they'd dispatched a team to investigate.

After that the story became muddled. Some said that the U.S. team arrived and fought a Nazi task force sent for the same purpose, and there were similar whisperings of a strange disaster that had wiped everyone out.

At which point the world had forgotten about the obscure island again until a few years ago when its existence became impossible to deny—the ridiculous TINA policy notwithstanding.

According to Eleanor, furthermore, the battle between the American and German forces had indeed happened.

"Even I'm not aware of everything," she admitted, "but I have reliable sources for much of it. Both of the military task forces vanished after meddling with something buried within the island. This idea that our excavation team has—the one about a dangerous power surge from Atlanticore crystal—is the best explanation I've heard so far, but there is still much unknown to us. Please, use extreme caution in your investigation. We don't wish to lose you or anyone else. Over."

Daria nodded although Eleanor couldn't see her. "I understand. I'll be bringing one of the academics with me to study the team's findings, and we'll have someone standing by to haul us up if we must get out in a hurry. I'll check in with you when I can. Oh, and give Executioner Katakura my well-wishes. If he, ah, survives, perhaps one of us can help the other once we finish. Out."

"Yes, of course. Good luck, Executioner. Out." Eleanor switched off her radio, and Daria did likewise.

The conversation had ended not a second too soon. Dr. Gaje Gurung had approached the excavation site and was talking to someone next to the winch device. It appeared that the workers did *not* appreciate his presence. A cluster of them—arguably a small, angry mob—formed and began to seethe and roil.

"Damn," Daria grumbled. She checked to ensure that her pistol still rested in its holster and laid her Uzi on the seat of her truck, covered with an empty sack. Then she leapt down and rushed across the grass toward the scene.

A good half-dozen of the laborers were shouting things at Gage, much of it unintelligible since they kept talking over one another. Many of their comrades were glaring at the man, too.

Things could get ugly. Although, judging by the hard look in the small scholar's eyes and his attitude of absolute calm combined with total awareness, Daria was more concerned about the crowd's wellbeing than she was about Gage.

Either way, she wanted to avoid a bloodbath.

"Excuse me," she began, in a loud and clear voice that was a tad short of an outright shout but still penetrated the growing din. "Is there a problem? We had agreed that this man would accompany me during the investigation."

The noise softened to a vague rumble as most of the assembled pairs of eyes turned toward the newcomer.

The malcontents seemed to be spearheaded by a trio of women Daria hadn't noticed before. She'd assumed that the workforce was entirely male but probably should've known better.

All three of the women looked tough. Two were big and beefy with their hair tucked under caps. The third, who stood in the center and seemed to be their leader, was smaller but wiry and hard-looking, with frizzy brown hair tied back in a puffball of a ponytail.

She looked at Daria and barked, "Horseshit. He's one of them. He pulled a knife on Boucher. You're only bringing him along so you can make us dig again. Aren't you?

"Yeah. That's the plan. You go down there, do nothing but poke around for ten or fifteen minutes, then say that everything's clear, get back to work. The next time three, five, or ten of our people die, you'll say you don't know how it could've happened."

She pointed at Daria's chest as she spoke. Her two friends behind her rubbed their knuckles.

Daria shook her head. "No, that's not the case at all. I'm here as an investigator, not a strikebreaker. Dr. Gurung is the best person to help me figure out what happened to your friends. You will not be asked to start work again unless we determine that it's safe."

Resentful murmurs and sidelong glances were her response. They were all skeptical. They didn't trust anyone in authority, anyone they associated with Atlantica's notoriously treacherous and predatory elite class. Daria couldn't entirely blame them.

Still, she had a job to do.

"I made a deal with your foreman," she reminded them, holding up a finger and putting on a faintly haughty air of command. Trying to be nice and reasonable had failed. "He agreed to it, you all heard, and no one seemed to object to it at the time. If any of you are somehow unable to do what seems like a rather simple job, get out of here and send me someone else who can handle it. Anyone? No? Well, then. Please prepare to lower us."

Gage moved closer to Daria's side. His face was surprisingly neutral for a man who might've been no more than five minutes from being beaten by an enraged gang—provided that any of them got past his kukri alive. There were enough of them that it was within the realm of possibility.

The crowd hesitated. They seemed to be waiting for the mouthy woman to weigh in.

She did. "Oh, lower you, eh?" She sneered and put her hands on her hips. "Yeah, sure. But we're tired, and some of these guys had a few too many drinks. Myself, lowering that weirdo grease-ball down there," she pointed at Gage, "I might have an accident and drop him down the shaft. Tragic stuff happens, toots."

Daria stared at the woman. She took a couple of steps closer, allowing her face to fall in a feigned expression of anguished desperation, as though she were about to apologize with profuse gestures and remorse before begging for their cooperation.

It threw the salty woman off-guard. She was completely unprepared when Daria dropped the fake expression, and her fist shot out, straight from the shoulder and elbow, and connected with the woman's nose. The soft flesh flattened under Daria's knuckles, and it sounded like part of the cartilage might've crunched. A little. She didn't hit her *that* hard.

"Urgh!" The frizzy-haired woman stumbled back into the arms of her two bigger friends and shut her eyes in pain and shock. Blood trickled from her nostrils, and she sneezed, spraying crimson droplets across the grass. "Goddammit!" Her whole body trembled with rage.

The other workers, all men, gawked or squirmed, surprised and uncertain. Before any of them could do anything, Daria threw back her shoulders and chin and flashed a stern glare around the group as though daring them to act. When they hesitated, she looked back at the woman she'd slugged.

"You. Go back to the camp, have another drink, and put something cold on your nose. You're not fit to contribute to this simple task. Let someone else handle it."

The two beefy ladies behind the frizzy-haired woman's elbows took her by the shoulders and guided her away as she cursed, sputtered, and complained. Mercifully, it didn't take long for the string of obnoxious noises to die down, drowned out by the noise of the camp, the machinery, and the natural sounds of the surrounding forest.

Daria focused her gaze on the rest of them. It didn't look as though they were going to attack her or do anything else blatantly stupid. However, there was still a lingering, glowering resentment, a suggestion that they might rebel soon if not properly motivated.

"As I said before, prepare the winch." Daria waved and snapped her fingers, "Per Boucher's instructions, you're to lower us into the shaft at once. Ignore what that foolish woman said. If anyone so much as *thinks* of dropping either of us, you'd best eliminate me first since I would react *very* badly to anyone dropping Dr. Gurung."

She allowed a hand to hover near the pistol at her hip. Then she added, in a lower voice, "Once I crashed into the ground below, you'd better flee this place and hop onto the next transport off Atlantica—the earliest one you could find, even if it meant swimming out into the bay to catch it. Because if I don't report back soon, my contact will be highly curious about what happened to me."

By now, Daria could tell that the point was beginning to sink in. The defiance and hesitancy were melting away. It was time for the final blow. It was time to convince them to abandon this foolishness once and for all.

"When my contact grows curious, she'll react by sending my partner in to look for me. Executioner Katakura. Yes, *him.* I'm certain you've all heard of him. He would be most displeased, which would be unfortunate for all of you since he's not as patient as I am.

"He investigates disappearances by shooting people who refuse to answer questions. You're lucky he wasn't the first one sent to deal with this little problem. If you cooperate and respect the wishes of your foreman, your luck will continue, and Katakura won't need to deal with you at all."

Half the faces before her blanched with horror. Among the other men, eyes widened, and heads nodded. They'd all heard of Ty. While the specifics of Daria's threat were little more than a bluff, they grasped that the essence of it was true. The Executioners wouldn't allow anyone to trifle with them.

Sighs and mumbles accompanied their return to work as they prepared the winch, double-checked the distances they needed to cover, and set up lights to shine down into the darker recesses of the caves. The illumination went beyond what the sun alone could offer.

Gage caught Daria's eye. In her peripheral vision, she saw him nodding in what she assumed was appreciation, and his full lips rose in a faint smile. "I, too," he stated, "have heard of Executioner Katakura."

Daria shrugged. "Perhaps I'll be so fortunate and become as famous as he is. I'm not above mentioning his name. And what I said was no lie."

There had been no specific arrangement with Eleanor or Ty to have him check on her, but if Daria were to disappear, what she'd threatened almost certainly *would* happen, regardless.

Three or four minutes later, right as Daria was about to slip into her harness and let the workers attach her to the winch, someone approached. They were coming from the west side of the valley, where the academics' encampment was.

Daria cursed under her breath in Polish. The last thing they needed was another interruption. Especially by...

"Stop! Do you people have the *slightest* idea what you're doing?" Akshara Limbu yelled, waving as she stormed forward. Behind her were two other scientists, a man and a woman, both blank-faced and sheepish. The man carried an armload of random tools and equipment.

Gage's nostrils widened as he exhaled through them, trying not to sigh too obviously. Daria narrowed her eyes and set her face in a cool expression of mild inconvenience.

The entire crew stopped what they were doing. Daria suspected that they all grasped that the good doctor would interfere mercilessly with everything they did until she'd spoken her piece and run out of steam.

Dr. Gurung stepped toward her. "Hello, Dr. Limbu. We were about to go down. You gave me permission to accompany Executioner Barruk, yes?"

Ak placed both hands on his shoulders and stared into his eyes. "You are to gather the greatest possible amount of data while you're down there. We cannot afford anything less! That idiotic foreman has stalled enough. With all the time we've lost, and the dig paused until these people's ridiculous demands are satisfied, we *must* make up for it by taking the opportunity, *now*, to gather samples. Here!"

She reached over into the load of stuff carried by her male subordinate and produced a trio of vials along with small packets and what looked like utensils.

"You are to collect no fewer than three types of soil, composed of three different varieties of rock or clay, from three different locations within the tunnels. We must know the chemical composition of each stratum of the ground and how the Atlanticore is affecting it. And!"

After dropping the vials and instruments into Gage's hands, she reached over again and pulled free a rather bulky camera.

"And, you are to take pictures of everything, particularly the carvings in the excavated chamber where the disappearances occurred. Wait to observe, in each case, to determine if the bulb flash damages the surface in any way. Some materials are sensitive to light. If there is trace Atlanticore present, it might react to any form of photostimulation or electromagnetic power."

She stuffed the camera into Gage's arms. He blinked and awkwardly pocketed the vials, holding the camera in one hand to prepare for what came next. He raised a finger on his free hand

and opened his mouth to offer a suggestion, but his boss cut him off.

"Furthermore," Ak rambled on, "take these devices and measure the ratios of all artificial surfaces within, in case there is a secret mathematical formula at work that has escaped our notice so far. We cannot discount such possibilities! Our previous readings were cut short by the foolishness that has threatened to undo this entire expedition."

Gage accepted a ruler, measuring tape, compass, and a couple of other things Daria didn't recognize, struggling to handle them all at once. When Daria tried to take the camera from him and hold it, Ak jerked spasmodically toward her, shouting at her not to break it. Daria held the camera steady in both hands while staring straight ahead at nothing in particular.

Dr. Limbu concluded, much to the relief of everyone present. "Finally, we must collect artifacts. You must be vigilant. Pottery fragments, crystal nodes, anything that could be wiring, vessels made of metal, and any form of tool or weapon—you must gather all.

"We know that the chamber was for human usage, so objects of that sort must be present. Do not return to the surface without them! Collecting all of the above would greatly improve our ability to make up for lost time. Do not disappoint me, Dr. Gurung. You are one of the few intelligent people present. I am counting on you!"

Gage exchanged a glance with Daria. Ak, consumed in her emotions and obsessions, barely even noticed. Then he looked back at his supervisor. "Yes, I shall do my best, Dr. Limbu. It will depend on what we find. And, of course, on safety. If all goes well, I, ah, should be able to accomplish all of that or at least some of it."

Daria realized that Ak must not have been into the tunnels and had only the vaguest idea of what lay in the chamber. She was now operating on wishful thinking, *hoping* that everything she'd requested would be readily available, and demanding that Gage make her hopes come true.

The small man's sidelong glance told the whole story. Daria knew that Dr. Limbu would have to live with a certain amount of disappointment.

Fretting and talking to herself in Tamil with random English words sprinkled throughout, Ak turned away and trudged back toward her terrace, her unspeaking assistants trailing at a safe distance.

Once she was gone, one of the workmen cleared his throat. "Executioner, ma'am. We're ready. Put this harness on, and we'll get you secured. If you want to check the winch for safety or have, uh, Dr. Gurung do it, that's fine."

"Yes," said Daria, "we will, but thank you."

The man nodded. "We also found a second cord, so if you two would prefer, we can lower both of you at about the same time. It'll have to be slow going if we do it that way, though. More strain on the machinery, easier for things to go wrong. Oh, and uh, let's see if we can find a bag for all that stuff. Might make life easier."

Gage smiled with relief. His hands bristled with random pieces of scientific hardware. "Undoubtedly."

CHAPTER NINE

Despite the increased risks, Daria and Gage had agreed that they would prefer to be lowered together rather than separately. It meant that neither of them would be alone at the bottom, waiting for the other. Plus, it created a situation where the risk was shared equally by Gage, the representative of Dr. Limbu's team, and Daria, the representative of the Executives funding the whole operation.

Thus, there was double the incentive for the workers to be careful and avoid any unintended mishaps.

One of the men above called, "Whoa! Easy there. Try not to make sudden movements or swing around. We got to keep you both steady so you don't get twisted around each other."

Daria swayed. She'd tried to adjust her position since the harness was digging into her armpit and now swayed back and forth in the darkness and clammy air, her legs dangling and kicking at nothing.

She came close to Gage, but he held still and narrowly avoided her bumping into him. The workmen stopped the winch for a second until the Executioner's position stabilized. "All right." She aimed her voice up. "You may start again."

The metallic whining of the machine resumed, and the pair's descent into the depths of Atlantica continued.

Since the shaft was at an angle rather than straight down, they sometimes found their feet connecting with stone and had to carefully step into the void to continue the journey. The slope's degree was irregular, though. Sometimes it was approximately a right angle. Other times it was close to being a sheer drop.

Daria felt that the harness was secure if nothing else. It had fit her properly with a bit of adjustment. Gage had checked it thoroughly. He'd been lowered into the tunnels before, after all, so she trusted his experience.

She was far from a mild-mannered or easily frightened woman, but Daria had to admit that she was uncomfortable.

It was the lighting, more than anything. When she'd looked into the shaft earlier, she'd badly misjudged the distance and depth. It was a far longer drop into the subterranean hole than it had appeared at first.

Plus, the sun's angle had shifted so that less natural light was available to illuminate the deeper reaches. The electric lamps the team had set up, as well as the flashlight Daria carried, seemed pitifully inadequate to the task of banishing the thick blackness below them. The shadows in the cave were like a substance, something with a material existence rather than simply the absence of light.

Daria considered striking up a conversation to make the descent less ominous. Her new partner beat her to it.

Gage cleared his throat. "If I may be permitted to ask, Ms. Barruk, do you have your own hypothesis? About what happened that terrible day. I am curious to hear your opinion."

Above them, the metal whining of the winch seemed far away, while the dark, cavernous tunnel below was growing bigger as if in welcome.

Daria paused, thinking. "I don't know, Dr. Gurung. I'm no expert on such things. Without knowing more, my guess is no better than that of any other person. Most of what I've heard is curious. Strange, I mean. It doesn't make sense unless there is something else yet for us to discover.

"The idea that it might've been too much power surging through the Atlanticore crystals...it makes *some* sense. Atlanticore is volatile. But I don't know. What about you? You seem almost more like a fighter, but you're a scientist. Why is that?"

She looked at him, waiting for his answer. Partly, she'd asked to take the pressure off herself, to avoid having to think too hard about what might await them down below. She also wondered about the small man's background. There were things about him that he didn't advertise to the world.

"Oh." Dr. Gurung turned his face away from hers. His shoulders hitched up a notch, and it looked like there might've been a flush in his dark cheeks. "I am withholding speculation for the time being. We must study the chamber more. I was not there the day the team disappeared, which was also the first day we tried to do a serious examination of the carvings."

They came to another area of the shaft that was more gently angled, and their feet found purchase on the rock as they half-walked down it before once again pushing off into the air. The temperature was dropping rapidly. The day's warmth was all but gone, and Daria wished she'd brought a hat and gloves.

She prodded him further. "I see. That is wise, perhaps. I'm curious, though. The first I saw of you was when you stepped in to protect Dr. Limbu from the foreman. I had to wonder—where does a scholar of your mature age get a knife like that? Of still greater importance, where does he learn to use it? Most scientists cannot make similar claims."

Once again, the man tensed within his harness. Daria felt a twinge of remorse for making him uncomfortable. He'd been nothing but nice and helpful to her.

She had to know. Not only to satisfy her curiosity but because when working with people—and potentially trusting her life to them—she'd always found it useful to know what they were capable of and who they truly were.

"I was a Gurkha," he confessed. His tone was hesitant. Daria took it for embarrassment at first, but that made no sense. She decided, instead, that it was humility. The man didn't want to seem like he was bragging.

She kept her tone neutral. "Oh, really?"

"Yes." He paused, once again unsure how much he should divulge. "A damn good one. If I may say as much."

Daria laughed. The statement sounded a bit silly in the man's heavy accent, yet mostly it was his commingled desire to take pride in himself and his desire not to be crass which had struck her as so funny. There was no malice or mockery in her laughter, though.

"I suspected as much. I've heard of the Gurkhas, and I recognized your kukri. Now that I think about it, I've never heard of a Gurkha who *wasn't* damn good. They have an impressive reputation. The British speak very highly of them. Of you."

Gage didn't respond, perhaps unsure what to say given his ambivalence and humility. "Well, yes, we do our best. I served in the Second World War in many places throughout Asia. I saw battle quite often in Indochina and the Philippines.

"I might have participated in the invasion of Japan if the Americans had not dropped their bombs first and ended the war. When it was over, I returned home to Nepal. For some few years, I farmed the land, as my family always has."

Daria frowned. "I thought Nepal was too mountainous for farming."

Her companion chuckled softly. "Parts of the country are very high and icy. There are many low plains as well, with a warm climate and fertile soil. Like India, our neighbor."

"I see." For all the illicit merchandise she'd handled from every corner of the world, Daria couldn't claim to be an expert in the minutiae of geography. "How did you become a scientist?"

"It is a most boring story. Far less exciting than the war, I am afraid. I saved money from my military pension and farming until I could afford to attend university. I studied archaeology and earned my doctorate. Atlantica offered me many opportunities to work on things that few others have had the privilege to study. So I came here and joined Dr. Limbu's team."

Daria didn't find it boring. She blinked in the near darkness, reflecting on how interesting the man's life must've been and how far he'd come after striving so hard. He'd matter-of-factly relayed everything without boasting or otherwise behaving as though he were anything special.

Before Daria could comment or offer her congratulations, though, he asked a question.

"Tell me, Executioner Barruk, about your experiences. Were you...ah, forgive me if this is rude to ask...were you old enough to do anything exciting during the war?"

His attitude had grown sheepish again. Despite genuine curiosity, the awkward hesitancy in his voice meant he knew he was potentially treading into territory that his new friend might not wish to discuss.

He was probably also worried about misjudging her age in one direction or the other. Daria was used to it. She'd retained a relatively youthful face for closing in on forty, at least in the right lighting conditions, but her graying hair sometimes made her look older.

Mainly, though, her mind simply came to the threshold of many things she didn't want to think about. None of which were Gage's fault.

"I wasn't quite old enough to serve in a military capacity," she told him. "I found more 'excitement' than I wanted, all the same. Like everyone else during those dark times, I did what I had to do to survive. That's all."

In her dealings with all manner of people over the years, she'd learned to calibrate her tone to get the desired effect nine times out of ten. If she succeeded in this case, Gage would grasp that she didn't want to talk about it and that she wasn't angry at him.

He hesitated, needing a moment to digest her words. "Oh, yes. Forgive me for prying. I am glad you made it here, today. Let us focus on the present instead of the past, then."

"Thank you."

The floor below them grew closer, and as the slope flattened out somewhat, their feet came down against an uneven rocky surface near the shaft's bottom. From there, they could walk the remaining short distance to the horizontal tunnel, which would lead them to the mysterious buried chamber.

Daria strolled forward. The line hooked up to her harness went a tad slack, and she reached around to unhook it.

Gage noticed what she was doing and insisted, "Wait. There is a stone here for us to put the lines on. Then they will be secure when we return."

"Ah, good idea," she conceded.

Forward they walked, past the rougher edges of the hole dug through the cliff and into the beginnings of the finer, more orderly hallway beyond. The pale beam of Daria's flashlight found a stalagmite that she assumed to be the rock Gage mentioned.

The Gurkha went ahead of her, detached the cord from his harness, and looped the hook around the stone spire so that it lay taut against it. Daria did likewise. Then she turned and called, "All right. We're at the bottom. The lines are secure."

"Good," a man's voice replied. "We'll have someone waiting. Holler when you're ready to come back up or if you need anything."

She would have to trust that they meant it, but it was impossible not to perceive the undercurrent of fear and loathing in his tone. Not hatred of her at this point. Of the place itself.

Daria looked ahead and shone the flashlight around, illuminating the hallway ahead. It seemed to end at an irregular stone mass, as well as the branching path off to the side that presumably led to the chamber. Their footfalls had a disturbingly flat, muffled sound. She'd somehow expected that everything down here would echo.

As they drew closer to the chamber, she stopped. The atmosphere was all wrong. Around the corner, she glimpsed what looked like an intricately carved wall. The indistinct sight of it, and knowledge of its burial on this forgotten island for so long, drove her to stillness.

The sheer antiquity of the place—the sense of it having been hidden by intentional or semi-intentional design, only to be stumbled upon now by people who could scarcely comprehend its secrets. Daria grasped at once why the workers were afraid.

The chamber gave off an air of the sacred.

Not sacred in a way that was lovely or comforting. It was a judgmental, wrathful kind of sanctity, a sense that she was trespassing somewhere mortals and sinners weren't supposed to tread, and their insolence might well be punishable.

Unbidden and unwanted, memories welled up from the deep pools at the bottom of her mind. They were things from her childhood before her parents died…before Europe became an abattoir of barbed wire and scorched earth for the second time in as many generations.

Her mother and father had been deeply religious and had insisted on raising their daughter with a firm grounding in the traditions and rituals of Judaism. They kept kosher, observed the Sabbath, attended synagogue regularly, and sent Daria to a *yeshiva* when she was of the appropriate age. They had also read to her from the Torah, nodding with its words and looking into her eyes to ensure she was paying attention.

"Listen," her mother had intoned, "for this part is important, Daria. The Holy of Holies, within the Tabernacle in the First Temple. No one was pure enough to enter, save the High Priest, and he only once per year on Yom Kippur. He must be holy enough to stand before that which dwells within. Any who were impure would be struck dead by the power of the Lord."

That part had always frightened her, but she got the message. The feelings she'd had as a little girl, listening to her parents discuss such things, had remained dormant for many, many years. The things she'd seen in real life had banished all thought of superstition—or faith—from her mind.

Or so she'd thought.

It took Daria a short time, a few thumping heartbeats' worth, to notice that Gage was looking at her. Examining her, although his expression wasn't unkind.

"Try not to have fear," he suggested, raising an open palm and attempting a smile. "There is something strange in the air down here. We all felt it. Our best guess is that it is like an electrical charge in the air, as from a thunderstorm. But not true electricity; the energy, rather, that is generated by the Atlanticore crystals."

Daria nodded, blinked, steeled herself, and put on a mask of relaxation. She couldn't allow her dread to interfere with the task at hand. In truth, though, Dr. Gurung's explanation had changed nothing. The powers of Atlanticore were as miraculous, as close to supernatural, as anything she'd witnessed.

Still, for the sake of giving herself more time to adjust, she suggested that they start by going straight ahead and briefly examining the unfinished dig area at the end of the hall. Then the chamber.

Gage nodded. "Very well. We found nothing there, but perhaps it is worth another look."

Keeping her eyes focused forward, Daria strode to the end of the passage. It seemed longer than she'd anticipated, but given the distortion of her earlier view from the surface, the extra distance wasn't really surprising.

She also noted that the walls in some places showed flat, smooth masonry where the crew had chipped away enough of the native rock and dirt to expose it. How big was the complex? Had they discovered a mere shrine, a small treasure vault? Or was this the edge of an entire underground city?

At the end of the hall, there was nothing but bumpy, jagged rock. Dust covered the floor. The walls showed nothing they hadn't already seen.

Gage said, "The workers, and Dr. Limbu, thought this hall might bend around toward the chamber from the other end. Alas, the accident happened before they could finish their dig."

"Yes." Daria inhaled. "Let us go." There was no use putting it off any longer.

She allowed Gage to lead the way and kept her eyes unfocused until they finally stepped into the strange room where five souls had vanished and where the beating heart of the mystery seemed to be.

She looked up and around. Her flashlight was almost unnecessary since a soft blue luminescence bathed the entire chamber. What she saw in the glow sent her face into slack-jawed wonder. She could only stare.

Almost the entirety of three walls were carvings and friezes, intricately whorled like artistic interpretations of real-life scenes interspersed with the hieroglyphics of a long-lost script. The bulk was concentrated near the latitudinal center of the walls, about a meter and a half from the floor. Similar work formed all the corners, including those by the ceiling and in thinner strips above and below.

What truly stunned her was the crystal. It was Atlanticore, without a doubt, interwoven with the friezes like a cascade or current that ran from scene to scene and phrase to phrase. It cropped up in large swells of azure here before thinning to a wire-sized line in other places and pulsed with light.

Daria blinked and whispered, "Have you discovered what this place was for? What are the theories so far?"

Gage stepped in. "I am sorry, but no. There is still too much we do not know. The accident cut our progress short as things were growing interesting. We do not even understand how this chamber could be. Especially concerning the crystal. Look."

He pointed, tracing the tortuous path of the bright blue vein through a frieze that seemingly depicted figures arranged in celebration. "It is continuous. What is the word...seamless. As though it were all a single, great, smooth piece behind the walls.

"It does not have a truly crystalline structure with different facets. Whoever carved this room would also need great skill to shape the Atlanticore in such a fashion. It is nearly impossible for this to occur by the work of nature alone."

Shaking her head, Daria advanced, running her fingers along the stone but avoiding the crystal itself. It was beautiful, and for a moment she was lost in wonder.

Then she looked toward the far wall and the floor in front of it. Daria stopped. Ahead of her was something she'd expected to see, but it still wasn't pleasant.

Three long, irregular scorch marks marred the surface, patches of black soot and burnt stone in roughly ovoid shapes with ragged edges that bespoke the sudden violence that had created them. They weren't shaped like human beings, exactly. However, a full-grown man could've laid down inside one and found it a cozy fit.

Gage sighed. "Yes, I am sad to say, this is where it happened. Those poor people. I had tried to make friends with all of them. They were good men and women."

Daria moved closer and squatted to examine the centermost mark. Next to it, and to the other two as well, were small lumps of what looked like scorched deadwood and twisted fragments of metal.

"Tools," she breathed. "These are what's left of the tools they were using to excavate and study the chamber." A shudder ran through her, and she stood so the motion made it less obvious.

She wrapped her arms around her torso, conscious once

more of how chilly it was this deep underground. That was far from the only reason she shivered, though.

The wonderment and awe inspired by the carvings and odd continuous vein of Atlanticore faded, replaced again by the childish fear of the unknown and the dread of punishment. Seeing the tools somehow made it worse. It seemed more real, more personal. If the wrath of God was a thing that truly existed in the world, the evidence of it lay right at her feet.

Gage stood by her side. He did and said nothing, but there was an unspoken offer of help or support if she requested it. Otherwise, he waited for her next reaction.

Daria only stood at the faceless patches of blasted stone.

Her mouth opened, and almost without conscious thought or choice on her part, a passage from the Talmud came out. "'And fire went forth from before the Lord and consumed them. And they died before the Lord.'"

CHAPTER TEN

Gaje Gurung asked the obvious question. "What shall we do, Executioner?" He unslung the bag he'd carried over his shoulder, the one containing Dr. Limbu's ridiculous profusion of scientific instruments.

Daria glanced at him. "Well, I would say that you should record anything you can, or take measurements and readings if you can do so without damaging anything or potentially starting another...reaction. We don't want to end up like these people." She gestured at the scorched floor.

"Of course," Gage agreed. "If I may suggest, it might be best to simply draw out the carvings in a notebook so that we may study them from afar. I could try to take a photograph, as well, but I worry about how the crystal would react to the flash. See how your light affects it?"

Daria moved the flashlight's beam slowly over a larger area of the glowing blue stone and noticed that it shone brighter, as though somehow absorbing the rays and feeding upon them. She moved it away, and the crystal returned to its normal intensity. "Yes. Use your pen and notebook. If Ak tries to curse you out when we return to the surface, I'll happily tell her to shut up."

Her partner's mouth clamped tightly shut, although his chin and lips moved weirdly, as though he were trying not to laugh. "Very well. Let me know if you need help with anything."

He fished around in his bag and patted the pockets of his shirt and pants until he found a small pad of paper and a pencil, then he set to work transcribing the runes and friezes. He drew quickly, making notes in the margins, and sidestepped from place to place, intending to do the main central carvings first before moving to the less prominent upper and lower ones.

Daria stared at the three scorch marks. Something wasn't right. With a faint but rising sensation of nausea, regret, and long-repressed fear, she grasped that she would need to dig once again into the mental grave of dark memories.

Seeing how these people had died and what remained of them —or should have—took her back twenty-one, perhaps twenty-two years. More than half of her lifetime ago, back in Poland. It didn't seem that long.

Daria had still been in her late teens during her time in the camp. She wasn't a child—she'd been caring for and supporting herself before then after her parents died. However, many of the other inmates had still thought of her as a "young girl" and had doted on her accordingly. At least, the ones who weren't so reduced to animalism by their brutal conditions that they thought of her as nothing more than a potential rival for their next meal.

Sometimes, the camp authorities requested volunteers to perform certain tasks. Those who offered their labor for these extra jobs might receive small rewards; an extra crust of bread, for example, or simply time spent doing something different from the endless forced labor pressed upon them all to wear them down while serving the Third Reich's war machine.

Daria had initially wanted to volunteer, more out of curiosity than anything. But she was a late arrival, and an older man—she was fairly sure his name was Julius—had stepped in and forbidden her from doing so.

"No, Daria. You stay here. I'll go instead. It isn't the sort of thing a young woman like you should have to do. Maybe later, when you're more worn down, and there's nothing else for you if it comes to that. Keep your innocence for now."

She'd protested, thinking he was patronizing. She considered her period of innocence to have ended years ago. Still, she could tell that he was legitimately concerned for her as well. He'd been adamant, though, and the other inmates—the ones who'd already been there for months or years—had backed him up.

Julius had gone off to help carry the corpses to the incinerator. Daria didn't find out that was what the job entailed until her fifth or sixth week. By then, the other things she'd seen or experienced were already numbing her to the horror of it all.

One night, Julius had begun babbling about the details of his extra volunteer gig. He was growing bony and probably had a fever since the weather was growing cold by then. While Daria tried to sleep, he talked and talked about the responsibility he'd taken on himself. She lay in her bunk, staring at the ceiling, and his words never entirely left her.

He'd particularly described how he began to think of bodies as piles of ash in waiting. Based on the person's size at their time of death, he could usually predict how much ash would be left over when the business finished. If he had to clear out an incinerator after someone else had filled it, he could usually guess the size of the person disposed of.

The other inmates told him to shut up, and after some minutes, he did. The damage had already occurred, though.

Daria blinked. Her whole body shuddered, and she felt sick. However, she'd learned to banish the episodes quickly enough over the years, and she forced the memories back down into the dark pool at the bottom of her mind. She'd retrieved the information she required for the task before her.

"Gage," she began in a soft voice. She didn't bother to look up but heard him stop moving and scrawling. "Something isn't right here. There isn't enough ash for even one person left in these spaces, let alone three people along with their clothing. There would have to be more. It makes no sense."

He walked across the chamber and stood behind her shoulder. "I had not thought of that. Do you think it could have... No. Not underground."

She nodded, assuming he meant the wind. "There's no breeze down here. No rain, no weather conditions that might've scattered, dispersed, or washed away the remains. Any remnants of these people should've stayed right here on the floor. Yet, there's almost nothing. Only the scorch marks on the stone and the fragments of their tools."

Gage was silent as he rubbed his eyes. He murmured something in his native language, then added in a hushed tone, "Why, yes. That is true."

He seemed legitimately surprised, but Daria had to be thorough if she was to conduct a proper investigation. "Did you, or anyone else on the research team, or any of the workers, *anyone* —did you gather up the ashes or remains of these people? Did anyone disturb them, or does anyone remember what they saw?"

The Gurkha knelt and examined the scorch marks more closely. "No, we did not. We did not even stop to extinguish the flames on the burning clothes or gather up the tools that were left. The workmen who were down here will give you the same story as what I have said. I asked them myself."

"Tell me more," Daria insisted. "Recount what happened, exactly as you remember it."

He'd already told her earlier. She recalled most of the details, but at the time, they were both more concerned with the overall chain of events. Now, what mattered were the specific factors pertaining to the vanished scholars and workers. Those were what Daria focused on and what she pressed him to discuss.

After the flash of terrible light and the echoing screams, it took a couple of minutes before either the people from the encampments or the workmen blocked off in the other corridor could reach the carved chamber. Everyone, including Gage, had risked falling by descending the shaft more quickly than they should've. They all knew it was an emergency.

They'd spent only a moment examining the chamber. They saw nothing except the burned patches of stone and the flaming coveralls that had belonged to the three unlucky laborers. Everyone was terrified that another flash might be forthcoming, and they would suffer the same fate.

The group that had crowded into the depths in the hope of rescuing their comrades had fled for their lives. No one else had been down the shaft ever since—until now.

Daria rubbed her chin. She wanted a smoke but was leery of how the curious charge in the air might react to fire, clove fumes, or anything else. Not to mention she might need to climb out of this shaft in a hurry, and it would help if she didn't impair her lungs.

"Dr. Gurung, Gage," she intoned, "I hate to agree with something Ak says, but in this case, I'm afraid I must. It's at least *possible* that some or all of those five people might still be alive. I know it sounds mad. There's simply no good evidence of their deaths to prove otherwise. These dark patches couldn't be their final resting places unless someone removed a great deal of ash. Do you think it possible that someone might've snuck down here at night, after the incident, and done that?"

Gage shrugged. "Perhaps? It seems doubtful to me. No one wanted to come down here. No one had any reason to do that."

Daria was inclined to agree with his assessment. Nevertheless, she made a mental note to interview the workmen who'd been in the shaft when the flash occurred, as well as the other researchers who'd joined Gage on the impromptu rescue mission.

While she was thinking it over, Gage wandered over to the

chamber's far side, where chunks of stone and dirt still clogged whatever further portion of the carved complex lay beyond. "There is no way someone could slip through there. They could not replace this rubble behind them so quickly. But look! There, at that marking. I had not seen it before."

Daria's eyes followed his finger to a particular spot on the wall. "Marking? What do you mean by that?" It was possible that his intended meaning was something else, but he didn't know the proper English word.

He grimaced, his mind racing as he thought of the best way to express himself. Daria gave him a moment while she studied the wall.

Gage had pointed at a portion of the bas-relief that banded the center of the walls. It showed an image of what looked like human figures gathered around a tree whose branches extended in multiple directions into the sky. Blue crystal filled the tree's outline, aside from a single major branch on the left.

"That." Gage indicated again. "The place where there is no crystal. Do you see? It should be there. We saw that formation previously. I recall noting it myself, yes. Crystal filled all of those branches. It is gone now. And...look more closely."

Daria leaned in, her gaze fixed on the empty tree-branch carving. There were slight deformations in the surrounding stone, including some scuff marks and general chipping that looked sharp. Fresh, perhaps.

"Are those tool marks? Do you have instruments that would leave markings like that?"

"We do," Gage confirmed. "But it could have been made by other things, possibly."

Daria somehow doubted it. "Could it be that one of your people tried to break loose a section of the embedded Atlanti-core?" She paused, then added, "For study, I mean." It seemed wise to be charitable, to give the vanished researchers the benefit of the doubt and assume innocuous motives of them. So far.

Gage extended his arms and waved while shaking his head. "No, no, no. We would never do that. That would be a terrible error. Very bad ethics. Bad form. It could ruin everything. There was so much more for us to uncover here before we even knew how far the carvings go and what we are dealing with. To take a piece of it, at this stage, would be like..."

He hesitated, seeking the right simile. "Like peeling a piece off a fine painting before you have seen the full picture! Our team would not do such a thing."

Daria nearly pitied the Gurkha. He was a good man. Despite his wartime experience and globetrotting, he was perhaps operating from the naivete one might expect of someone who *hadn't* spent most of his adult life in the company of smugglers and criminals.

Unlike Daria. She was less forgiving in assessing people's motives. The time for giving the benefit of the doubt was over.

"Such a strip could be worth a great deal of money," she grimly muttered.

She took another step closer to the frieze and risked shining her flashlight around the edges of the crystal bas-relief to get a better look at the damaged area.

Up close, the havoc wrought upon the stone was more serious than she'd thought at first glance. Someone had sheared away an entire hand's breadth of stone—a fact confirmed by pebbles and dust near her feet. It appeared that something had been driven deeper and deeper into the rock until small fissures opened all through that portion of the wall. Hairline cracks ran through nearly a third of the carving.

Daria motioned Gage over to look at it more carefully, then inquired what could've caused it.

The look of disappointment on the small man's face, the dawning realization that his coworkers might not have been as upstanding as he'd believed, was a bit sad. Daria couldn't afford to entertain people's pleasant illusions if she was to get to the bottom of this.

Gage let out a heavy sigh. "I see now. I cannot be certain. If I must guess, I will say that someone probably did this with one of the small backpack jackhammer units, which the workers carried. Not a proper tool for this sort of archaeology. It is for breaking stone, not taking delicate samples."

Daria frowned. "I was afraid of that. It might've been one of the workers, then, instead of the scholars. Or perhaps two people agreed to collaborate. Maybe all five." She looked around the chamber, taking in the totality of the place and weighing her options.

Dr. Gurung had taken out his notebook to double-check his prior sketch of the tree carving. After confirming that the whole thing had been inlaid with crystal before, he turned back to the Executioner. "What now, Ms. Barruk?"

She tapped the ends of her fingers on her lips and swiveled toward the scientist. "I have two things that we must do next," she explained, her expression grim, "and I don't like the thought of either of them."

CHAPTER ELEVEN

Riding the winch back up wasn't as eerie or intimidating as the initial descent had been. Rather than being lowered into a black pit where uncanny deaths or disappearances had taken place, they were returning to the normal world of light and life. Still, the increased physical difficulty almost canceled it out.

"Oof," Daria grunted. Her gaze snapped up toward the square of fading daylight up above. "Be careful! Slow down. You aren't pulling us straight up, remember?"

A brief chorus of slurred voices attempted to respond, but she couldn't distinguish the words. Somehow she doubted she was missing anything important.

Gage, next to her on his line, seemed to be having less trouble than she. Despite being older and slightly overweight, he was surprisingly agile and had good stamina. He hovered as close to her as he could while being polite, as though waiting for her to ask for help but hesitant to offer it of his own accord.

The winch *buzzed* and *whined*. Since the shaft was at an angle —or rather, a series of angles—returning to the surface was less an example of being given a ride than it was a case of mechanically assisted rock climbing.

On the shallower portions of the slope, the endless tug of the cord simply helped propel them forward. When the rock gave way to short, sheer cliffs or steeper ridges, the pair had to seek out the best handholds and footholds before the winch dragged them straight into solid rock, bashing them against it or scraping them along. So far, Daria had avoided either.

It wasn't easy. She cursed herself for not quitting smoking when she was younger.

Gage glanced sidelong at her. "Are you all right, Ms. Barruk?"

They hopped over a disturbingly jagged shelf of rock, and the lines pulled them more or less into empty air for a moment before they reconnected with the earth. "Yes," she retorted, trying not to grit her teeth. "I'm perfectly fine. In particular now that we're almost to the top."

The small crew left to operate the machine watched them with a faint mixture of amusement and concern, although tired boredom dwarfed both of these emotions. Despite the fact that there was little real work for them to do, it had been a long day. The sun would set soon. They probably wanted to get back to their tents, their drinks, and their card and dice games.

At last, the pair came close enough that the darkness of the excavation shaft fell away behind them, and two of the workers stepped forward to offer them each a hand and pull them the rest of the way up. The winch machine fell silent, and the crew helped them out of their harnesses.

Daria thanked them and told them that they could go back to their camp. "Please tell your foreman that I would like to speak to him soon. I'm sure he's curious to hear what I have to say."

They looked skeptical and squinted at the prospect of disturbing their temperamental overseer at this hour, but they nodded in agreement before wandering off.

Gage lingered. Daria turned toward him. "Don't tell anyone what we found. I'm sorry to ask you to lie, but it's important that we not give everything away too soon. Show Ak your drawings. That should be enough to keep her happy for now."

The small man gave a deep nod. "Yes, I can do this. The others will be curious about everything. But I understand. You must find out more before we tell them everything. Will you be here through the night?"

Daria wasn't sure of that yet and said so. "I'll have to check with my employers and decide how best to handle this."

She stared at the horizon, then looked back at Dr. Gurung and squeezed his hand. "Thank you. I appreciate all the ways you've helped me."

By that, she meant more than anything Gage's willingness to keep Akshara Limbu busy and stop her from getting underfoot while Daria continued her investigation. Also his aid in everything else and his concern for her safety during the climb out.

His smile once more held a mixture of faint embarrassment at being put on the spot and legitimate pride in his actions. "It is nothing. You are welcome. We will speak again soon, I'm sure."

Daria watched him wander off toward the terrace. Perhaps it was her imagination, but she thought she could hear Dr. Limbu calling for him already.

Drawing a deep breath, Daria rushed over to her truck. There was no sign that anyone had molested it. The doors remained locked. She checked her Uzi, which was where she'd left it, hidden under the empty sack.

The entire crew had seen her brandish the gun earlier, so everyone knew she had it, but her threat of what Executioner Katakura would do must've cowed them all into leaving her vehicle and gear alone.

She contemplated trying to call Eleanor Cervantes on the two-way radio and reporting in. She could do that later. Daria concluded that it was far more important to get what she needed from the foreman—information. He would know better than anyone what to make of the jackhammer situation.

When Daria arrived in the workers' tent city, no one made any effort to greet her or direct her toward Boucher. She chewed her lip in irritation, not looking forward to a repeat of the unpleasantries from earlier.

"Excuse me," she announced. "Where is your foreman?"

The voices died down, and eyes turned toward her. This time, two men stood with relatively accommodating expressions. One even took his hat off. The other was among those who'd hauled her up from the hole.

The latter beckoned. "Ma'am. Right this way. We mentioned to him that you wanted to talk. He said he was busy but to send you over anyway."

"What could he be busy with? None of you are working, and it's getting dark anyway. Is he supervising the distribution of ace cards and shot glasses?"

The young man who'd removed his hat snickered at that, but neither of them ventured an answer.

A minute or two later they came to a tent toward the camp's rear, set a couple of meters apart from most of the others, and pitched between the thick trunks of two trees. A low ridge, perhaps two meters high, lay at its back. A faint orange light burned inside.

"Here," said one of her guides. "We'll fetch him."

After a short, shouted exchange, Boucher emerged from the tent, looking tired and irritable. "Well, I'm glad you made it out." He scanned Daria up and down. "If you need to discuss things, let's hear it. I need to make plans to resupply this damn camp, you know."

Daria smiled. "May we speak in private?" She glanced at the two younger men, who nodded politely and wandered back to the main camp.

Boucher scowled. "That doesn't sound good. This doesn't *look* good. Don't want the men to think you're doing me any favors, you know."

Daria raised a hand. "You need not flatter yourself. This is strictly business. I thought you might want to hear my findings. It was a productive day."

The foreman grumbled and motioned for her to follow. He held open the tent's door-flap, and she ducked in. A lamp sat near the edge of a table with a bottle of whiskey at the other end, along with two chairs. A bedroll occupied the far corner next to a small pile of effects and supplies. The men certainly didn't live in luxury here.

Boucher gestured for Daria to sit at the table. He did likewise, settling into the bigger of the two chairs.

"All right," he rumbled, laying his big knobby hands on the little table and leaning forward. The gesture was somehow both a sign that he was relaxing and an admission that he was steeling himself for the worst. "Let's have it. What did you find? And what do you need from me?"

Daria deliberately waited for three or four seconds before she spoke. There was no immediate rush, and she wanted to take a measure of the man's attitude.

He was at once skeptical and accommodating. The inner tension and defensiveness were still there, but he was beginning to warm up to the idea that Daria might be here to help. Her best guess was that he would be willing to aid her if she didn't threaten him or push him to do too much too quickly.

There was only one way to find out.

She took out a cigarette and gave him an inquisitive look. He waved vaguely; he certainly hadn't struck her as the type who would object to someone smoking in his presence. She produced her lighter and lit the end of the clove, taking a long draw before blowing it off to the side.

"Mr. Boucher. First of all, your people didn't miss anything obvious. They gave an accurate report about what was in those tunnels before they fled. However, there were two particular details which they overlooked in their hurry to get out. I believe that these things might point us toward a solution to this mystery. All I need from you so far is a bit of information."

He grunted and nodded. "Yeah, yeah. Go on."

She elaborated, telling him how they'd gone back into the carved chamber and examined the burned patches where the three workers had supposedly died, as well as the carvings themselves. She included the damaged portion that was missing its vein of crystal. She avoided spelling out her suspicions or conclusions. It made more sense to lay out the facts and observe the way he reacted.

The foreman had a rather good poker face, but she saw mounting discomfort. At first, she wondered if there was some guilt on his part, whether he'd had a hand in whatever wrongdoing had led to the fiasco underground and the stalemate between his team and the academics.

She doubted it. The man's low-simmering hostility was more likely a defense against suspicion laid against his men. Or, of course, the sheer weirdness of the case.

Daria wondered if Boucher was a believer in the supernatural. The toughest and most no-nonsense of men could sometimes be frightened with surprising ease by anything that suggested magic, ghosts, curses, unknown creatures, or sheer uncanny bad luck.

His hands began to dig into the surface of the table. "So, what are you trying to say? You think one of my guys tried to steal this crystal and it blew up and killed them all? Or that they all faked this whole thing? I don't know how they would pull *that* off."

Daria finished her cigarette and extinguished the butt between her fingers. She noticed a rusty metal bucket in the corner of the tent and flicked it in with the rest of the garbage.

"I'm not certain yet." It was the truth. "I hope you can help me narrow down the possibilities. Regarding the damaged carving, Dr. Gurung tells me that it looks as though the tool was a portable jackhammer, which the workers sometimes employed.

Do you know where these devices are and at what times? Is one of them missing, by any chance?"

Boucher shook his head. "None of my people would be stupid enough to try and loot something from a dig. Particularly not one like this, where no one knows what the hell we're dealing with, and half the crew is spooked half the time, anyway. If you're looking to lay the blame on someone, look somewhere else."

She raised her eyebrows. "You sound confident, even though you haven't checked any of these things yet. Were jackhammers being used by the crewmen that night?"

"No," the foreman insisted. "I hadn't checked those things out to them that night. Would've made too much noise while the rest of the camp was trying to sleep. People try to take stuff like that into consideration around here."

He was lying, Daria realized. Or at least omitting part of the truth, playing innocent to cover for his lack of certainty. Her suspicions rose, but she told herself to be patient and not leap to any conclusions.

His last sentence was interesting. It implied a kind of loyalty among the crew. The standoff, the impromptu strike, was happening under Boucher's orders, from a desire to protect the people who worked under him.

At last it clicked. Now, he was trying to protect his employees from *her*.

Thus far, Daria had adopted a cool demeanor, open to discussion but with the implication of threats lurking behind her. They'd seen her punch or elbow two unruly workers in the face, they'd seen her guns, and they knew the reputation of the Executioners in general. It was pointless to remind Boucher or anyone else of the harm that might come to them if they did anything too stupid.

What she needed to do instead was reassure him.

"Mr. Boucher. I can tell that you're trying to protect your people, and I respect that. You're worried that I plan to cut someone's head off for all of this. I would prefer to avoid that sort of thing.

"Far more important, first of all, is finding out where these people are. Assigning blame isn't my main purpose. We must discover what happened, especially because some of the five who vanished may still be alive. If you help me uncover this mystery, we might save their lives."

Muscles along the foreman's jaw rippled, and there was a flash of emotion in his eyes as he glanced to the side, looking at a bare patch of canvas. He kept his eyes there as he started talking.

"Two of the portable jackhammers are missing," he admitted. "The thing is, nobody signed for them, so I can't prove who took the damn things to begin with. Or what they were doing with them. So I got questions about all this, too."

Daria responded with a single nod. "What's your opinion of the three men who were in that chamber the night it happened?"

Boucher rolled his head back toward her. "If we're being honest, ma'am, then if anyone here was gonna do something sketchy, I'd wager it would've been one of those three. That's why we stuck them on the graveyard shift. So they wouldn't get in everyone else's way.

"Everybody was worried, scared. Thought the poor schmucks might be dead. Saying they were lowlife dipshits didn't seem right. Now you're saying maybe they *aren't* dead, after all."

"Correct. That's interesting." She filed away the facts in her mind, confident they would prove useful soon.

The foreman readjusted his position in his chair and sat up straighter. "So, if they're alive, where in God's name are they? There was no way out of that cave."

"I don't know." Daria shook her head. "They might be dead somewhere else, for all I know. What I'm certain of is that they didn't burn to ash in that chamber. That's worth looking into further. Is it not?"

The man's eyes were dark and clouded. "Yeah, I'd say so. We

can all agree, something fishy as hell is going on here. We should've bailed as soon as we found Atlanticore. Anytime that blue shit turns up somewhere, trouble follows."

Recalling all the death and destruction that she and Ty had dealt with after Sector Twelve had turned up a deposit, Daria had to chuckle.

"Frequently, yes, it does. It's too valuable to be any good to most people. I appreciate your honesty, sir. Tell me, though.

"Have you noticed those three speaking to anyone suspicious? Or any of their friends, their frequent work partners? Anything that could suggest a 'business arrangement?' After all, snatching pieces of Atlanticore only makes money for those who have a buyer ready and waiting. Or at least, accomplices to help them cover up their theft."

Boucher shook his head. His gaze swept across a bottle of whiskey in the corner and lingered on it for a second before he looked back at Daria.

"No, no. Nobody. We've been out here for weeks, and there hasn't been a single soul who's come and gone aside from the porter. Only people we see are the archaeology team and each other.

"Before you ask, the porter is always the same guy. I know him, and it's always the good doctor or me talking to him. He doesn't linger around and chat up the guys. We give him lists of the supplies we need, and that's it. He hits the road."

Daria rolled her tongue around the edges of her front teeth. "Hmm. No prostitutes? It won't shock me to hear about it if that's the case." Prostitution was common on Atlantica, and hookers and their pimps could stand to make a great deal of money off a group of men out at a worksite for weeks on end.

Boucher's ears turned slightly red. "No. The guy from the Executives who hired us was pretty specific about that. Hookers always talk to lots of people, and they didn't want anyone knowing about this dig. They're paying us well enough to make up for it. Plus, half of these guys have families. You know, morals."

"I see." Daria pushed her chair back and stood. "Again, I thank you for cooperating. I'll continue looking into things. I might need to leave but will be back tomorrow if so. Don't allow anyone else to leave until I return. You might wish to take account of the people you trust the most, and assign them to keep watch over the rest. But don't be too obvious about it."

The man frowned. "I don't like where this is going, Executioner."

She supposed she couldn't blame him. "I'll do what I can to resolve things peacefully. Oh, one final suggestion. Don't spread the word that the three disappeared men might still be alive. Part of this is so we don't share false hope, which is a cruel thing to do."

Again, the unwanted memories from Europe two decades ago bubbled to the surface. Daria commanded them to go away. She focused instead on the job.

"And," she added, "we don't want information getting to any accomplices of theirs. If there are guilty parties here, they must not be able to prepare themselves too well. We want to catch them unaware." She extended a hand to the foreman.

He took it and gave it a good shake. His attitude remained guarded...but they'd made definite progress.

"Okay, ma'am. You got yourself *another* deal."

CHAPTER TWELVE

It had been a long night, and Daria had spent far too little of it on actual sleep.

The truck bounced and rumbled down the track toward the valley. Once she arrived, Daria would know at once if the foreman had kept his word and if the rest of them had stayed away from each other's throats. There would likely be little more than a burned patch of earth otherwise. A few of them would be too drunk to have noticed the conflagration, and Dr. Limbu would probably be standing on a rock and delivering impassioned speeches to the sky.

It was an optimistic hope, she knew. Everyone in the camp was near their boiling point. Still, a girl could dream.

After leaving the valley last night, Daria had taken her truck back to the city. She'd had the opportunity to stock up on a few supplies, and more importantly, to pass on information to people she knew from the smuggling world. Individuals she trusted to find out things that might be of use and to relay their findings back to her through discreet channels.

In some cases, that might mean having her friends from the underworld get in touch with Eleanor Cervantes. They hadn't seemed enthusiastic about the idea. Daria had assured them that Cervantes was trustworthy and devoted solely to the pragmatic accomplishment of tasks. She had no real agenda, at least none that Daria could discern.

Then there was the matter of the other Executioner.

Ty had successfully killed his way out of the problems he'd encountered. That didn't surprise her much, but it was still a relief to learn. However, he hadn't finished yet. The destruction of one cell of the arms dealer's ring didn't put down the whole operation. Ty would be plunging back into the fray today.

Daria wished him the best of luck—she'd grown attached to him in the handful of months they'd known each other. As a friend.

Finally, Daria had collapsed onto her bed back at her house. She'd risen soon after dawn, washed down a muffin with a cup of strong coffee, then piled her things into the truck and headed back up into the hills. Now, as she rounded the final bend and entered the mouth of the valley, it was clear that something was extremely wrong.

The combination of distance, the lay of the land, and the rumbling noise of her engine had blotted out the rowdy, chaotic scene before her. The furor of dozens of shouting, arguing voices became audible as she slowed down.

Daria tensed, focused, and mentally switched herself "on." She had long experience with instantly making the transition into the mindset that accompanied danger and violence.

Her immediate, split-second guess was that another argument had broken out between the two camps, that the abrasive head scientist and the curmudgeonly foreman were butting heads again. She soon saw that whatever was going on was different from the scene she'd witnessed after first arriving yesterday. It was also more complex.

The entire team, laborers and researchers alike, had clustered in a giant roiling mass around the excavation shaft within the cliff. Some people shifted around to get a better look, others tried to talk to one another, and individual arguments broke out here and there. Those who were closest to the hole seemed to be leaning over it and pointing down.

Daria muttered a cursing lament. Nothing could ever be easy, smooth, or simple. There were always complications, always disasters waiting to happen.

She pulled the truck off to the left of the road's mouth and parked about halfway across the clearing toward the shaft. It was far enough away that she wouldn't be surrounded by potentially angry people the instant she stepped out the door, but close enough that it would be only a short jog to offer help.

She grabbed her Uzi and slung it over the back of her shoulder, letting it hang there in case she needed it—and as a sign that she wouldn't tolerate any shit beyond a certain threshold. She wouldn't brandish it in hand unless things took a turn for the worse. So far, the situation looked less like a deadly brawl than a cross between a team debate and an accident site in a crowded town square.

At the same instant that her mind produced the "accident" analogy, it occurred to her what had probably happened. Someone had fallen down the shaft.

Turning off the engine and pocketing the keys, Daria jumped to the ground and hustled directly toward the crowd. She planned to stop a few yards back from the edge of the brouhaha, see if she could get everyone's attention, and talk some sense into anyone about to overreact.

If she had to intervene directly, she would. The Uzi was loaded, as was her pistol.

A handful of the assembled personnel had noticed her arrival, but they acknowledged it with little more than glances before turning back. No one, irritatingly, tried to consult with her. Perhaps they might've under better circumstances, but for the time being, everyone was distracted.

Closing the distance with long fast strides, Daria got a better look at what was going on. She picked out Dr. Limbu and Mr. Boucher near the center of the whole mess, next to the winch before the shaft's opening. Both were shouting and gesticulating at each other.

As for everyone else, they seemed divided into three main groups. Those pressing close to the hole and peering in, those arguing with one another, possibly on behalf of their respective factions' leaders, and those essentially standing around glowering and waiting to see if things turned ugly.

Daria stopped about two yards behind the old workman closest to her. She drew a deep breath and yelled, "Hey! What's the problem here?"

The man jumped, startled by her volume. Rather than turn and speak to her, he walked deeper into the crowd and vanished. A couple of other heads glanced at her with sympathetic eyes. No one did anything. The clamor of voices was impenetrable.

Daria tried getting their attention twice more through merely vocal means. When that failed, she decided that she'd had enough.

She drew her pistol, aimed it up and angled a bit off to the left, and squeezed the trigger. No one pretended to ignore the miniature thunderclap that echoed through the vale.

The noise died down. The hustle and bustle gave way to shifting postures and turning faces. Half of the assemblage granted the Executioner their full attention. The other half were finally beginning to realize that someone had arrived to take charge of the situation.

Daria stood and waited. Once things were silent and calm, she lowered her gun and shouted again, "What's going on here? I'm sure I can help. I'll need someone to explain what happened. Dr. Limbu? Mr. Boucher? Perhaps one of you can start."

By drawing the leaders out of their conflict with each other, Daria figured she could neuter the hostilities before they grew worse. The downside, of course, was that one or both might simply turn their combative tendencies toward her.

That was exactly what happened.

"This is all their fault!" Akshara cried and waved her thin arms. "The fools have attacked one of my researchers, and now, look at the results. Madness!"

She stormed toward Daria, forcing aside everyone else between them. It occurred to the Executioner that, for the first time, the doctor seemed to appreciate her presence. Probably because she expected Daria to take her side.

Boucher growled, "Bullshit!" He folded his thick arms and stood his ground beside the winch.

Daria frowned. Ak would be upon her momentarily, but she had a short time to reexamine the crew. For the first time, she noticed that Gage was nowhere in sight. A pang of panicked worry hit, and her stomach fluttered. She clamped down on it. Emotions wouldn't interfere with her professional response.

"Dr. Limbu, please tell me your side of the story." Daria braced herself for the worst.

Ak wasted no time. The rest of the crowd all seemed to hold their breath and look at the ground as the ranting began.

"As I said," the archaeologist repeated, "one of my team, Dr. Gaje Gurung, was attacked by these idiotic reprobates and chased into the ground! He is down there now. How could they have done this?" She wrung her hands and looked skyward, perhaps for answers.

Daria started. If Gage was in trouble, she wanted to do something about it immediately. "Is he all right? Is he still alive?"

The foreman was the one who answered her, calling from the other side of the crowd. "We're not sure yet. Again, the good doctor's version of the story is horse manure. Nobody attacked Gurung. An argument got out of hand, and he started acting crazy."

It was sorely tempting to allow her face to fall into her

opened hand and shake her head while pinching her nose, but that would look bad. Daria remained stony-faced and only nodded. Determining the course of events and who was at fault wasn't going to be easy. It sounded as though both group leaders had fallen back into simplistically blaming the other camp for everything.

She walked past Ak, who sputtered about what she was doing and why, and pushed through the throng of men and women toward the pit. When she stopped next to Boucher, she met his eyes for a second, hoping that he remembered their deal.

He probably *did* remember it, Daria grasped, but the current situation had little to do with what they'd discussed last night.

Daria stepped past him and peered into the shaft. Only one spotlight shone down into the depths, disclosing little save a half-dozen irregular outcroppings of rock along the slope and a small portion of the tunnel floor at the bottom. The sun wasn't yet high enough to illuminate anything else.

It was silent. There was no trace of Gage, whether by sight or sound.

She cupped her hands around her mouth. "Dr. Gurung. Are you there? Are you all right?" Her voice echoed down the shaft and vanished into the tunnel itself, the surrounding earth muffling it out of existence.

Frowning, she turned back to the foreman. "Mr. Boucher. Please tell me your version of the story. Start at the beginning and relate everything you can remember. Leave no detail out. I must know as much as you can recall."

The big man drew a deep, ragged inhalation, swiveled his head a bit to crack his neck, and began.

"Gurung was out here, doing something last night. I don't know what. Anyhow, four of my workers came out to do a routine check on the equipment. We have people on the grave-yard shift anyway, so we have them do that every night before dawn even though we ain't working lately. Last thing anyone needs is for the equipment to die on us.

"So they comes out here and bumps into Gurung, and I don't know exactly what happened or how, but everyone starts shooting their mouths off, trading insults and stuff, people lose their tempers. *So then,*" Boucher raised his voice and grimaced, "your boy, the doctor, comes right at one of them, this Chinese guy named Wing, with his pistol drawn, and *bang!* Shoots him."

Daria's nostrils flared. She found it difficult to believe that Gage would've shot a man over a minor verbal argument based on what she knew of him, but perhaps she was wrong. "Is Mr. Wing still alive?"

"Yeah," said Boucher. "Shot him in the side, kinda. He's all messed up, but he might make it. Our medic wants us to get him to the hospital. Says he's okay for now, but that could change. We figured we'd let you handle it, or the porter, who might show up today. But it's a bumpy ride, and that might be bad for the poor bastard."

Daria had to confess that she wasn't sure what the best course of action would be. "Have your medic check on the man again and report back. I'll decide if we should risk moving him or give him time to recover. I need to determine how to deal with Dr. Gurung's situation as well. Please, continue with the story."

"Right," the foreman agreed. He turned and nodded at a man with a big salt-colored mustache near the crowd's periphery, presumably the medic, who ran off toward the tent city to check on the wounded laborer.

Then Boucher looked back at Daria. "Okay, so. After Gurung shoots this guy, another of my men gets scared and pulls a pistol. He had this little .32 down his pants. He pops off about four shots, doesn't know if he hit a damn thing, and the doctor turns and runs."

Daria would have to interview the men involved in the confrontation to estimate the likelihood of Gage taking a bullet.

The foreman hadn't mentioned how far away they'd been from each other or how good a shot the man with the .32 was.

The foreman went on. "He runs to the winch, slams the damn controls to start feeding the cable down, only he sets it to this reckless speed that nobody in their right mind would use for going down a shaft like that. He grabs the cable, runs to the mouth of the tunnel, and jumps right in."

The more Daria heard, the more she was sure that either someone was lying or that there were strange variables at work that no one had yet uncovered. She wondered if Gage had been drunk. Simplistic an explanation though it was, it was the only thing, so far, that would've made the slightest sense.

"The guys go over to the winch," Boucher added, "but then two shots come up from down below. From Gurung, they figure. There's nobody else down there, right? So that holds them back.

"Anyway, after the first shot—when the Gurkha shot Wing—I woke up, got out of bed, and ran out to see what the hell the problem was. I got out here right after Gurung takes his two potshots at the guys from halfway down the shaft. They tried to tell me what's going on, but I figured most of it out. Someone lost their marbles and started shooting, and a guy is going down into the caves on the winch.

"So they tried to shut it down, but I stopped them. Because at the speed it's going, a sharp stop like that could knock the cable out of Gurung's hand and send him falling, and he'd crack his damn head open on a rock. Since he shot their buddy, the guys seemed perfectly fine with that happening. I told them no, we got to try and keep him from dying in the process."

Daria noted the low mutterings of discontent from some of the workers at this part. Meanwhile, Boucher looked sharply at the malcontents, glaring at them until they shut up.

She said, "Thank you for saving his life so far." If Gage had been hit by one of the other man's panicked shots, though, he might well be dying, if not already dead.

"Yeah, yeah," the foreman grumbled. "I made you a promise that I'd help you get some answers. So we need the guy alive. The Gurkha, I mean. Letting him die, we might never find out what went wrong.

"We started to slow the winch down. That takes a minute. By the time we gets it slowed down enough to stop it and reverse it, it had to be at the bottom. Or at least close enough because it seemed light when we brought it back up. When it arrived, no Gurung. Either he got to the tunnel floor and waltzed off before we reversed it, or he was willing to risk jumping the rest of the drop. Either way, he was long gone."

Daria glanced up at the sky to ascertain the position of the sun. "You said that this happened shortly before dawn? So, about three or four hours ago?"

The foreman confirmed as much. Since then, they'd alternated between focusing on keeping Mr. Wing alive and trying to decide what to do next about Gage.

"All right," Daria told him. "Thank you for your input." She turned toward Dr. Limbu.

Ak realized that she was about to be called on. She marched forth, stopping about a meter from the Executioner and conveniently positioning herself so Daria blocked her view of Boucher.

Before Daria could ask, Ak immediately began talking. "No, no, no. This is all wrong. It's a distorted account of the events that clashes with everything we saw and experienced. My team can corroborate everything." She put her hands on her hips and swiveled her head around.

Dutifully, the other academic team members trudged forth, weaving through the jumble of workers to stand closer to their boss' side. Once they got close enough to contribute to the conversation without shouting, Ak resumed her spiel.

"We rose early this morning, before first light, and were making our preparations for the day's work. The others were busy with various tasks." She gestured at them.

"I was going to find Dr. Gurung myself. I wished to speak with him about a project that I wanted him to begin as soon as possible. Exceedingly important work regarding our study of the crystal devices, you see. I saw everything from the start of the shooting until now."

Daria noticed that some of the workers cocked their eyebrows or turned their heads to gauge the other men's reactions. They must not have been aware that Dr. Limbu had witnessed the whole event.

"Yes," Akshara went on, "it was most terrible. The rest of my team didn't make it out to the shaft until after Dr. Gurung had made his descent. But! I witnessed a chain of events that began well before that point.

"What I saw was Dr. Gurung running from your workers in fear for his life, Mr. Boucher—they were chasing him down and shooting at him! He was clearly frightened. His manner wasn't that of a man who'd started a fight himself. I saw no gun in his hand. If he lowered himself into the shaft, it was only to escape the unwarranted attack launched against him."

A chorus of groans, sputters of disbeliefs, and throaty sounds of anger and indignation rose from the mass of the laborers, and Boucher fumed and chewed on his lower lip while he adjusted the cap on his head.

Daria also noticed the other scientists out of the corner of her eye. When Ak had related her version of the events, half of them —notably Johnson, the Englishman who'd helped Gage demonstrate their research yesterday—had made sour faces or blinked in surprise, although they kept their mouths shut. All of them went pale when Dr. Limbu turned to stare at them.

There was one final detail. Daria had seen it before, but until now, her mind hadn't truly registered it as significant. Ak had a large bruise on the side of her face. It looked recent.

It seemed, for an instant or two, that peace would settle in. A curdled, resentful, confused, and smoldering peace, but at least that everyone would agree to disagree on the nature of what had happened. Which would mean that it would fall to Daria to solve the mystery, as it should.

Then a man's voice from somewhere within the cluster of workers barked, "We didn't do a damn thing, and that *ain't* how it happened, you lying—"

Someone shoved him, and Akshara screamed and wailed in irritation and feigned terror. A ring of bodies around the edge of the group expanded to make room for the two men who'd started fighting. Someone ran toward Dr. Limbu, waving a hammer. Daria was about to draw her pistol on him when another man tackled him from out of nowhere.

All hell broke loose. Everyone was yelling at everyone else, and other fights were breaking out, including one between Johnson, the scientist, and a scrappy-looking worker who'd tried to seize him from behind.

Rather than fleeing as she ought to, Ak waded into the melee waving her arms and screeching at everyone. Boucher shouldered and elbowed his way through the mass, barking at them to stand down, only to take a fist to the jaw and stagger back against the winch.

Daria gritted her teeth as her eyes darted around, frantic but controlled. Somehow she perceived everything at once. She saw blood flowing from busted lips and noses, the morning sun reflecting off the blades of knives or the surfaces of tools and even handguns.

Ugliness was coming.

The buildup to serious violence was always like this. Heightened senses and emotions combined with a weird slowdown of time itself and the awful, half-nauseating sensation of being pulled over a waterfall. Beyond that, normal means of solving problems were no longer possible. She'd failed to deal with the camp's tensions the diplomatic way.

Over the years, Daria had grown good enough at keeping her

exterior persona cool and collected that most people didn't notice or even suspect how frightening and sickening deadly combat still could be for her. Yet there was an element of exhilaration to it. Sometimes it was justified, causing her no great degree of guilt.

Still, it was never *normal.* It always represented something beyond the fringe of extremity, something that happened when everything else had failed.

As her eyes took in the whole crowd at once and her fingers twitched against the sleek metal surface of her submachine gun, she wondered who she would have to take down first. At least she was a good shot.

Then someone else opened fire first. With a cannon.

"Shit!" Daria stumbled back a step and blinked at the brightness of the incredible flash of light. Her brain reeled, processing the new information as fast as possible while the men and women around her froze, faltered, or cried out.

It wasn't a gunshot. Or a cannon shot, or even a bolt of lightning. Something had erupted from within the depths of the earth, issuing forth from the mouth of the excavation pit—from the chamber.

Although everyone was half-blinded by the flash, they all seemed to know what it was.

CHAPTER THIRTEEN

The blue-white flash receded as quickly as it had appeared, leaving the normal light of day seeming dull by comparison. Everyone blinked, and Daria saw multicolored spots in front of her eyes as they struggled to adjust to the expulsion of power they'd witnessed.

Her ears rang, as well. It was strange. The flash hadn't been accompanied by a thunderous crack or a deep boom, exactly. Rather, there had been a kind of ringing, a semi-audible sound like that from an obscure musical instrument with its volume and force amplified to terrible levels. Struggling for a way to describe it to herself, Daria decided that the sound was crystalline.

She tried to summon her senses back to full functionality and scanned everything around her. She might still need to act with immediate haste. Lives might still be in danger.

The fight had gone out of the crew. Mere seconds ago, half or more of the gathered workers and scholars were ready to kill each other, but the bizarre explosion had cowed them all.

Something else was happening. Gazes had turned softer now

that they'd drained of anger. They were still grim as people glanced back and forth and examined the looks on one another's faces. Apprehension, fear, and horror were the paramount emotions. No one spoke. For a moment, no one seemed to breathe.

The unspoken message was obvious. They all assumed that Gaje Gurung was dead, that the same awful surge of light that had taken his friends and coworkers had taken him, as well.

Daria's default instinct was to believe them, to join in their palpable despair. Another instinct asserted itself instead. One she'd *learned* through many long years of hard and bitter experience.

She knew what it was like to be given up on, to have people assume that her case was hopeless and leave her to the proverbial wolves. After the war, she'd re-established contact with people she'd known before when life was still relatively normal. At first, she'd been glad to see them. Then she'd been disgusted to learn that they'd written her off as dead. It had never occurred to them that she might still be alive and fighting somewhere.

No, she decided, she wouldn't write Gage off in the same fashion. Or those who'd disappeared in the chamber, thus far without a trace. Until she saw their bodies and confirmed their deaths, she would recognize the possibility—however perilously slim—of hope.

"Move aside, please." Daria squeezed between two crestfallen laborers and made a beeline for the shaft.

She would trust no assumptions. Only her own eyes. Besides, she'd intended to inspect the tunnels chamber below, regardless. The strange flash of light only gave her that much more justification without having to argue excessively with Limbu or Boucher or arouse suspicion in the rest of them.

"Excuse me." She pushed her way through throngs of gawking men and women, conscious that hostility might simmer among some few of them and trying not to be antagonistic. By the same token, though, she wouldn't allow them to obstruct her. "Move aside, please. Thank you. Excuse me..."

The last traces of the weird pink and yellow spots in front of her field of vision vanished as the winch came into sight and beyond it, the pit itself.

Much to her dismay, the passage from the Torah came back into her mind. Fire from the Lord and those who died by it. She shuddered briefly and banished the thoughts, asking the Lord instead for strength and clarity.

Boucher noticed her, finally. "Hey," he began, raising a meaty hand and moving toward her, "you're not planning to go down there again, are you, ma'am? I didn't think you were *that* crazy."

Daria tightened her jaw. "I have to. No one else will, it seems. It's my job and duty to find out what's going on here. Besides, I was starting to like Dr. Gurung. I don't want him dead if it's within my power to save him."

The people around her scowled. Given the bad blood between themselves and Gage, and by extension, the researchers in general, she might've made a tactical error in mentioning her burgeoning friendship with the Gurkha. She didn't care. She was growing tired of these people's hostility toward each other, combined with their trepidation toward a mere hole in the ground.

She raised a hand and snapped her fingers. "Prepare the winch if you would, please. Get me a harness and rig me up. I'm going down."

Someone in the crowd chuckled mirthlessly and quipped, "If you say so, lady. The tunnel is all yours. Stay down there as long as you want."

Boucher looked sharply in the direction the voice had come from. "Who said that? Shut the hell up!" He faced Daria again. "Ma'am, I don't think it's a good idea. But if you insist, well, we'll see what we can do. I'll keep some men here to watch the winch and hoist you back up right away if anything happens."

Daria managed a polite smile. "Thank you, Mr. Boucher. I appreciate that. If possible, I would appreciate it even more if you supervised the team monitoring the winch yourself. We've all heard that English expression about who to trust if you want something done right."

The foreman's account of how his workers were ready to let Gage fall to his death hadn't left her memory. Most of them seemed halfway decent, but the labor force here contained a handful of characters to whom she would prefer not to trust her life.

Rumbled mutterings and shuffling noises came from the men as the implications sank in. She ignored it, looking around instead for a harness.

Boucher sighed. "Yeah, okay, I can do that. We were trying to investigate stuff on our end, though, remember?"

She did remember. The foreman alone was the one she wanted to handle looking into the available information on the portable jackhammers. But...

"This is more important, for the time being. If Dr. Gurung is still alive, it's my responsibility to try to save him."

A shrill voice yelled, "Wait! Wait—it's too dangerous." The bodies in the crowd shifted again as someone pushed their way through toward the winch.

Daria narrowed her eyes and waited for whoever it was to arrive. It sounded like Dr. Limbu, but it seemed odd that she of all people would care much about the Executioner's safety.

Two men at the edge of the throng parted as Ak stepped through. "You must not go alone, Executioner Barruk," she proclaimed. "It's not safe for a lone person, especially since you'll be unable to communicate with anyone on the surface. Yesterday, we had Dr. Gurung accompanying you. To go down there alone would be entirely different. Far too much risk after what has happened."

There was another ripple of tension through the small sea of workers. Someone grunted, "Aye, so the bint's sendin' one of us down with 'er? That's a job no one'd volunteer for. Hah!"

Boucher looked up and held a fist skywards to shut the men up. "Hold on. Dr. Limbu has a point. *Does* anyone want to volunteer? Makes sense to ask before we go jumping to conclusions, don't it?"

Daria wasn't sure she *wanted* anyone to accompany her, with the possible exception of Dr. Johnson, and he'd said nothing so far.

While the personnel figured it out among themselves, she turned to Ak. "Yes, you do have a point, Doctor. Hooking me up to a communications device will be helpful. Does the team have radios? Walkie-talkies? I have a portable radio in my truck that I might be able to bring with me and tune to the frequency your team is using."

Boucher rolled his tongue around his teeth as he thought it over, meanwhile grabbing his cap and tightening it around his head. "Okay, we can do that. Everybody! Did you all hear that? We need to get our radio out and some walkie-talkies. Winch crew, get over here and start that whole process. Radio crew, do your thing. Ms. Barruk, go get your radio also, and we'll begin."

Daria nodded. "Thank you, foreman. I'll need a few minutes to contact my superiors as well as my fellow Executioner. Don't worry. No one is in trouble yet. I merely need to check in with them."

She'd added the second part in case anyone within earshot assumed that Tyler Katakura would be showing up, sword in hand, to wreak righteous vengeance upon them all. Daria hoped that would prove to be unnecessary.

Nodding as she passed Dr. Limbu, who had a curious, expectant look on her thin face, Daria trotted back to her truck, unlocked it, and turned on the radio. It seemed to take a full minute or more before the static died down and Eleanor's voice came through.

"Hello, this is Cervantes. Executioner Barruk? Is everything all right? Over."

Eleanor sounded calm, Daria decided. The woman was good at masking her emotions and staying professional most of the time. Still, they'd worked together for long enough by now that Daria was confident in her ability to judge Eleanor's moods.

"I'm fine, but there's been a disturbing development. One of the research team had an altercation with the workers and disappeared into the excavation shaft. I'm going in to look for him directly and will be using this radio to stay in touch with the personnel at ground level. Is Executioner Katakura okay? Is he still busy? Over."

Eleanor made a faint throaty sound as she digested the new information. "Thank you for reporting that. Once again, please use caution. As for Katakura, he's still engaged with his campaign against the arms dealers, but as of one hour ago he was still alive. He generally tends to survive situations like that. Over."

With a grim smile, Daria reclined in her seat. "Yes, I'm aware. If I finish before he does, I'll report in and request a transfer to his area of operations to offer him backup. If, on the other hand, he completes his assignment first, I might request that you send him here.

"So far I haven't encountered overwhelming opposition of the sort he thrives upon. However, there are enough tensions throughout the camp that his mere presence might have a cooling effect. When I brought up his name, everyone fell silent. Over."

Eleanor let out a small laugh. "Yes, that's to be expected. I'll relay the message. Also, if you need extra supplies, we can have a car sent out there to drop things off. Please let me know. Over."

It didn't seem necessary. They weren't *that* far from civilization, and bringing extra parties into the equation—particularly if it was a random civilian whom Daria didn't know—could only complicate matters.

"I don't think so, but thank you for the offer. I'll be switching over to the workers' frequency now. Out."

As Daria was fiddling with the dials and trying to find the appropriate channel to tap into the team's walkie-talkies, someone wandered over toward the truck. They moved with soft steps but a rather hurried and furtive gait, as though they were trying to avoid anyone seeing them but didn't want to appear too blatantly suspicious if they *were* sighted.

Daria looked up. It was Johnson, the amiable British scientist who'd helped Gage show her their discovery regarding the disc and its interactions with electricity versus Atlanticore. He approached the driver's side and stood near the window, positioning himself so the vehicle's body mostly blocked him from the view of the general crowd.

"Hello, Dr. Johnson," she greeted him in a soft voice, sensing his desire not to attract attention. "How can I help you?"

He nodded. "Good day. I might not have much time to speak, but there are some things you must know. Of course, I would appreciate it if you didn't divulge that I told you." He wore an uncomfortable, almost pained look, and his tone held an undercurrent of profound dread.

She had a fairly good notion of what he was about to discuss. Her left hand reflexively gripped the steering wheel tighter. "Yes, of course. Go on."

The blond man sighed, and the Executioner felt the stress and worry sloughing off his shoulders. "Dr. Limbu's account of what happened last night, or this morning, rather, isn't accurate, I'm afraid."

Daria clenched her jaw. "I'd suspected as much."

Johnson nodded and went on. "What transpired was this. I, and everyone else, awoke in the wee hours of the morning to a heated argument between Dr. Limbu and Dr. Gurung.

"It sounded like part of it was in English, but we couldn't make out anything substantive, only a few random words. Otherwise, they used a different language. I believe Hindi since they both speak it as a lingua franca despite hailing from different ends of the subcontinent. At the point when Dr. Limbu noticed that the rest of us had awoken and were coming to check on them, she sent Gaje out of the camp so they could continue their spat in privacy."

Daria frowned. She'd *known* something was wrong with the story—the workers' version had sounded suspicious enough, and Ak's had been still worse. She didn't have a specific reason to trust Dr. Johnson more than anyone else aside from his simple politeness, but there was no reason to *distrust* him either.

The man continued. "Before Limbu went to have it out with Gaje, she lingered a moment to give the rest of us a tongue-lashing. We were standing there, bleary-eyed and half-awake, simply wondering what was going on and hoping we could get back to sleep before the day's work commenced.

"Akshara wouldn't have it. She accused us of being slothful, foolish, lacking in vision, and essentially treasonous, you might say. I believe her exact words were that we were 'not dedicated and loyal to this project.'

"Then she seized her radio and dashed off into her alcove, where she had some kind of whispered conversation with... Well, I don't know. With whoever was on the other end."

Daria offered a single slow nod but could think of nothing to say. Ak's near-fanaticism was obvious, but Johnson's account was raising more questions than it answered.

"Then," the scholar concluded, "Dr. Limbu headed out into the clearing to speak to Gaje herself. We didn't follow her or overhear much of anything. We all thought that she was simply being, ah, emotional, and we were eager to return to sleep.

"Right as I was about to drift back off, though, was when we all heard the gunshots. The rest, so far, is history." He frowned and his eyes went vacant. Then he shrugged as though ashamed that he couldn't offer more.

"I see." Something occurred to Daria. "Was Dr. Limbu armed?"

Johnson shook his head. "Mm, no. I've never seen her carry a gun, or a knife, or anything else for that matter, and we've lived in close confines for many weeks now. If she were carrying a weapon, it would come as a great surprise to me and likely to the rest of us."

Daria glanced out the windshield to check if anyone was taking an interest in what she and the scientist were doing. Everyone seemed distracted, either by the preparations they were making on Boucher's orders, or by more petty arguments, or by sheer laziness.

She looked back at Johnson. "Thank you, Doctor. May I ask why you chose to tell me all this?" She wasn't suspicious of his motives but wanted to gauge his reaction all the same.

He looked a little ruffled by the question but elaborated, "Well, because what Limbu said simply isn't true. You're here to uncover the truth, aren't you? I only mention it because she told you that she went out looking for Gaje, as though he'd ventured out on his initiative, when in fact she was the one who sent him out."

Yesterday, Daria's impression of Johnson and Gurung was that the two were friends, or at least "friendly acquaintances," so it made sense.

Before she could thank him again and get on with the mission, however, he added one last thing.

"Oh, also. To be frank, Dr. Limbu has been behaving in an increasingly erratic fashion for the last three or four weeks. She was always something of a flamboyant and eccentric character, I suppose, but her recent behavior has been, ah, concerning.

"We've all grown worried that she's on the verge of a complete mental breakdown. Due, I suppose, to how much we've discovered, yet how far we still have to go before the dig can be considered a full success." He shrugged as though out of empathy with the frustrating and tedious pace of his chosen profession.

Daria said, "Thanks again for... Wait."

A slender figure had emerged from the bustling throng and was standing at its edge, looking toward the truck. It was Ak.

Grimacing, Daria looked back at Johnson. "Your boss has seen us. Or she's seen me and will see you when you go back to the camp. If she asks, tell her that you were lecturing me on the properties of Atlanticore.

"She didn't stick around for your and Gage's demonstration with the discs yesterday, so she cannot know what we talked about. Say that you were repeating what we discussed then in preparation for what I'll observe in the chamber. I'll confirm the same thing if she asks me. And please, watch your back."

Johnson gave a curt bow of his blond head. "I will do so, Executioner. Thank you for your time—and good luck."

He turned and strolled back toward the crowd. There was no way to leave the truck's vicinity without being seen, so he wisely sauntered straight across the clearing in as casual and conspicuous a fashion as possible.

Daria stalled another minute or two and gathered up her radio, noting that it was bulky and heavy enough to be a nuisance if she had to carry it in her arms or on her back while making the long, steep descent into the earth. Still, Dr. Limbu had been correct. It would be better to go in with an extra means of calling for help.

When she left the truck and strode back toward the winch, two-thirds of the laborers had departed since they were superfluous to the operation at hand. Boucher had remained to observe and to impose order and efficiency on the remaining tasks.

All of the scholars were gone as well, with one notable exception. Akshara Limbu had remained near the tunnel's mouth.

Her narrow face lit up with an excessively wide smile. Given the purplish bruise on her cheek, it looked painful. "Executioner Barruk, I've decided that I will accompany you into the tunnels."

Boucher started in place, turned, and stared bug-eyed at her. "What? Why the hell do you want to do that? It's going to be dangerous, and we'll have to delay a couple more minutes if we need to set up another harness and cable. Pardon me, Doctor, but you're better off sitting this one out. Go have a cup of tea or whatever."

Ak bristled, her hands trembling. "Don't tell me what is and isn't a good idea! This is my dig, you realize. Someone simply *must* accompany her. I possess greater knowledge of what lies down in that chamber, after all, than anyone else here."

Daria's stomach churned at the thought of having Ak breathing down her neck the whole time. Not to mention, Johnson's version of the story had only heightened her suspicions that something was seriously amiss.

"Dr. Limbu," the Executioner began in a patient yet firm tone, "Mr. Boucher is right. We don't have time for this. There is no need to risk yourself.

"Dr. Gurung and I already examined the chamber in substantial detail, so there is unlikely to be much new information you can contribute. I mean no offense. It would be better for you to stay on the surface. If by some chance I need your help, I'll radio for it."

Ak's mouth opened and closed. She balked, clenching and unclenching her hands. When she spoke, she was far louder than she'd been a moment ago.

"Dr. Gurung is my friend as well as my professional associate! I worry for him. Am I not responsible for his safety and well-being as the project leader and chief archaeologist here? All of this began *when I set out to look for him* this morning! I must see the task through. For his sake!"

Her sudden outpouring of emotion and the way she swayed

and wrung her hands was so melodramatic that Daria almost burst out laughing and had to bite her tongue. It reminded her of a stage performance or something from an old silent film. Perhaps the scientist was partly sincere, in a way.

Daria couldn't help being skeptical. Dr. Limbu had seemingly regarded her employees as mere accouterments to her objectives until now.

Before she could speak, though, Ak pressed on with her importunes and pleas, targeting the foreman more than the Executioner.

"Mr. Boucher! Have you no compassion?" she urged. "Even if it was your workers who drove the poor man down there to begin with, I will be willing to forgive you if we can yet have the opportunity to find him. To save him!

"You must agree with that much. Allow me to look after the welfare of my subordinate. Cannot you see how much this pains me, thinking that he might be dead after all that has..."

Daria watched them both and saw the foreman's smoldering anger once again rising. He got in a couple of words edgewise, trying to dismiss the archaeologist's concerns and reassure her that Daria could handle things by herself. Ak kept talking over him and deliberately trying to annoy him.

She was attempting to force Daria into a position of having no choice but to take her side against the big, short-tempered man. Failing to give the woman what she wanted would only stoke the fires of conflict and potentially bring things to open violence between the factions in the camp at last.

Mentally cursing the doctor, Daria stepped in. "Fine, fine. Yes, Dr. Limbu, you may come with me. Please defer to my judgment if there is anything dangerous to deal with, however. Danger is my area of expertise, as science is yours. Mr. Boucher, please prepare a second harness for her."

The foreman stared at Daria as though she'd gone utterly mad.

Daria coughed. "It will be easier this way. Trust me."

Sighing and muttering, Boucher turned away from the women and waved, shouting orders to his men in between subaudible swearing.

The archaeologist only stood in place, abruptly silent, and smiled.

CHAPTER FOURTEEN

Daria double-checked her harness and had one of Boucher's more trusted men triple-check it for good measure. The man then similarly examined Dr. Limbu's fastenings, grunted his approval, and stepped back.

The two women stood nearly at the brink of the precipice. The yawning darkness seemed somehow larger and more encompassing than the mostly clear blue sky above them.

Waving his meaty arms, the foreman bellowed, "All right. They're going down. Everyone in position! Step back. Make ready. Do we got the radio working?"

Daria unhooked the microphone. The device was on. She flicked it and heard a bit of static. "Yes, it's working on my end. Can someone send a test message?"

One of the workers, the gangly individual selected to operate the team's radio, fiddled with a dial and spoke into his microphone. "Check. Check. You hearing this?"

Daria heard him *without* the radio, but his voice was nonetheless eerily replicated by the device in her hand. "Yes. The walkie-talkies?"

Those, too, worked. Anyone in the camp with a walkie-talkie

could hear any message sent by Daria through her radio. They'd also given one to Dr. Limbu at her insistence. Just to be safe.

Daria inhaled deeply. "Good. Mr. Boucher, we're ready. Please lower us. I'll check in when we reach the chamber."

"Yeah, sounds good." The foreman pulled the cap down on his head. "Lower 'em! Be careful. Nice steady pace. This time, try to keep that damn spotlight shining a little below their feet the whole time. The good doctor doesn't have as much experience at getting down there safely, after all."

The bitterness and contempt in his voice were obvious, but Daria didn't *think* he would go so far as to sabotage Ak's descent. She would have to trust him to do the right thing, for now.

The machine started. Its mechanical whining seeming louder than it had before, and the pair began their slow drop into the black depths of Atlantica. Daria noted that it seemed to be at a slightly slower speed than had been the case yesterday when she and Gage had gone down together.

First, they clambered down the short initial slope, then there were a couple of minutes of dangling in the open air as the winch did the work for them, their legs pointing the way through the dark, musty air, and the guy manning the spotlight doing his best to illuminate their course.

Dr. Limbu hadn't spoken much, but she was giving in to her various nervous habits, seeming twitchy and anxious in general. Being next to her under circumstances where one or two minor slip-ups could result in the deaths of them both wasn't pleasant or encouraging.

Daria decided that as long as there was time to kill, she might as well gather more information and break the proverbial ice of their mutual awkward silence.

"Pardon me, Dr. Limbu, but if I may ask, how did you get that bruise on your face? Are you injured or feeling unwell? A bump hard enough to cause a mark like that can cause more problems than it might seem at first."

The archaeologist's first response was a barking peal of nervous laughter, as though she were an air bladder filled over pressure, and the question had somehow punctured her, letting out its contents in a loud, obnoxious rush.

"It's nothing," she stated, her tone incongruously sharp after the laughing fit. "I fell in the dark early this morning. While I was rushing out to make sure those stupid workers didn't kill Dr. Gurung. Poor, poor Gaje. My friend."

Daria narrowed her eyes and looked downward as a shelf of rock approached. The "stupid" workers up above might well have heard her remark.

"Oh. You fell, as in, you tripped over something first and collided with the ground? Or did you smash your face into a solid object first, *then* fall?" It was a pedantic question. But asking questions that forced people to think hard about their answers was part of her strategy.

Dr. Limbu reacted much the way she had before to inquiries she didn't like. She didn't truly speak or make much noise but somehow said volumes regardless by the way she shook her head, hitched up her shoulders, and clenched her hands.

"I said it was nothing," she snapped. "Why is it necessary to repeat myself? Especially when discussing something so tragic and unpleasant. You're behaving as though I'm obligated to defend myself from some accusation when I had a simple accident. I don't wish to talk about it further. Let us focus on—*oof!*"

The rocky shelf came up on them faster than they'd anticipated, and Ak was too distracted by her rantings to prepare for it. Her knees bent quickly to account for the impact. She scrambled over the edge faster than was necessary and dangled again by the cord on her back.

Daria watched with alarm. Her dislike of the archaeologist notwithstanding, she didn't want to get her killed by distracting her. "Pardon me." Her voice echoed a short way down the shaft. "I agree we should pay attention to what we're doing. Be careful."

Limbu said nothing in response. They made the rest of their descent in silence. Mostly.

Between the metallic *whining* of the winch above them, their feet sporadically scraping against stone, dirt, and gravel, and the occasional *crackle* of radio static, it was difficult to hear soft noises. Yet, Daria could've sworn that Ak was talking to herself. During brief instants of relative silence, the woman's querulous voice spiked out of what was otherwise a series of breathy whispers. It was impossible to determine if she was speaking English, Tamil, Hindi, or anything else.

The one thing of which Daria was sure was that Ak wasn't talking to *her*.

Furthermore, the scientist's eyes kept darting around, her head making stiff yet rapid movements, somewhat like a bird or lizard, as though she expected to see something leaping out at her from the shadows.

Daria wasn't sure what to make of it all. It could mean that Ak had malevolent intent and was nervously waiting for her plans to come to fruition. Or it could be an innocent and understandable reaction to the stress and tension of the day so far, combined with the generally creepy atmosphere of the shaft and the ominous knowledge of what had happened in the chamber.

Or it might mean that Dr. Akshara Limbu was completely crazy.

As they came to the next area of elevated rock, Daria moved a little closer to her new partner to make it easier to offer aid in case Ak tripped or otherwise had difficulty. The archaeologist had refocused on the climb and did far better than she had a minute ago.

Soon, they reached the bottom. Daria sighed gently in relief that the process was over, although what lay ahead of them in the chamber might be worse. She unhooked the cord from her harness and looped it around the stalagmite as she'd done the first time with Gage and showed Ak how to do likewise. Then she called up the shaft, "We're at the bottom. All is well."

Immediately she felt a bit foolish for yelling instead of using the radio. A second later, a man's voice responded. "Good. Call us if you need anything. Good luck."

Daria nodded and turned toward the hallway that led to the crystal-lined chamber. Thinking of what was to come, her spirits sank.

Gaje Gurung was probably dead. A gunshot might've wounded him to begin with, and the powerful blue-white flash didn't portend anything good, given what had happened to the five-person crew many days past. Daria hadn't known him long, but she'd grown to like him all the same.

If indeed he'd perished like the others, it meant she'd failed to protect him—that the situation here had grown worse since she'd arrived.

"All right." She drew herself up to her full height and checked on her unwanted companion. "Let us go. We move slowly, observe everything before we act, and if I say *stop,* or *get down*, or *get back,* you must do it. I say this not to throw around the weight of my authority, but for your safety, Doctor."

With a cool, skeptical gaze, she waited for the reaction.

Dr. Limbu looked back at her more or less blankly, though a bizarre smile was making its way onto her face. "Yes, I under-stand. After you." She extended a hand toward the hallway.

Nodding, Daria stepped out in front. It suddenly occurred to her that she ought to have checked Ak for weapons, despite Johnson's insistence that the woman was unarmed. It was too late to rectify the oversight now without causing a scene.

The catacomb was as dim and silent as ever. The hallway leading back wasn't very long, but the dark space before it branched off to the side, where the blue-glowing chamber lay, nonetheless was swathed in total blackness. Daria clicked on her flashlight.

Nothing. Whatever they were to find most likely lay in the carved room.

Although she didn't want to dwell on the thought, what they would probably find was another human-sized scorch mark on the stone floor, all that remained of the pleasant little man from Nepal.

Other than the ashes. Or, rather, the absence thereof. Daria still had no explanation for it.

She rounded the corner and shone her flashlight into the chamber with the friezes and veins of crystal, then *clicked* it off to avoid disturbing the Atlanticore and drew in her breath. Preparing for the worst while hoping for the best, as the Americans said.

Behind her, Ak panted, "What is it? What do you see?"

Daria blinked and allowed her eyes to slowly open wider, taking in the sight of the entire chamber. She took two steps, then three, closer to the threshold. "So far, nothing. It...it looks the same as it did yesterday. Let me go in and examine it further."

Dr. Limbu made vague muttering and whispering noises as the Executioner advanced into the room, head on a swivel and hand near the pistol at her hip. She'd all but forgotten the radio on her back.

Gage was nowhere in sight. Daria stared at the floor, but there were still only three scorch marks, the same ones left there the previous day. She knelt and shone her flashlight on each of them, checking for any differently colored patches or other irregularities in case the flash had incinerated Gage's body in the same spot as one of the workers, and the two burn marks had overlapped.

There was no sign of any such thing. Like the scholars who'd been with the ill-fated laborers, Dr. Gurung had vanished with nary a trace.

Inhaling through her nose, Daria stood and turned back toward the head scientist, who'd come to the chamber's threshold and now stood there between the Executioner and the exit. She was glancing around at random.

"Nothing," Daria reported. "He's not here. There's no sign that he ever was. Like your two researchers, it would seem he's...missing."

Akshara's gradual scanning of the chamber heated up and sped up. Her calm examination became a frantic shuffle. She whipped her head around while her hands and lips trembled.

Then, as if in total rejection of what she saw, she stamped one foot. The fall of her boot on the stone didn't have much force behind it, given the woman's willowy frame, yet in the dead silence of the subterranean chamber, it seemed far louder than it should've.

Daria stared at her, half-dreading whatever outburst was to come.

"Where is he?" Ak demanded. She directed her inquiry at the chamber itself, her voice warbling into the stale air and dissipating against the carved walls. Then she looked at Daria and repeated herself. "Where is Dr. Gurung? Why is he not here? It's ridiculous! Have you done something with him? What is this nonsense? He should be *right here!*"

Daria gawked at her, mouth hanging partway open. She was truly amazed. She'd expected Dr. Limbu to overreact to their mutual disappointment and frustration in failing to find Gage. Daria had figured the woman would begin yelling and pointing fingers.

What was stunning, though, was how a scientist could so easily reject evidence, logic, and common sense when it personally inconvenienced her.

Daria cleared her throat. "We're both standing in the same chamber, Dr. Limbu," she pointed out and rotated her hand with the index finger extended. "We both see the same things. If you see no trace of Gage, neither do I. My guess is as good as yours. Perhaps worse since I have less experience with this place."

Ak again lost control of herself. A tremor of incoherent rage threatened to overwhelm her before she made herself stand still and breathe deeply. The only point of activity was in her eyes, which blazed brightly and darted around the room.

"They were *lying*," the archaeologist concluded, folding her hands in front of her. "Yes. Those oafish workmen must have been lying to us. We should leave since this has quickly become no more than a waste of our time. They never saw Dr. Gurung descend into this shaft. It was all a fabrication on their part."

Daria bit her tongue then quipped, "There were parts of the story that didn't have the ring of truth to them. That much, I'll agree with. I seem to recall you saying that you saw Gage climb down into the hole, as well. Did you not?"

Ak's head and eyes snapped toward her. "It was dark. Perhaps it was someone else. There was no way to be certain it was him." She sniffed.

"Well." Daria sighed. "If someone *else* had come down here, regardless of who it was, we would've found them. Instead, we've found no one at all. We can check the end of the hallway, where the men were still excavating the rubble, but I doubt we'll find anything there, either."

Dr. Limbu started to say something. She opened her mouth. The beginnings of a strange, garbled noise came out, and she raised her hands as she often did during outbursts. She stopped herself at the last instant, clamped her lips shut, and lowered her hands.

Then she spun on one heel toward the wall. Something about her attitude and the gesture's nature reminded Daria of a pouty child who'd lost an argument with an adult and was now determined to ignore them by way of retaliation.

Leaving the scientist to her fuming and muttering, Daria took a moment to reexamine the chamber for further clues. She'd already checked the floor for any trace of poor Gage and was confident none was there.

The walls, though... She wanted another look at them. The carvings and the solid sheet of Atlanticore in particular.

Daria went first to the particular section of the frieze that she and Gage had studied previously. The one depicting the various figures gathered around a massive tree of crystal. She stared at it for a moment, seeing it and recognizing that something was wrong, but without fully comprehending the problem.

Then it dawned on her. The branch where someone had cracked off the crystal was as blue and shiny as the rest of the tree. Either Daria had accidentally looked at a duplicate carving on the other side of the room—which she doubted—or the Atlanticore had *grown back* by some astonishing means.

She shook her head, the motion slow and deliberate, while her eyes remained fixed on the carving. "They couldn't leave it alone," she whispered, and her field of vision seemed filled by the smooth, glowing azure surface.

She raised a hand and let the tips of her fingers trail along the stone. The fleshy pads went cold against the sleek, hard, heat-sapped material, and the chill seeped into the bones of her hands and wrists. It wasn't unpleasant, though. She traced over the lines of the runic inscriptions, the crudely humanoid fingers, getting closer to the crystal without fully comprehending it.

Then Daria withdrew her hand sharply, drawing in a sharp gasp of breath. A faint but definite tremor had gone through the wall and up her arm. It reminded her of the feeling that immediately preceded an electrical shock.

Nothing had happened. So far.

"Damn." She turned and froze.

Ak was standing right next to her, the tip of her nose little more than a hand's length from Daria's face. The other woman's expression was blank but weirdly intense. Her eyes were wide and staring.

Instinctively, Daria's fingers found the edge of her pistol's grip, nestled securely at her waist. A pang of fear and disturbance seized her, and not only because the scientist standing so close was inherently odd and unnatural.

It was also because she hadn't heard or felt the slightest trace of her partner moving up on her. Daria prided herself on being alert and perceptive. It was rare for *anyone* to get the drop on her. Akshara Limbu hadn't struck her as one of the few individuals who might be able to pull it off.

"What?" Ak queried, a curious smile beginning to spread across her long face. "They couldn't leave *what* alone? Hmm?"

Something in the woman's cold, querulous tone set off multiple alarms within Daria's brain. They were close to the corner, with little room to maneuver, so the Executioner acted on her lifetime of smuggler's intuition and simply shoved the scientist away with her upper left arm and shoulder. Her right hand stayed on the handle of her gun.

Ak staggered back, making another of her characteristic sputtering noises, but she didn't move far and recovered her balance more quickly than Daria would've liked. Suddenly, a metallic object appeared in her hand.

Daria drew her pistol, bringing it up in a flash and pointing it straight at the doctor's chest. Both women froze in place. In the moment's hesitation, Daria saw what the archaeologist held. It was one of the smooth metal discs they'd shown her back at the scientists' camp, complete with wire tail attachment.

Narrowing her eyes and drawing her lips back from her teeth, Daria snarled, "What the hell are you doing? What is that? Keep your hands to yourself, Doctor. I don't know what your game is, but now is the time to stop it."

Akshara only continued to stare, and the unpleasant, inscrutable smile widened, showing her teeth. "Now, now," she said. "Watch."

She raised the disc in her hand and pressed the end of the twisted wire tail against the solid crystal vein within the carvings.

The sound that resulted was essentially the same as what

Daria had heard yesterday, during the little demonstration put on for her by Gage and Johnson. Now the musical hum was far louder, as the quantity of Atlanticore in the chamber greatly exceeded the modest sample they'd had then. The humming became an oppressive drone. Louder and louder it grew and more menacing.

At last, Daria understood what was happening. Her eyes bulged, and she aimed the pistol at the scientist, beginning to squeeze the trigger right as an unseen force lifted her off her feet and into the air.

Akshara giggled madly. "All of it to myself. *All of it to myself!*"

Daria's trigger finger pulled back, and the gun went off at the same instant she was hurled backward. The crackling report was painfully, deafeningly loud in the enclosed underground space. She saw the bullet tear through the thin layer of flesh along Dr. Limbu's shoulder.

Then she saw nothing else. Her midair speed picked up, her head spun, and it felt as though her stomach had stayed behind in the corner while the rest of her hurtled toward the far wall. She braced herself for a crashing, bone-shattering impact that never came.

Instead, all was light. Brilliant, blue-white, and eye-stabbing bright.

CHAPTER FIFTEEN

Daria's consciousness returned to her only after the pain had mostly receded.

She had a faint memory of the torment, a dim, implicit awareness that it had occurred. Still, it had been so intense, so overwhelming in its agony that her mind had simply blotted it out and not allowed her to perceive it happening. For a fraction of an instant, she wondered if she was dead.

She could feel her body again, or so it seemed. Now what she experienced was the echo of the pain, the last pangs of its departure, which themselves were unbearable though fleeting. Even that was so horrible that whatever had happened to her before must've been the greatest suffering a human being could experience.

It was within this awful final echo that oddly enough, she heard a familiar voice speaking in a casual and friendly register.

"Sorry, sorry. I'll be with you in one moment. Try to relax, please."

The light was fading, and the real world was coming back. The pain was over, although it had left her breathless and in shock. Blinking and gasping, Daria asked, "G-Gage? Dr. Gurung?"

When the terrible light had erupted from the tunnel's mouth while everyone had been arguing on the surface, Daria recalled that it had messed up her vision and left her seeing spots when she blinked for a good minute after that. At present, having been within the heart of a similar blast, the effects were far worse.

Everything she could see was indistinct with swirls and bursts of yellow and pink radiance that flitted away if she tried to focus on them. The details of normal reality seemed dull and indistinct.

The worst of it was ending, though. She fixed her gaze on a person-shaped silhouette. The lights slowly faded away. Balance and order gradually reasserted themselves.

She gulped and breathed deep. To her surprise, she realized that she was standing. She'd somehow braced her back against a wall, and though she leaned awkwardly, both feet remained firmly planted on solid ground.

The dimensions of her surroundings became clear. She was in a stone room, not too dissimilar from the carved chamber but smaller. In front of her, the human-shaped silhouette could only be Gaje Gurung.

He was standing next to a shimmering wall that appeared to be nothing but sleek, solid Atlanticore crystal. It was breathtaking at first. The flash's lingering effects, which was too bright for human eyes to comprehend, had initially masked its blue glow. With her normal sense back, the crystalline wall was plenty brilliant enough.

Gage wasn't looking at Daria. He held something to his ear, a small object that she couldn't identify at first. His back was to her. He stared intently at a section near the center of the wall where oddly enough a stone disc appeared to be suspended over the crystal.

Daria swallowed what little spit was left in her mouth and willed herself to take a step forward. As she moved, her head swam, and her muscles tingled. Plus, she was hot. Her face felt flushed, sweat ran down her body beneath her heavy armored uniform, and there was a generally oppressive sense of muggy heat throughout the chamber, as though it were adjacent to a sauna, furnace, or boiler room.

She ignored the discomfort for now and pressed on, taking a couple more steps. Her pistol remained clutched in her right hand. She returned it to its holster.

Coming up behind Gage's shoulder, she could see the strange stone disk in front of him. There were images in the center of it. She focused on them, baffled about what she was witnessing.

It took a second or two for her to grasp that the disk functioned a little like a small television screen. The moving images within it, she surmised, were of another location nearby.

Unless she was mistaken, the scene was of Akshara Limbu in the chamber of friezes. The colors were dim, though, and the details blurred. Furthermore, the shapes, especially the humanoid one that resembled the archaeologist, were outlined in a dark corona of sorts.

Ak was down on her hands and knees, crawling around the floor near the periphery of the chamber and groping around. After half a minute of fruitless activity, the slender woman's hands found a wall. Then, moving slowly and carefully, she used the solid surface, notably the indentations around the carvings, to grab hold of and lift herself back to her feet.

Daria squinted. "What's she doing?" It was mystifying. Ak didn't seem injured, and assuming it was the same room they'd been in together a moment ago, she ought to still have the light of the crystals to guide herself. She was moving the way a blind person would.

It made Daria wonder if the terrible flash had impacted the scientist's vision as badly or worse than it had impaired hers.

Gage didn't answer. Daria repeated her question and again received no response. She thought about putting a hand on his shoulder and shaking him, but for obscure reasons, it seemed unwise to disturb him. Whatever he was doing required concentration.

Daria glanced at the object in his hand. It resembled a seashell, an abstract carving of one that took the kind of artistic liberties that often showed up in both ancient and modern art. That he would be holding it to his ear was bizarrely appropriate.

She waited, breathing in and out and turning her attention back to the scene playing out on the disc. At last, Dr. Limbu wandered out of view, leaving the chamber empty. The view provided on the disk didn't move with her. It was fixed in place as though tied to a stationary camera.

Gage waited a minute to see if his boss returned. When she didn't, he nodded, mumbled something in his native tongue, and lowered the stone shell away from his face. He fitted it carefully into a grooved slot in the stone circle, which Daria hadn't noticed before.

With the shell returned to its resting place, the entire disk gave off a low hum and glided through the air over to the wall's corner. Daria stared at it, marveling at the properties of Atlantica's buried secrets, but unable to be fully fazed after everything that had happened to her.

Dr. Gurung turned and greeted her with a mild, sheepish smile. "Forgive me for that. I needed to pay attention to what I was doing. Performing reconnaissance."

Daria raised her hands to her face and rubbed her eyes, which still stung from the blinding flash. "All will be forgiven, Dr. Gurung, if you'll kindly tell me exactly what in the holy name of God Himself is going on here."

She could use a nap before facing the truth. Her lack of quality sleep last night came back to her, nettling her with acute discomfort. There was no time. Whatever the hell had happened, she had no choice but to deal with it on its terms.

Gage nodded. "Yes, it's understandable that you would be

confused. I was, too. Still, not everything makes sense. Things have been...strange."

"That is perhaps an understatement. But yes. I arrived back at the camp this morning and heard that someone chased you into the tunnels after a fight. Then there was another flash of light, so I descended the shaft to look for you. Unfortunately," she lowered her voice, "Dr. Limbu insisted on accompanying me."

The small man bobbed his head again, acknowledging what she'd said, but when he resumed speaking it was as though he were picking up directly where he'd left off. He could probably guess the general nature of the discussions that had taken place on the surface, so he launched straight into his version of the story.

"Last night," he began, his face grave but distant, "Dr. Limbu asked me to uncouple the Atlanticore crystal—the one we had in our camp, which I showed you—from its harness. I was doing as she'd requested. She came upon me in the middle of the job, and out of nowhere, immediately began to call me names. She was most angry and hostile. More than usual, I mean."

Daria brushed back a lock of her hair that had come loose. She'd tied it back that morning, but the experience of being blasted through space by the blinding light had ruffled her. "Yes, I see." It was good to know that Gage was perceptive enough to grasp that something was seriously wrong with his boss beyond her typically abrasive personality.

"She called me things like *thief* and *traitor*, which was unusual. Most of the time, she only insults my intelligence, my work ethic, and so forth. These slurs were new to me. I didn't fully realize what was happening, though. Dr. Limbu is often difficult to work with."

He sighed. "I tried to remain calm and explain to her that I had done nothing out of the ordinary, and nothing which she had not requested. But she persisted. Then she insisted that I must go outside and wait for her. So that she could yell at me more, I thought."

Daria was impressed by the man's self-restraint. Most individuals wouldn't have been able to put up with working under such a person. Gage had protected her against an angry Boucher earlier that same day, no less.

The Gurkha continued, "She was hysterical, very emotional for reasons I did not understand. Because she was so...agitated...she did not notice that I kept the Atlanticore crystal with me and put it in my pocket. I took it with me, out to the clearing below our camp, and waited for a short while."

Daria noticed definite pain in the man's voice, although he was doing a good job of keeping it under control. The pain that came with betrayal, with being—as the Americans put it—screwed over.

Dr. Gurung explained that while he was waiting for Ak to come out and finish her ranting, a handful of workers from the camp appeared from their end of the clearing. They walked toward the shaft, which he was also close to at the time. He'd assumed that they were simply there to check on the equipment and prepare things for the coming day.

Then, one drew a pistol and shot at him. He tried to flee toward the scholars' camp, but Akshara had appeared from the darkness, flailing her arms and hissing, "Get him, quickly!"

Daria's gut clenched at that. She was beginning to suspect that all of them—herself, Gage, Johnson, Boucher, and perhaps the Executives—had been played for fools.

Gage continued, "I drew my revolver and made the quick decision to fire a shot in the air to deter my pursuers and frighten them off. The men from the work camp did hesitate, and half of them dropped to the ground in fear. Then Akshara was upon me, and she had a pistol. She fired at me. But she missed and hit one of the workers instead."

Daria nodded. He meant Wing, the Chinese gentleman they'd

tried so hard to save. He still might need to go to the city for treatment.

Gage went on. "I was most frightened, and because I knew they meant to kill me, I did something I would never have done otherwise. I punched Dr. Limbu in the face. This knocked her down, and she lost her grip on the gun. Then there were more people coming from the labor camp... I thought I would die if they reached me. It seemed as though everyone had turned against me, but I did not know why.

"The winch machine was close. I slammed down the gears and took a cable, simply holding it in my hand since there was no time to attach it to a harness. Which is terribly dangerous.

"I was not certain I could make it very far down. They might have reached the machine and stopped it or cut the cord before I could attain the bottom. Still, it seemed my chances would be better than if I stayed on the surface, where an angry mob would tear me limb from limb."

At this point, Daria realized, Gage's story corroborated what everyone else had said. It was only the first half that differed from what Ak and the workmen had told her previously.

"It was clear to me that Dr. Limbu had been conspiring with others in the camp, although I did not know what their purpose was. With all that had happened, I could think only of getting away from them. I went very fast down the shaft, almost falling several times. I made it quite far before the winch stopped. When it began to draw me back up, I took the risk of dropping." He frowned. "Unfortunately, the fall was greater than I had guessed. I do believe that I broke my left ankle."

Daria blinked and looked at his leg. She hadn't noticed anything until now, but upon closer examination, he appeared to be favoring it, and she thought she saw swelling beneath his half-torn pant leg.

She was about to suggest that he let her inspect it, but he held up his hands. "I have already bound it. Thank you. I learned such things in the military."

"Ah, I forgot, if you will pardon me. Please, finish your story."

Gage obliged her. After his hard landing, he'd limped down the tunnel and made his way into the chamber of friezes. He'd waited for the mob to come after him and prepared to make his stand. No one came, and he heard nothing topside to suggest that they were preparing an expedition to do so. For the time being, it had seemed that they would leave him to rot.

So, out of boredom and the natural curiosity that afflicts all scientists, he found the tree carving that he and Daria had studied the previous day. Upon observing the empty branch that should be inlaid with Atlanticore but was bereft of it, he recalled that he still had a crystal in his pocket.

The man found it difficult to describe what had happened next, and Daria struggled to understand his meaning. It had been truly bizarre; that much was clear. Although his English was fairly good, he didn't possess the fluency that would've been necessary to explain the occurrence.

Gage had touched the crystal he'd brought to the damaged branch slot in the wall, and somehow, it had flowed into the carving and reconfigured itself to fill the space. At least, that was Daria's best guess.

"Then, there came a terrible flash of light," Gage concluded. He cringed.

Daria nodded. "We saw it. Everyone in the camp was out near the shaft when it happened. We all thought you were dead, although I preferred not to leap to that conclusion until I'd seen your body."

The man chuckled. "You see it now. I think I am still alive. Yes, there was great pain, and I was confused until I found myself here. In the time since I arrived, I have studied all of these things to the best of my ability." He waved. "I made several interesting discoveries..."

He'd ascertained that the stone disk which had descended from its position high on the wall gave him a remote view of the chamber of friezes, and the seashell carving allowed him to hear what happened within. He wasn't sure how they worked, but it was a simple operation once one grasped its essence.

Dr. Gurung's voice trailed off. His mind seemed to be momentarily preoccupied with the mysteries of Atlantican technology. Daria decided to butt in.

"Gage. Were you the one who started the process that brought me into this room? Was it connected in some way to that disk or the shell thing?"

The Gurkha shook his head. "No, I'm afraid that I had nothing to do with it. That does remind me of something. Odd symbols made of light flashed over the image upon the disk when I saw you being thrown into the air by the device. They had vanished by the time you appeared in this room. I guessed that you would be joining me after that, and I was correct."

The device, he'd said. By that, Daria assumed he meant the other metallic disc that Akshara had activated with the wire.

"Did you know it could do that? The thing Dr. Limbu had, the disc. I wasn't sure if it caused me to be here, but it must have."

Gage shrugged. "I was not aware. We had not tested the device in this chamber. Perhaps the idea came to Ak only today, or perhaps she had one of the others test it before when no one else was paying attention. I do not know."

Daria thanked him and turned away, looking around the room. It was featureless aside from the wall of crystal and the remote-viewing disk...and one other thing, so important that she was surprised she hadn't noticed it until now.

A line ran through the stone on the wall behind her, where she'd been leaning after she'd regained consciousness. Rather, three lines—two vertical and a horizontal one above it, connecting them. Like a doorway cut into the rock.

She beckoned for Gage to come over and pointed at it.

"Ah, yes, I saw that. I have not been here very long. There was not yet time to try it."

Daria almost laughed. She would never understand scientific types. Banished to a mysterious chamber under deadly conditions, Dr. Gurung had busied himself learning how to operate an ancient gadget before he'd bothered trying to find a way to escape.

"Well, we might be able to get out. You haven't seen anyone else in here, have you?"

"No." Excitement was kindling within him. He was probably reaching the same conclusion she was.

She nodded. "So, do you think that what has happened to us is also what happened to the others, the ones who went missing? Could they be here too? Or somewhere else within this cata-comb, perhaps."

Before Gage could offer his opinion, the door slid open with a smooth motion, making no more sound than the gliding of cloth over wood.

CHAPTER SIXTEEN

Daria's hand went automatically to her gun, the fingers wrapping around the grip, but she didn't draw it yet. Two people emerged from the portal beyond the stone rectangle. They would've looked out of place amid the workmen. Scholars, without a doubt.

Gage perked up. "Oh, hello! It is good to see you two again. We were all worried. How are you?"

Daria relaxed. At least at first. Once the initial shock faded, she grasped at once that the pair weren't doing well and were mentally frayed to dangerous levels by whatever had happened to them.

On the left was a pale, stocky man of average height, with black hair and a matching goatee. He'd obviously not shaved in many days, so the rest of his stubble was threatening to catch up and form a full beard.

On the right was a woman barely five feet tall with blond hair and freckles. The latter had likely appeared in conjunction with her deep tan, although it was fading after spending so much time underground. She wore noticeably crooked wireframe glasses.

The man licked his cracked lips. "Ah... hello. Gage. Yes." His voice was dry and hollow.

The woman nodded, and her right eye twitched. "Dr. Gurung. Dr. Gurung! So this thing caught even more people, did it? Wow. When? When will enough be enough? Ha. Ha, ha."

Daria stood where she was, waiting for an introduction. Neither of the scientists had paid much heed to her so far. Physically, they seemed about as well as could be expected—tired-looking, unwashed and smelling like it, growing emaciated and probably dehydrated, but mostly functional. Their mental health was what concerned her.

Gage took a step forward and clasped the hands of his colleagues, then turned toward Daria and extended his arm. "I would like you to meet Executioner Daria Barruk. She has come to help us with our little problem. Do not worry. She has not killed anyone yet. Ms. Barruk, this is Dr. Carlos Hurstett, and Dr. Diana Fields."

The scholars stared at her blankly. She smiled, stepped forth, and shook each of their hands in turn. "Dr. Hurstett. Dr. Fields. Are you both all right? You must've been down here for quite some time now."

"Yes," Hurstett replied in his raspy, sighing voice. "Yes. A long time. What did you do to make it angry? Why did it catch you, too?"

Daria's skin crawled. It occurred to her that, in addition to the pair's convenient and sudden appearance right as they were examining the door, she also had no way of being sure they weren't in on Dr. Limbu's plot, whatever it was.

She cleared her throat. "It? What do you mean by that?" She had an idea, but their responses might prove informative.

In nearly perfect unison, the two raised their hands and pointed at the shimmering crystal wall. Then each gestured to the side, indicating the frieze-carvings that lined the walls of this room as they did the other chamber. The carvings here, too, held veins of Atlanticore.

Fields went back to staring at the solid crystal wall. "That thing." Then she shivered and averted her eyes. Hurstett had barely looked at it, as though he didn't want to draw its attention.

Daria and Gage exchanged a glance. It was impossible to read the Gurkha's exact thoughts, but he looked as disturbed as she felt.

Before Daria could suggest the same, Dr. Gurung spread his hands. "Now, now. There is no reason to be afraid. But please, tell us exactly what happened to you. The more we know, the more we can help."

The two scientists drew closer together, nearly hugging one another as though seeking safety from the external world with each other. Daria wondered if they'd been a couple, but there was nothing romantic about the gesture. It suggested primitive fear and desperation more than anything else.

Dr. Hurstett gasped, "We made it...angry. We shouldn't have done so. But...mistakes occurred."

"I'll say. I'll say!" Dr. Fields added. Her eye twitched again as she snuck a furtive peek at the crystal wall.

Gage exhaled slowly and grimaced, flexing his hands as he tried to think of how to approach such a bizarre situation.

Daria had dealt with people who were unable to think normally after terrible experiences. "Please, understand that no harm can come to you from a...wall. Dr. Gurung and I are here to help and protect you.

"All of us can get out of here if you explain what happened. Please start at the beginning, and leave nothing out. Tell us what it did to you and all that has occurred since you were, ah, sent to these chambers."

Dr. Hurstett closed his eyes and shook his head. His lips trembled.

Dr. Fields still hung onto his arm. She looked at him. "No. No, right?" She glanced back at Daria. "No! It might hear! Come on." She yanked on her colleague's sleeve with surprising force, and his eyes opened again in time for him to burst into action.

Before Daria or Gage could do anything, both of them had spun and fled, scampering back through the doorway where they'd entered and vanishing around the corner of a hallway beyond.

"What the hell?" Daria lamented. "This is becoming far more difficult than it needs to be. Gage, have those two always been this, er, strange?"

The Gurkha pushed his glasses up his nose. "No, not quite. All archaeologists are somewhat strange, of course. But not like this. Something is bothering them greatly."

"I've noticed," Daria grumbled. "Let's track them down. I doubt they could've gone far."

As she started over the threshold of the open stone door, two unpleasant notions collided simultaneously in her head.

First, she recalled that Gage had probably broken his ankle. He might not be able to keep up with her. If by some chance the pair of disturbed scholars had a vast amount of space in which to flee, finding them could be a long and arduous process.

Second, she had no idea what lay beyond the current room. She could see a corridor past the doorway, similar to the one that led into the first frieze-chamber the team had uncovered. There might be an impassable labyrinth of similar halls and rooms. Or a cavern full of pitfalls and loathsome subterranean wildlife. Or a grotto opening into an undiscovered body of water.

Furthermore, what had spooked the two so badly? The effect of the bright flash followed by being transported to a different room was undoubtedly weird and disconcerting. For professional scientists to have reverted to childlike superstition— ascribing personality and volition to inanimate objects— suggested other things were lurking within these ruins that Daria hadn't yet seen.

And might not *want* to see.

CHAPTER SEVENTEEN

Past the doorway, the corridor extended straight for about two yards before turning to the left. There were no paths in other directions thus far. Daria turned back to check on Gage.

He hobbled along. To avoid undue pressure on his left ankle, he essentially walked with the right leg and dragged the left one up behind it. Daria felt a pang of guilt, and she frowned.

"Forgive me. Here, let me help." She reached out for his arm to support him.

He held up a flattened hand. "No, it is quite fine. I cannot move very fast, but I will manage. The ankle does not hurt too much, as long as I do not press down upon it hard."

Daria shrugged. "So be it. Be careful. I'll scout ahead. If I say to stop or turn back, don't question —for your sake."

"Yes, yes. Of course." He shuffled forward a couple more steps as Daria trotted down the hallway, her ears open for any noise made by the two fleeing scholars.

Oddly enough, there was none. Unless a trick of acoustics was masking their movements, they must've retreated only a short distance and stopped somewhere to hide or take refuge.

Around the corner to the left, then the corridor bent again to the right and seemingly opened into a room or chamber. So far there were no intersections, no multiple paths. Daria advanced toward the opening. She briefly scanned the walls. Carvings here were minimal, and there were only occasional small flecks of crystal that kept the corridors in relative darkness.

She glanced back at Gage, who was making better speed than she would've expected. "So far, all is clear," she told him. "This way."

Drawing a deep breath, she strode forward another three steps and pivoted into the next opening, her hand hovering near her gun as a brighter blue glow engulfed her.

The chamber beyond was similar to the one they'd left but a bit larger and differently furnished. The carvings still circled the walls in bands but weren't inlaid with Atlanticore. Instead, the illumination came from what looked like windows filled with panes of shining crystal that admitted broad beams of azure light into the chamber. It occurred to Daria that, despite being underground, the effect was curiously similar to daylight in a house on the surface. Only bluer.

At the far end of the chamber was another stone door, much like the one through which Hurstett and Fields had first emerged. It was closed. The two scientists themselves had crouched into a corner near it. They held each other's arms and looked vacantly into the air, not noticing Daria's entrance.

There was one final feature of the room that demanded attention and set it off as different from the others. Three stone troughs, or perhaps sarcophagi, rising from the floor. Daria couldn't yet see what lay within them.

Behind her, Dr. Gurung approached, his shuffling footfalls slowing. Daria advanced farther into the chamber to make room for him, and after crossing the threshold, he stood beside her, coming to an abrupt halt and gaping wide-eyed at the sights around him.

Daria glanced at the scientists. They hadn't moved and

seemed vaguely aware of her and Gage's presence but weren't reacting to it. She decided that they posed no threat to her, Gage, or themselves for the time being.

She turned her head to the Gurkha. "What do you think, Doctor?"

Gage appeared awestruck by the chamber's ingenious design, particularly the false windows and their evocative streams of light. His slack-jawed expression was one of clear wonder—tinged, however, with dreadful trepidation.

Her face must've looked much the same when she'd come into the first chamber of the friezes. She recalled her unwanted trip into the depths of memory, the juvenile fear of God and His works and powers.

Gage once more readjusted his glasses and drew a long breath before he spoke. In the deep silence that had fallen over the chamber, his respiration sounded like a moderate gust of wind.

"We had assumed," he began, his eyes taking in everything at once, "that the ancient Atlantican peoples were simpler. We felt, based on what we knew or had learned since we discovered this island, that they had not advanced to nearly this level. Everything I see in this place defies that assumption."

Daria had nothing to add. It would never have occurred to her, either, that there would be a true civilization buried here, one far more sophisticated than they could've dreamed or imagined.

Dr. Gurung went on, "Our best guesses of what we would find in Atlantica's prehistory did not include anything like this. We must reevaluate all which we know. We thought that they simply used the Atlanticore crystals as sources of light, and no more."

Daria deduced that Gage was talking about the remote viewing disk in the other room as much, if not more, than the impressive windows in the present one. It was as though the magnitude had only fully struck him at this moment, the reaction delayed by the strangeness of their circumstances or by his specific focus.

He continued, "We did not think they possessed wiring. Without it, we presumed that they could not use Atlanticore at its full potential. We thought they regarded it as a simple phosphorescent material instead of the energy source it truly is. In fact, we lacked understanding. We had no way to know that somehow, *somehow,* the crystal itself can function as the wiring."

Daria watched as the Nepali went to the nearest frieze and pointed at the thin veins of blue stone, tracing their course and showing how they connected the windows and other major concentrations of Atlanticore within the buried complex.

"Incredible," he commented. "It was so obvious, and yet I did not see it. The crystal is threaded all through this place, like an electrical grid."

Daria asked, "What about that humming, floating disk thing? The one you used to watch Dr. Limbu in the first chamber."

When she'd first observed the thing, coming off the frightening and agonizing experience of being blasted through space, she'd taken it in stride. Now the fact of how incredible it was fully impressed itself on her mind. A people who had probably gone extinct thousands of years ago had created things that could compete with the most advanced technology of the present day.

Gage had difficulty answering the question directly, perhaps because his guess was as good as the Executioner's. He went off on a brief tangent about how the Atlanticans might've been far more aware of the relationships between the crystals and metal or the crystals and electricity than suspected. By this, Daria gathered that he was referring to the demonstration back in the camp, where the disc had reacted differently to a battery than it had to Atlanticore.

The Gurkha concluded with, "It was only a theory—pardon me, a hypothesis. That perhaps they understood these relationships. But ahh, I was foolish. I vastly underestimated the Atlanticans."

Daria walked farther into the room, keeping one eye on Hurstett and Fields. "What is all of this? By that I mean, how is it that the same substance can have so many different uses?"

Gage shrugged. "The crystals are like electronics, but perhaps far more advanced. Like the display monitors of television sets, they might connect via all of the crystal wiring to other machines that lay deeper within this structure. We might have only scratched the surface."

Although not a scientist, Daria found it impossible not to burn with curiosity over the questions her new friend had raised —and his enthusiasm was infectious.

Still, they had other things to focus on. "Gage, let's check on your colleagues. And those troughs over there..."

He agreed, and she moved slowly toward them, keeping her eyes on the pair but maintaining a neutral, unthreatening demeanor.

"Are you all right?" she asked them. No response. She took another step. As the angle of her perspective shifted, she could see into the tops of the tall, trough-like structures.

In each of them lay a naked human body suspended in liquid. Daria tensed but tried not to react in any obvious way that might alarm the disturbed scholars. She felt cold—but not only as a reaction within her body. There was an unpleasant void of heat near the troughs, a virtual aura or miasma of coldness rising from the liquid, so intense that it made Daria's skin ache.

Her winter in the camp, the suffering and privation came back to her. She'd nearly lost toes and fingers to frostbite, time and again. She shook her head, rebuking the memories and pushing them back down and away.

"Gage, come and look at this. Do these individuals look familiar to you?" She beckoned him over.

He seemed a tad nervous, and she couldn't blame him.

However, his face lit up as he saw the suspended forms. "Yes, they do. These are the three workers who were with Carlos and Diana. The ones whom we thought were burned to ash by a power surge."

Daria nodded. At this point, it was abundantly clear that all five had been transported elsewhere within the complex by the powerful flash, not unlike themselves. That raised the question of what, precisely, had happened to the three laborers. Daria found it difficult to imagine that they'd willingly climbed into stone coffins filled with liquid ice.

Daria caught the attention of the kneeling and distraught pair on the floor. "Excuse me, Dr. Hurstett and Dr. Fields. Again, allow me to reassure you that you are in no danger. But we are curious, how did these three end up...like this?"

She wondered if they were alive, though it seemed doubtful. The substance within the troughs had likely frozen them solid.

Diana Fields looked up, and her eye twitched. "They offended it. Offended it! Made it even angrier than we did." While she spoke, she flapped her hand at the troughs but refused to look at them. Daria suspected that the pair had crouched specifically to keep their eye level below the edges of the sarcophagi to avoid looking at the people within.

Carlos Hurstett raised a withered finger. "They are the lucky ones," he intoned.

Daria's stomach turned over with uncanny loathing as she stared down at the motionless bodies. They stared up at the ceiling with blank, glassy eyes.

"What do you—" she stopped herself, her breath cutting itself off with a sharp *hiss*.

One of the three men within the liquid had blinked. Slowly enough that it hadn't been obvious at first, but his eyes, opened at first, were now closed. Then they opened again, and the eyes had shifted position. They looked directly at Daria.

She took a step straight back, the skin on the back of her neck crawling and the tips of her fingers teasingly fluttering over the hilt of her weapon. "They're still alive," she stated. "Those three are *not* dead."

Gage was coming up next to her. He puffed and coughed as though someone had knocked the wind out of him with a kick to the gut. Daria wondered if he still had his revolver on him. She hoped so.

For a second or two, she wanted to turn and run. A crude, primitive, infantile part of her mind told her that there was no way the men could've survived immersion in that liquid, that they were now returning from death as dybbuk-possessed corpses, as vampires.

"No," she whispered. "Things like that don't exist. If they're still alive, they need help."

She forced herself to take two steps forward, coming right to the edge of the nearest trough. It contained the gaunt man who'd blinked in slow motion before turning his eyes on her. If the substance within the trough hadn't killed him, it probably couldn't harm her, either.

Probably.

"Gage, stand by to make me a tourniquet in case I lose a hand." She gritted her teeth and plunged her left hand into the liquid.

The cold struck her at once as a deep, sharp ache that ignored her flesh and went straight to the bone, an anti-burn that was like blood loss or desiccation. She wouldn't be able to bear it for long. Nonetheless, she moved her fingers toward the man's neck, feeling for his pulse.

The substance certainly wasn't water, nor was it truly a liquid. It was a thin, gelatinous solution that slid across and encompassed her hand and wrist but without adhering to the skin.

Strangely, the initial pain faded rather than intensified. There was no buildup to a horrible, agonizing burn, as was the case when one shoved one's hand into a bank of snow. Still, she was rapidly losing sensation, and her motor skills were slowing down.

At first, she felt nothing, but wasn't sure if that resulted from the man having no pulse or the gel's frigidity dulling her sense of touch. Then, through the clammy flesh of the worker's neck, there was a soft thump. His heart rate had decreased to an incredible slowness, but it still beat.

Daria pulled her arm back. Her hand emerged from the solution amazingly clean; none of it stuck to her flesh or clothing. The comparatively warm air of the chamber tingled around her fingers and knuckles as sensation returned and the dull pain vanished.

"How is that possible?" she mused, staring both at her hand and the naked, motionless man beneath her. "How?"

Gage came up beside her again, not wanting to get too close and be in her way but near enough to help her if she needed it. He examined the floating body. "A kind of suspended animation? I have no other suggestions to offer. I know basic medicine from my military days. But I am not a medical doctor or a biologist."

Daria scoffed, not out of contempt for Gage, but at the sheer unbelievability of the whole situation. "Suspended animation. That sounds like something from a dime novel about spacemen and aliens."

No sooner had the words left her mouth than the two crouching scholars burst into fits of unhinged, erratic giggling.

Fields exclaimed, "Yes! That's what we said. Ha! Ha... Science fiction stuff. Pure silliness. But the longer we've been stuck here, the more we discover that we know nothing. *Nothing!*"

Hurstett added, "Years of research and understanding, lost and wasted. Now that we finally get to see it all, we cannot understand it. Worse, we know that we'll die without being able to share it."

Daria frowned and chose to ignore the latter part of Hurstett's statement. "I'll admit that it's difficult to adjust to all of this new information. I don't think human beings are supposed to learn so many bizarre things at once."

Finding the two missing scientists had given some clarification to the overall mystery unfolding at the site. Then again, Daria had never paid much attention to such things or found them important to her life.

By contrast, the scholars had lives, careers, and worldviews tied up in these matters. The kind of discovery they'd made here on Atlantica might be enough to shatter their minds altogether.

As though he knew what she was contemplating, Gage chimed in with, "We might have to, ah, reevaluate everything. All that we know. The entire foundation of modern science."

"The foundation," Hurstett interjected, staring vacantly at a point beyond Gage's head, "of *reality*."

At that, Fields burst into a fit of nervous giggling while staring at her hands.

Daria refused to admit how unsettled she was, not only by how crazy the researchers had gone but by the possibility that they might be correct. The fine hairs on the back of her neck were standing straight up, and she tried not to look at the man beneath her in the trough of cold gel. She decided to change the subject.

"All right, yes, all of this is fascinating, I'll agree." She raised her voice, cutting off the gibbering of the pair on the floor. "We need to consider one thing before any others. Where is the exit? How do we get out?"

Dead silence fell, and both Hurstett and Fields stared at her. Then they both erupted into manic laughter, with the man's guffaws coming in dry, raspy waves while the woman's were a seemingly endless metronome of snickers and tittering.

Daria wasn't proud of herself. She wanted to draw her gun

and shoot them both. It took most of the self-control she had left to keep from doing so. Beside her, Gage fidgeted in confusion and discomfort.

Before she could decide what to do instead, however, Dr. Hurstett stopped laughing for long enough to look straight at her and gasp, *"There is no way out!"*

CHAPTER EIGHTEEN

Daria stared at them, her mouth shut but her eyes wide. She *wanted* to dismiss what the archaeologist had said, to tell him that he and his partner were being ridiculous, and to keep thinking of them as too maddened to say anything sensible.

They'd been down here for many days. No matter how badly their experiences had frayed their minds, there was every reason to assume the pair had tried to escape and had looked around thoroughly.

The worst possibility was also the likeliest one. Hurstett was telling the truth.

Daria swallowed a mouthful of acrid spit. She raised her hand, pointed at the doorway behind the two huddled scientists, and asked the most obvious question. "What about that door? What's behind it?"

Dr. Fields shot a rapid, furtive glance at it and went back to looking at the floor. "Rubble. Lots and lots of rubble! We checked before. It goes on a few feet, and it's blocked the rest of the way. No other exits. Ha, ha. Don't you think we tried? Ha..."

Daria's eyes drifted closed. That was exactly the reply she'd both feared and expected. Still, it was always best to verify things oneself rather than to solely trust the word of others.

She strode past them to the section of wall marked off by the narrow rectangular outline. Behind her, Gage hobbled ahead several steps and paused beside his colleagues.

Daria laid her hand on the door, which was barely even recognizable as anything other than another part of the smooth stone chamber's side. She was about to ask Fields and Hurstett how to open or otherwise operate it when she felt a faint tingling under her fingers and heard a low *hum*.

She retracted her hand as the stone moved, swinging away from her with a perfectly smooth motion and barely making a sound. She couldn't tell how the door was attached or what mechanism controlled it, but it was clearer than ever that the Atlanticans had been skilled engineers. Skilled enough for things to keep working after the passage of entire millennia.

There wasn't enough room for the door to swing all the way out. Toward the end of its arc, it struck something. Daria peered into the square beyond, which was dimmer than the room it was attached to, but still partially lit up by the blue crystal glow.

The researchers hadn't lied. Nor were they mistaken. The corridor beyond was piled from floor to ceiling with a tightly packed mass of chipped stone, dirt, rock clusters, dust, clay, and gravel. Without proper digging or cutting tools, getting through it would take days upon days of intensive, finger-shredding labor.

It was impossible to tell how deep it went or where the hallway led, anyhow. They might nearly kill themselves trying to clear it by hand, only to discover after a week of effort and agony that the corridor was a dead end.

Hurstett let out one of his dry, rustling chortles. "You see? It's hopeless. We're trapped here. It won't let us leave."

Daria turned to Gage. "We need to double-check this chamber, the hallway, and the first room for any other way out." She exhaled. "We probably won't find anything. Still, let's look first before we jump to conclusions."

The Gurkha nodded. "I agree. Since I have been in the first room longer, you will have fresher eyes. I will search this room while you look through the hall and the chamber of the blue wall."

Daria touched the man's shoulder for a second. It was good to have him around. Then she set off into the multi-jointed corridor that had led her to her current location.

She still had her flashlight. Fortunately, it had transported into the chamber of the crystal wall along with herself, her clothing, and the rest of her gear. She wondered how that was possible but decided not to dwell on her relatively good fortune. There were other things to worry about.

A final glance showed Gage shuffling to the nearest wall and inspecting it before moving gradually to the side. She supposed that, to some extent, his decision to handle the current room himself had to do with his ankle. What he'd said made sense regardless.

She crossed the threshold into the hall connecting the two chambers and clicked on her light. The thin veins of blue crystal gave off *some* illumination but not enough to examine the place's finer details. She swept the beam across the walls and looked for any signs of doors and switches, hidden or otherwise, but found nothing.

Nothing. The hall was only a hall. There was no indication whatsoever of an entrance or exit that they might've missed.

When she got back into the chamber of the crystal wall and the stone disk, the results were much the same. The only way in or out, as near as she could tell, was the same doorway that Hurstett and Fields had first used to greet them and which she and Gage had used to pursue them.

Sighing, Daria turned and trudged back to the room with the three troughs. She shuddered once, fighting off the creeping, bile-rising sense of desperation, claustrophobia, and general panic that was setting in as the awfulness of their situation became increasingly impossible to deny.

When she stepped into the trough chamber, Gage had almost finished his circumlocution of the room and was peering at a wall about three hundred and forty degrees around from where he'd started. The strained yet morose look on his face suggested that he'd been no more successful than she had.

"Dr. Gurung," she called, "have you found anything? I saw nothing." She pointed at the door she'd opened a short while earlier. "It looks like that blocked hallway is the only way out."

He stopped what he was doing and looked back at her, trying to compose himself. "No, I'm afraid I have not seen anything that would be helpful to us."

"See?" Dr. Fields interrupted him. "It's hopeless. Ha. We're trapped here. Trapped!"

Daria glared at her. She couldn't blame them for all but giving up hope, but she wished they would keep quiet.

Then, looking at her and the man who clutched her arms, something else occurred to Daria. It was so obvious she wanted to smack herself in the face for not having thought of it yet despite all the commotion and distractions.

There was nothing in this catacomb to eat or drink. Certainly no food. No water, either, unless the two had managed to collect moisture runoff or found a tiny pool or trickle that Daria hadn't seen yet.

As such, physical deprivation was likely destroying their minds' ability to function as surely as despair, fear, and isolation were. Hurstett's lips looked like ancient, crumbling paper. Both were skinny to the point of gauntness.

The notion sent her gut lurching toward the wall, or so it felt. She'd eaten nothing since her light breakfast hours ago. And she was thin enough that she wouldn't last too long in conditions with zero nutrition. Overweight people had an advantage in that regard.

She might never leave these two rooms and the angular hallway that connected them alive.

Gage was looking at her. She met his gaze and waved vaguely behind her. "Come with me, Dr. Gurung. Let's, ah, examine that crystal wall again. We should reflect on everything we know. It might be useful for us to think back on every single thing that has happened since we were last in the carved chamber. I can think of nothing else that might point the way out."

The man looked skeptical—the horrible reality of their situation was beginning to dawn on him as well. He only shrugged and hobbled forward. This time, Daria helped him, ignoring his polite objections and holding his arm to help him keep his balance as they moved back down the corridor together.

Neither of them spoke during their slow jaunt toward the first room. Daria couldn't clarify her feelings, which churned within her in a chaotic mass like a storm cloud roiling before the wind and unsure when to unleash its payload of rain and thunder.

She'd been through things that some people could scarcely imagine. She'd survived events that many might regard as impossible. If they'd been in the same dire straits, perhaps they would've found the will to carry on, or perhaps they might've given up. And died.

Daria didn't think her situation was hopeless. What she feared was the long period of doubt, uncertainty, and abject suffering she might have to go through before she reached the end and emerged with her life.

They came to the first chamber, and her eyes went at once to the wall of solid blue crystal. It looked like solidified water from the tropics, or perhaps like exceptionally thick ice from the

Arctic Ocean, where icebergs took on an azure hue under the sun's glare or the sea's reflection.

What did the crystal have to do with the incomprehensible process that had sent them away?

Daria helped Gage to rest against the back wall next to the doorway. Then, grateful to be relieved of the burden of helping him along, she stretched her limbs and paced across the middle of the room.

Gage watched her. "Ms. Barruk. What is on your mind? Some of it, I can guess. It seems as though something else is bothering you, which you have not told me so far. If you think it would make you feel better to explain..."

She waved but kept marching to and fro. "I'm thinking only of what we can do to save ourselves. We must start from the beginning. You already told me your story. What was it like? When you went from the other chamber to this one. I rose in the air as though pulled up and to the side by a great invisible hand or rope attached to a truck, or something like that. Did you experience this?"

"Yes. Then a great light, white or blue, and too bright to look at. Painful. Terrible, terrible pain...I could not think or remember much after that."

Daria nodded. "It was the same for me. It was only after the pain faded that I found myself here. I was hot and sweaty, and I couldn't see at first. I could barely move. It was as though I hadn't been able to use my body for a very long time, and it seemed that only seconds had passed."

Gage shrugged. "I do not know how much time it was for me. For you, I watched everything on the disk. You disappeared from the chamber where you were with Dr. Limbu. I heard you appear behind me almost instantly. There was...no delay of which to speak. Whatever power makes this happen, it acts with great speed."

Across from him, the crystalline wall glistened as though it had somehow acknowledged his words.

Daria dismissed it as a trick of the lighting. At first. An idea was growing within her mind. Under their current circumstances, which became more desperate by the minute, it was worthwhile to entertain even the most ridiculous-seeming notions.

She clasped her forearms with the opposite hand and swiveled at the waist to look back and forth between the Gurkha and the mass of blue stone. "So, it transports people instantly. Like a machine, which has an automatic reaction once it's engaged. One turns the key, and the engine starts. The mouse takes the cheese and the trap springs.

"Yet your fellow scientists spoke of this thing as though it were alive and had intelligence. Why? What do they know, what have they seen, that we have not?"

"Probably nothing," Gage offered. "They did not seem to understand how the disk worked. Or so it appears. I believe they are simply going mad after being here so long, especially with no water or food."

Daria glanced at the disk. "That had occurred to me also. Yet, some things make no sense. How far is this chamber from where we were before? What space did we pass through to get here? Why and how did we come here, and why is this room a destination when other places aren't?"

Dr. Gurung's eyes were going distant as he reflected on it all, and he pursed his lips as he sank within himself, thinking deeply about the many strange possibilities unfolding before them.

"I have wondered about such things myself," he admitted, "but there are no good answers. We know that the Atlanticans had technology far more advanced than anyone has dreamed. Do you know anything about computers? Robots? I am beginning to think about things like that. People sometimes say that robots and computers behave as though they are alive."

Daria knew very little about things of that nature, but the concept disturbed her.

Gage went on. "Maybe our friends, Hurstett and Fields, believe that all of this," he waved at the chamber, "is controlled by a machine that can think or that can imitate human thought. One which can behave like a living thing with its own will."

The notion sounded absurd on its face. Trapped here in an ancient catacomb surrounded by wondrous things lost for thousands of years, it was easier to consider it than it might've been under the natural light of day.

"But why," she mused, "would it always choose to send people here? What does it have to do with the crystals and their power? Why did those three workmen end up in the troughs with that strange, cold gel? Ugh. There are too many questions."

Gage held up a hand, palm outward in a gesture of conciliation. "No, no, it is good to ask questions. That is the essence of science. To always question things and never assume that we know everything, for we do not. Perhaps I should speak to my colleagues again."

Daria didn't want to force him to make the trek with his injured ankle, so she offered to head to the other room and see if the scientists would come out instead. Begrudgingly, Gage allowed her to go.

When she arrived in the trough chamber, the pair were sitting against the wall. Their demeanor was more relaxed as though the worst of their irrational fears had subsided, and they were resting in preparation for whatever came next.

It didn't last. As soon as Daria raised the subject of determining the true nature of the power, entity, or autonomous machine that had banished them here, they once more cowered in terror, gibbering and covering their ears and eyes.

"Nope!" Dr. Fields protested. "We're not talking about that. Nope!"

Dr. Hurstett shook his head and moaned. "It's useless. We

would only anger or frighten it. It does not seem to understand us. It's too powerful and yet too simple. No, no. Please forget all about it. Useless..."

Daria ground her teeth, turned, and left without a word, leaving the two scholars to their blather and anxieties. As she stepped back into the first room, her mind processed what Hurstett had said.

Too powerful and yet too simple. What did it mean? It had to have some significance. He'd tried to tell her nothing, yet he *had* told her something regardless.

She reported it all to Dr. Gurung.

"Hmm, yes, yes," the Nepali murmured. "There might be something here for us to pursue."

Daria crossed her arms and tapped her foot on the floor. "Well. It would make sense that if the flash of white could move us from the first chamber with the carvings to this chamber with its wall of blue crystal, it could also do the opposite and move us back. Would it not? If it's like a living thing, maybe it could be...convinced."

She half-expected that the other two scholars would've already thought of this and tried it themselves. Scientists were people who made a career out of asking questions, trying to answer those same questions, and if nothing was forthcoming according to the established ways of doing things, making new shit up.

Gage sensed what she had in mind. "I will go and ask them. Please wait here for now. Since they know me, I hope they will speak like they are sensible, instead of acting like crazy people." He frowned. "I cannot promise anything."

Daria waved that off. "Do as much as you can. Don't hurt yourself. Watch out for your ankle."

"Those two will probably need time to recover in normal conditions before they're much help. Still, it's worth a try. Here, I'll help you down the hall and leave before they can see us both.

They might be frightened by me coming back to yell at them again."

She aided Gage once more, supporting him until the final corner when she hung back and allowed him to progress on his own. The room muffled their low voices, and it took nearly ten minutes for Gurung to start limping back.

Daria saw his face and knew at once that he got something useful out of the two. "What is it?" Her excited impatience was difficult to disguise.

His expression was one of grim satisfaction. "They have confirmed some of what we suspected. The power controlling this place, and the crystals, does things automatically, like a machine, but it also has a mind of its own. If that is true, and not only the ravings of madmen, this machine can do other things."

The Executioner's brow grew wrinkles as she scrunched up her face in concentration. "Such as sending us back. How would we communicate with it? Something completely different from a human being. The humans it would've known, those who would've given it life, lived thousands of years ago. A much different culture."

Dr. Gurung shrugged and spread his hands. "Yes. But people from different cultures can sometimes communicate. We can try talking to it. I can think of nothing else yet."

Daria was about to voice her skepticism, but she didn't want to discourage the man, so she kept her mouth shut. Instead, he leaned on her arm, and together they returned to the crystal room. Then he shuffled past her, moving carefully to avoid aggravating his ankle, toward the blue wall where the odd floating disk awaited.

He raised his hand and touched the edge of the circular object, which caused it to waft down to chest height in front of him. Then he took the seashell device from its niche within the stone and held it up next to his face. Daria noted how much he looked like a man about to speak into a telephone receiver.

He cleared his throat. "Is there anyone there? Can you hear me?" Then he waited.

As they'd both expected, the immediate response was silence.

As Daria was about to suggest something else, a metallic *hum* came from the shell device, not so much shattering the silence as gently pushing it aside. Riding the reverberations was a voice.

Gage started, and Daria stiffened. An icy trickle worked its way down her spine, and her senses instantly rose to full alertness.

The voice that came from the shell was harsh and guttural, yet it was more the result of noises surrounding it than the essence of the voice itself—like a child speaking through a mass of grinding stone, *clanking* metal, and sloshing water all at once. Not a single word of it was understandable.

Daria blinked. She hadn't expected an answer at all, and it would have been foolish to assume the Atlanticans spoke any modern tongue. Still, she scanned her brain for anything recognizable within the garbled, eerie statement. She spoke several languages, being fluent in English, Polish, and Yiddish, and was moderately proficient in German and Hebrew. Nothing whatsoever amidst the brief, disembodied response sounded like anything other than gibberish.

"Gage," she whispered, "do you understand what it said?"

His face had tightened in concentration. "No. Let us try again, in different languages. Perhaps it will understand one. Dr. Limbu thought that Atlantica might be related to the legend of Kumari Kandam, which is a lost civilization spoken of in Tamil myth. I speak little Tamil, but it is worth trying, and maybe it would understand Hindi as well."

Daria nodded. "If that doesn't work, it might know Hebrew through the Egyptians, perhaps." She doubted it, though. The North Atlantic was a long way from both the Eastern Mediterranean and the Indian subcontinent.

Gage repeated his simple request in every language he knew.

Each time, there was the same harsh, distorted, bone-chilling response, and Daria quickly grasped that the voice was always replying with the same phrase or sentence. She had no idea what it meant, but it was the same pattern of sounds in each case.

When the Gurkha gave up, Daria tried her repertoire of languages. The voice was even stranger but less intimidating when speaking into her ear directly. Still, at no point did it reply with anything other than its stock response.

She shook her head. "It's hopeless. It seems to know only one language, Atlantican, or some other people who might've been here long ago. Native Americans or perhaps the Norsemen. I can think of nothing else."

As she paused to gather her thoughts, the shell repeated its usual statement. She glanced at it and began counting. Every twenty-four or twenty-five seconds, it spoke again. But there was no way to comprehend it. She considered asking the two scientists in the other chamber, but it was doubtful they could help even if they could overcome their terror of the mysterious entity.

Daria sighed and turned her face toward Gage. "I'm sorry, but it seems we can do nothing. I'm going to hang up. Then we must think of—"

While her hand was in the process of placing the stone shell in its niche, the stone disk shimmered, and the random blobs of light that appeared coalesced into an identifiable shape. Daria gasped despite herself, and Gage shuffled two steps closer, stopping beside her to stare at the smooth surface before them.

The light formed into the unmistakable image of a human face. It lacked detail or individual features, but it represented something a person would recognize as one of their own. Its eyes were startlingly realistic, although the irises were rings of blue-white light like the glow of Atlanticore.

It looked at each of them in turn, the expression shifting subtly as though in acknowledgment of their presence. It *saw* them.

Daria was the first to speak and tried not to stutter. "Can you understand us?"

The mouth moved upward at the ends in a gentle smile. The face tilted a bit upward and reoriented itself, a foreign gesture but close enough to a nod that its meaning was clear.

Yes.

CHAPTER NINETEEN

Daria's mouth opened and closed as a hundred questions raced through her mind, all of them fighting for dominance. Her mind struggled to assign them priorities and decide which language to ask in—after all, if the face could somehow understand English, it might comprehend Polish or Yiddish.

Gage, it seemed, was experiencing a similar dilemma. He stammered and tripped over his words, beginning in English and lapsing into what was perhaps his native Nepali tongue, or possibly Hindi or Tamil. He gesticulated to better express himself.

When he paused, Daria slipped a question in edgewise. Since they'd first asked the face if it comprehended them in English, she opted for consistency.

"Who and what are you? Did the Atlanticans leave you behind? Can you send us out of here, the way you brought us in?"

Dr. Gurung tried pressing a few more inquiries along similar lines.

The face only looked back and forth between the two of them, smiling and staring vacantly. Daria despaired of receiving a proper answer from it. Not only did it seem unable to speak without the stone shell device to project its voice, but the placid, bemused look on its strangely primitive features suggested a lack of adult intelligence.

Daria fell silent as Gage continued his questions, though at a slower pace. Then, the face fixated on him, individually, and began to move its head up, down, or to the side after each thing he said.

"Wait." Gage looked at Daria. He hadn't realized that she'd stopped pressing the face for answers a moment ago. "It seems that it cannot understand too much at once, only one question at a time. It is replying with movements of its face. We must determine what each of those movements means if we are to communicate with it."

Daria breathed a sigh of relief. Dr. Gurung was a quick thinker. Assuming he was right, they could still have a chance to get out of the catacomb. "When it raised its chin like it was nodding upward, that seemed to mean 'yes.' How do we determine what the other motions mean?"

A jumble of ideas arose in her brain, but Gage had one first.

"I know." He beamed, obviously proud of himself. "We will ask it questions that can have only one possible answer which is true. That way, we will know what each gesture means in advance and can memorize them."

Daria patted the man on the shoulder. "Most excellent, Dr. Gurung. I can see why you became a scientist." Based on her long experience in dealing with different types of people and communicating under stressful circumstances, she might've come to a similar conclusion given enough time. For Gage to have reached it *almost instantly* was far better.

The man's smile dimmed a little, not because he was unhappy, but because she'd embarrassed him with praise, drawing out his humble and sheepish side. He rolled his shoulders and looked back at the glowing blue face.

"Am I speaking to you right now?"

The face took on a mild but pleasant expression and tilted upward.

Gage looked at Daria. "Very good. That means yes. Fix in your mind what it looks like, please."

"I have," she stated. "Now let us see how it expresses the opposite."

The Nepali returned his gaze to disembodied visage within the disk. "Are there three of us?"

This time, the face's pleasant expression dimmed to one of slight disappointment, and it tilted downward and a bit off to the left.

Daria smoothed out her hair, growing more excited by the second. "Up and a smile is yes, down and a frown means no. That makes sense. I wonder if it has other responses, like 'I don't know?' That might be too difficult, though. We should only ask it questions it can answer with a simple negative or affirmative."

"I agree. I will start at the beginning if you have no objections."

Daria did not, so Gage looked once more at their guest. "You. Are you the one who took us from the excavated chamber and sent us to this room?"

The face paused for a moment, and Daria feared that it might not comprehend the nature of the question. It was possible that it didn't recognize itself as a distinct entity, and therefore might be confused by the word "you."

Then, after the bluish light that made up its features flickered, it took on a bemused smile and nodded up.

Gage stroked his chin while squinting in concentration. "It is incredible. This thing must be able to read our facial emotions and tones of voice and perhaps trace parts of our languages to older root tongues. It is amazing for it to understand us since it cannot speak back in any language we would comprehend."

Daria had to admit that it was mind-boggling to consider. If indeed the face was a machine of some sort and not a supernatural being, the Atlanticans' technology might well have *exceeded* that possessed by the greatest scientific leaders of the modern world.

There would be time to ruminate on such matters later. For now, they had other concerns.

Daria stepped in and got the face's attention, posing the next query herself. "You sent us here. Are you able to send us back?"

Again, the head responded with its pleasant little upward nod.

Daria closed her eyes, exhaling in relief. There was hope, after all. They'd found a way to get out of their predicament alive. All they needed was for the autonomous machine represented by the face to cooperate, to acquiesce to their request.

Gage asked it, "Will you? Will you send us back, please? All of us that is. Including the two scientists and three workers from before."

The glowing face fell, its gentle smile became a frown of mild disapproval, and it nodded down and to the side.

Daria's eyes bulged. *"What? Why not?"* Her hands trembled with sudden anger, the frustration of being at the mercy of this strange, simple creature from a past era. It held nearly absolute power over their fate yet could barely communicate with them.

The face stared blankly. The Executioner fumed. She'd made an error since it was not a yes-or-no question, and the face had no way of replying to them.

Gage intervened and addressed the visage. "We must return to the first chamber. It is very important. You are saying that you cannot allow us to do that?"

It replied with its inoffensive little smile and upward nod.

Daria turned, threw her hands up in the depths of her fury, and clawed the musty air. She abruptly wanted to kick a wall or draw her pistol and fire a round at the crystal barrier or the smooth stone disk. She restrained herself. Either of those options would be beyond stupid and pointless.

Kicking a wall would accomplish nothing and might injure

her foot or leg. Shooting the wall or disk might frighten or anger the face or whatever intelligence lay behind it, not to mention it could cause a ricochet that might injure or kill Gage or herself.

Dr. Gurung remained calm and kept the entity under steady pressure from a stream of careful inquiries.

"Why is that? Do you think that something bad will happen if you do?"

The face replied in the affirmative.

"Why?" Gage went on. "Does it have to do with this place needing to be kept secret from everyone?"

Surprisingly, the face frowned and turned downwards. Gage seemed as confused as Daria was. The entity's motivations made no sense, and getting it to answer them solely through questions of yes or no might take an excessively long time.

Daria asked, "Is there some way you can show us or tell us why? What do we need to know to explain to us why we're prisoners here? You owe it to us to at least explain that much!"

The face held itself in a neutral, pensive expression, as though it were paying attention but had nothing to say and lost itself in reflection. Then its eyes brightened and stared back into the pair's faces and drew their total focus toward itself.

With that, it vanished.

"What..." Daria began in a low, gasping whisper. "Did we anger it?"

Gage raised a hand and made a sharp chopping motion. "Wait. Look!"

They both leaned forward, peering at the smooth disk. The face had disappeared, but the vague shimmering light that had constituted it continued to swirl. Daria deduced that it was reforming into something else.

It did. Once more it showed them a scene like that from a movie or television program, a view of the frieze-chamber where they'd started. It was similar to Gage's perspective while he spied on Dr. Limbu after Daria's banishment.

Both quickly grasped that they were viewing an event that had occurred in the recent past. Gage scrambled to grab the seashell device and held it up between his and Daria's faces so they could hear any sounds that might accompany the images.

Before them were the two scientists, Hurstett and Fields, and the three workers who now reposed in the gel-filled troughs. The scene undoubtedly depicted the day they'd all been laboring before their disappearance.

It was banal at first. The archaeologists prodded at things, dusted off parts of the friezes, and made notes in their little booklets while mumbling to one another. All they had to say sounded like no more than typical expectations of what they hoped to find, combined with scientific jargon that went over Daria's head.

Much of their dialogue was impossible to distinguish due to the racket from the portable jackhammers wielded by the three workmen as they sought to clear the remaining excess rubble from the chamber's far corner. Daria idly wondered if that corner led to the same hallway, still blocked by debris, that branched off from the trough chamber.

If not, it could mean that the whole underground complex here was far more extensive than anyone had imagined.

Things progressed without incident for about a minute. Then, one of the three laborers moved toward an adjacent wall. Fields and Hurstett were busy comparing notes in the opposite corner and paid him no heed. Daria saw that he'd put himself close to the carving of the many-branched crystal tree surrounded by human figures.

She more or less knew what to expect next. The man fired up his jackhammer and made a show of chipping off some protrusions of extra rock, then paused and slowly, carefully turned the tool's blade toward the luminescent blue substance itself. He made the motion so quick and furtive that had anyone seen him, he could've passed it off as an accident.

As the slim piece of Atlanticore fell into the man's hand, something happened that he probably hadn't expected. Flickers of light rippled across all the smooth crystal expanse throughout the room, and a faint *hum* rose to fill the confined space.

It was impossible to ignore. The man cursed under his breath and slipped the fragment into his pocket as the other two laborers glanced at him, and the two scholars turned and shouted in alarm.

"Hey, hey!" Dr. Fields began. "What are you doing? Did you damage the crystal?"

Hurstett looked at the carving of the tree and noticed at once that one of the branch portions was empty. "What happened there? You didn't chip that off, did you? We *must not* damage any of the architecture here, and especially not the crystal portions, given how unstable it is. Furthermore, you're all under contract not to remove any Atlanticore from the dig site."

He waved his pencil around with a stern expression while Fields ran to the other side of the chamber to ascertain how bad the damage was.

Daria's heart rate increased as she watched, intent on nothing else. To her surprise, the trio of workers didn't act sheepish, didn't deny the charges, and otherwise didn't bother to defend themselves. Rather, they blustered.

The other two laughed while the one who'd stolen the crystal fragment jeered, "Yeah, *under contract*, whoop-de-doo. There are other contracts out there. What're you gonna do about it, huh? You sure ain't telling anyone, *that's* for sure. All this," he waved and pointed at the tree-frieze, "is *just* how we all found it. Right?"

The trio advanced, still holding their jackhammers. Fields rushed to Hurstett's side. The two scientists stood their ground and tried to look courageous despite being cut off from the exit.

As it happened, the light on the disk that sketched out the whole scene changed. A pale corona formed around each figure, much as it had when Gage had watched Ak prowl around the chamber earlier.

Fields exclaimed, "Stop this at once! Or we'll tell Dr. Limbu. She will *not* be happy to hear that some of her workers are stealing from the dig and threatening her research team. You would all be kicked off the job and forfeit your pay."

The workers only laughed and exchanged knowing glances. Daria fumed inwardly. These three were, without any doubt, among those in league with Akshara and part of whatever plot she was pursuing.

Dr. Hurstett added, "Let's not forget Mr. Boucher. He promised us that he would run a tight ship and there would be no funny business. He doesn't seem like a man any of you would want to cross, now does he? So put those things down and come to your senses."

At this, the trio paused and appeared to hesitate. Then the man who'd taken the shard, their apparent leader, stomped forward, hoisting his jackhammer like a halberd. The others followed, reacting like cornered animals forced to defend themselves, even though it was they who'd cornered the scientists.

Dr. Fields screamed. Dr. Hurstett fell into a defensive stance, but the despairing look on his face told the whole story—as milquetoast researchers armed only with pencils, he and Fields would stand no chance against three burly men brandishing heavy power tools.

Something happened. As though the intelligence that had watched and recorded the scene were concentrating on the quintet, the coronas surrounding them changed color. Those surrounding the three workers turned smoky black, whereas the two scientists turned cherry red.

Then, with a bright white flash, all five of them were gone. The scene dissipated, and the blobs of light became mere shimmers on the disk's polished surface.

Daria shook her head. "That's interesting. It was the foreman they were afraid of, not Dr. Limbu. That's in line with what you've now experienced, yes?" She stared at Dr. Gurung, waiting for him to respond.

The small man seemed befuddled and disturbed. He didn't look back at her but had heard the question. "Yes, I am afraid it is." He cracked his knuckles in an absentminded way and kept gazing at the disk.

Daria's blood heated with simmering anger, but there was also the grim satisfaction of cracking open the case her employers had assigned her. The mystery was no longer so mysterious.

"It adds up when we review all that we know so far. Ak has a stake in this theft. She intended to loot some of the crystal from the dig. She has an arrangement with a portion of Boucher's workers. I don't know how many or what the deal is. Probably, they'll receive a cut of the profits after they resell the crystals on the black market."

Gage's face darkened as the fact of his boss' treachery became harder to avoid than ever. "But why? Why would she compromise the excavation? To destroy a site like this is terrible archaeology. To complete our study the correct way would be far, far, better."

Daria flashed him a grim smile. "For humanity and culture, and the posterity of our knowledge, yes, it would be better. For her pocketbook...perhaps not so much."

The Nepali hung his head and examined the floor, unable to speak. It wasn't only the betrayal that had nearly killed him, Daria surmised, but a profound disappointment in Dr. Limbu that disturbed him so much. On some level, he must've looked up to her as an icon, an upstanding scientist he would be honored to work with despite her abrasiveness.

Meanwhile, Daria recalled what Eleanor had told her before the mission. Powerful, wealthy, and influential people had invested in Akshara's projects. They must've expected a nice profitable return on their investment. As such, Dr. Limbu must've been under considerable pressure to produce evidence that would pay off.

All of the Atlanticore at the dig thus far had been interwoven into the priceless, ancient carvings of the buried complex. Removing it could become complicated. In the scene Daria and Gage had watched, Hurstett and Fields had objected to chipping off a single small piece. Stripping the whole labyrinth of its crystal payload would create an enormous scandal. Everyone would accuse the team of being grave robbers and plunderers, embarrassments to the world of science.

Furthermore, the revelation of the autonomous machine added an extra wrinkle to the whole inscrutable quilt of details— the strange artificial intelligence watched over the catacombs and manifested as a human face. The archaeological community would demand to study it in detail. Strip-mining the whole place for Atlanticore might kill the entity before they could do any such research.

No sooner had Daria had the thought than the light on the disk reformed into the face that had greeted them previously, its expression neutral and open.

Gage gasped. Not because he was surprised by the face's reappearance, but because something had suddenly occurred to him.

"It is a security system!" he commented. "You there. Your purpose is to stop people from being hurt. Is that it?"

The face smiled and nodded up.

Daria fixed her gaze on it and drew its attention. "So, you are only trying to protect us?" When it responded in the affirmative, she asked the obvious follow-up question. "Do you realize that if you keep us here for too long, we will die?"

They hadn't seen everything the entity was capable of yet since it shocked them both with an expression of profound horror and empathy. Then it reverted to its usual mild frown and downward headshake.

The Executioner and the Gurkha exchanged a glance.

Gage said, "Hurstett. He said it was simple. It has the mind of a small child. It means well, but it does not understand things."

"Yes, it seems that way," Daria agreed. "I wonder if that was intentional or because the original designers couldn't make it more intelligent to begin with. Or if it was smarter at first but has degraded over time."

Her companion shrugged. "It could be any of the three. I would be most curious to find out. Let us return to convincing it to free us."

Daria had no objections. They reengaged with the face, explaining that human beings needed food and water, and none was present in the underground labyrinth. Despite the entity's goal to keep them safe, it was killing them by cutting them off from the outside world and its necessary resources.

"And," Gage added, as the face listened patiently to their spiel, "we might need more oxygen, too. The air is stale here. Perhaps a small amount comes in from outside through cracks in the rubble, but with four of us down here now, we might breathe all the oxygen before it can replenish itself. One way or another, you must understand. If we remain here, we all will die."

The face again looked appalled at the idea. But it made no move, yet, to transport them back to the frieze chamber.

Then Daria thought of something. "There are others outside, too, who intend to do more harm. They mean to hurt one another—other human beings—and they also intend to damage the chamber and steal your crystal. Do you understand?"

It smiled and nodded. Then it flickered, and when its appearance stabilized, the light that composed it was dimmer.

Daria looked at Gage. "What was that?"

The small man examined the crystal wall beyond the disk. It, too, was not as bright as it had been mere minutes ago. "This system is old. Older than we can imagine. Nothing has taxed it for a long time. Now, we have placed great demands on it. It must be running out of energy. The crystals are draining from everything it has had to do since our team first found the chamber."

Daria blinked. Given how powerful Atlanticore was said to be, the prospect hadn't occurred to her, but it made sense. She looked at the face. "Are you worried that if you transport us all out of here, that you will run out of power and...die?"

It assumed a somber expression, then reverted to its usual pleasant gesture of affirmation.

Gage covered his eyes with his hand. "Oh, dear. This is bad. There may be no way to convince it. Or it might not have the strength to do it at all..."

Daria clenched her hands. Her mind raced. There had to be a way. She refused to give up so easily, not after everything she'd been through in life. Not when she'd sworn to uphold justice across this island, which represented the new best hope of humanity.

The concept of *justice*, she recalled, meant dealing fair outcomes wherever they were earned or warranted. Part of her duty was to protect Atlantica and its people.

She decided it stood to reason that her mandate included the need to protect Atlantica *from itself* when necessary. Now seemed like such a time.

She inhaled deeply, confronted the strange glowing face, and offered it a deal. "We can help you if you help us. You must have enough power remaining to send us back.

"I understand your concern at being overtaxed. We'll agree to stop you from having your strength taken away. We'll ensure that this team seals the chamber once more so no one can disturb your rest, and no one can take any of the crystal you rely upon to survive."

The shift in the face's expression was subtle and difficult to get a reading on, but it seemed to understand the general nature of her offer. Or, at least, it was listening and doing its best to comprehend it.

"And," she added, "as long as I have any say in the matter, the chamber will *remain* sealed, and you won't be bothered. I'm a person who has authority on this island, and my word is as good as law. Look; see the proof."

She pointed at her armored uniform and showed the face her shoulders, where the insignia of the Executioners, a skull and sword, gleamed with its mixture of majesty and foreboding. It was a symbol to take seriously.

The disembodied face's mouth opened and formed a circle as though impressed. Its childlike nature was never more apparent. She'd overcome its resistance and made her point.

Gage blinked. "Do you agree to our terms, then?"

The face smiled and nodded up.

Daria was about to suggest that they gather up Hurstett, Fields, and the three workers before returning to prepare for their brief but probably painful journey back to the original chamber. She never had the time.

Without warning, the face and the autonomous will behind it chose to fulfill its end of the bargain without delay.

Her voice caught in her throat as an invisible force lifted her and blinding light, blue-white and blazing with warmth, enveloped her.

"Wait!" she shouted, but the *hum* and the flash and the dizziness silenced her.

Then she could remember nothing; for how long, she didn't know, but it was all too familiar from her earlier ordeal. When she emerged from the flash, again there was terrible pain, an agony that must've been so intense her brain and body wouldn't allow her to remember it.

The first thing she saw through the mass of blinking yellow and pink spots was a carved frieze of a tree, but the Atlanticore laid throughout it was oddly dark. It had been drained of most of its power by the autonomous machine's repeated efforts.

The second thing she saw was the faintest trace of the enigmatic face, its light fading as it smiled and gave a curt upward motion of its head, much like a nod of agreement.

CHAPTER TWENTY

Everyone stood frozen in place and staring at one another. The sentient machine had arranged them in a perfect circle, all seven of them standing on their feet and facing inward, with arms down at their sides. They were back in the chamber of friezes, the first to be excavated.

That meant behind where Daria stood, around the short corner and down the tunnel, lay the sharp and jagged shaft to the surface. And escape. The possibility of survival in a normal life awaited them.

It took Daria another instant or two to appreciate the presence of the three workers. Their ancient benefactor had sent the trio along with the rest of them. Since their clothes had burned off when it had first transported them, they were still naked, in addition to looking groggy and confused after their long slumber in the frigid gel of the troughs.

The first of the group to break the stillness and silence was Dr. Fields. Her eyes, already wide, bulged incredibly in tandem with her face splitting into a crazy, silly, totally unabashed grin.

"Out," she gasped, her voice cracking with giddy exultation. "We're *out*. It let us go. It set us free! Oh, God..."

She turned and sprinted toward the doorway but stumbled and slowed down. She was too weak from hunger and thirst for her body to keep up with her excitement.

Daria realized that Fields would probably yell up the shaft for help, which would likely bring workers hustling to their rescue.

Yet, standing before her were three men who'd agreed to do terrible things. They still might be willing to finish what they'd started, as well. Daria didn't know how many of the others were in league with them.

She started after Fields. "Wait! Stop. We must discuss things first. Just a minute or two!"

The scientist was out of sight, but it sounded like her awkward, jogging footfalls slowed down. She didn't try to call for anyone to hoist them out yet.

Daria paused in the doorway and looked back over her shoulder. "You three," she said in a firm, sharp, and commanding tone, "stay right where you are. No one is going anywhere yet. Gage, watch them closely. I'll be right back."

Gage gave a short bow of his head and allowed his hand to fall to the hilt of his kukri. Dr. Hurstett stood in awkward and nervous silence.

The three workmen didn't react in any obvious way, but a vague look of comprehension on their faces, and a darkening of their eyes, hinted that they were coming back to full awareness of the situation. They were free of their unnatural frozen slumber, but someone had found out their scheme.

Daria didn't like leaving Gage alone with them. He was ferocious and probably an excellent fighter, but with his ankle injury, he might not be able to resist three men at once. Then again, the workers hadn't been around when the Gurkha had dropped into the pit and had no idea of his condition. This was the first they'd seen of him since the day the light had claimed them.

She plunged into the corridor beyond the chamber, trusting and hoping that her friend would manage for a minute or less without her. Dr. Fields had stopped only about three yards past the small intersection and was leaning against the wall, catching her breath. She was even weaker than Daria had thought.

"Dr. Fields. Diana," the Executioner began in a gentle voice. "Please wait. We've made it, and we'll call for help in a minute. But first..." She caught the smaller woman's eye and nodded at the chamber, hoping that Fields wasn't too maddened to understand what she meant.

The scientist gaped dumbly at her for a second, then nodded. "Yes, of course. But please. *Please* don't make us wait much longer. I'm dying for a drink of water. Dying!"

Daria didn't doubt it. Still, they might all die of backstabbing as surely as they would have of thirst if they didn't deal with certain issues first.

She put a firm hand on the smaller woman's shoulder and squeezed it. "It won't be long. We've almost finished here. Then it will be over, and you'll be safe and well. There's one major risk yet. Stay here, and don't make a sound. I'll be right back."

Fields trembled, squeezed her eyes shut, and probably struggled not to weep since rescue was so close at hand. Still, she was smart enough to grasp the wisdom of what Daria had said, and conditional insanity hadn't completely eroded her intelligence.

Daria left her in the tunnel and returned to the chamber. She tensed at once—Gage had drawn his big, intimidating knife and stood in a battle stance. As for the trio of workers, one staggered against the wall, groaning and drooling. Another leaned beside him and panted, while the third simply stood perfectly still in the same place he'd been when Daria left.

Gage explained the situation before she could ask. "Those two tried to move against me." He gestured at the pair who supported themselves against the wall. "They were too, ah, unwell from their slumber to move properly."

The Executioner nodded. "Good. Now would be an excellent

time to ask them a few questions." She turned her gaze on the three, and her eyes sharpened. "And to tell them how things shall be from here on." She allowed her hand to rest on her gun's grip, and they all saw it.

None of the men was stupid enough to try anything. Their physical faculties were still impaired since they hadn't fully recovered yet. Daria and Gage had the drop on them, with weapons, while they were naked and unarmed. If the maddened scientists jumped in against them, it would neutralize the slight advantage of one extra man.

Daria waved at them, the motion curt and imperious.

"You men. I know what happened, so don't attempt to lie to me. You endeavored to steal a piece of Atlanticore from the chamber, and you attacked Dr. Hurstett and Dr. Fields when they tried to intervene. You have a deal with Dr. Limbu, yes? I don't yet know the specifics, but your game is up.

"Now is your chance to cooperate and avoid severe punishment. If you tell me everything and don't attempt anything foolish, it will go far better for you." She drew her upper lip away from her teeth. "I guarantee it."

The one who'd leaned his head on the wall, barely avoiding the touch of the Atlanticore, spun around, gasping, and looked at her. She recognized him as the group's apparent ringleader by his high cheekbones—the man who'd taken the crystal shard and started the whole mess.

"Yeah," he huffed, "we get it. I don't know what the hell happened to us, but it must've been bad. Get us out of here, and we'll talk. Who are you, anyway?"

Daria moved her eyes sidelong, taking in the other two before returning to the man with the cheekbones. "I'm Executioner Barruk, partner to Executioner Katakura, and responsible for dispensing justice on Atlantica. The Executives called me in to investigate after you three and our two scientists disappeared.

"Now my investigation is nearly complete. So, talk. There will be time for all the details later. I want to know how many of you are in Limbu's pocket and what the rest of her plan is."

Behind her, there was a faint whimper of impatience from Dr. Fields. Daria ignored it. The woman could wait another minute or two while the corrupted workers divulged their secrets.

The leader, who gave his name as Ben, didn't waste time.

"Ak paid off about half of the men on the crew," he stated. "Or maybe a little less, like four out of ten, something like that. We're supposed to get as much Atlanticore out of this place as possible. It has to be a secret, she says. Can't be too obvious about it and can't reveal that she was involved."

Daria nodded. Most of that was no surprise, but it disturbed her that so many laborers were in on the plot. No wonder it had been as difficult as it had to make any progress on finding out the truth. The entire operation was essentially rotten.

The man who'd stood in place added, "She said that she had to protect her, uh, academic credentials. She's this big, esteemed archaeologist and it would fuck up her reputation if people knew she was a thief, out to grab all that precious blue crystal like all the other thieves on this damn island." He gave a sardonic chuckle that turned into a hollow, raspy cough.

Gage muttered something under his breath in his native language. He kept the kukri in his hand. Beside him, Dr. Hurstett's face was aghast at the revelation. He must not have suspected such a level of duplicity from his boss.

Daria gnawed on her lower lip. "What motivated her to do all this? Why is she so desperate?"

The sardonic fellow shrugged, and the others stared blankly. Ben said, "Beats me. Money, I guess? She already had a bunch to throw at us. So who knows. None of my goddamn business."

The Executioner frowned. "It makes no difference, then. We'll stop her and bring her to justice. I'll see to it that you men aren't killed or otherwise mistreated, but you'll probably be shipped off Atlantica with little more than the clothes on your backs and whatever you might have at home. After that, your lives will be yours, for better or worse."

Ben glared at her, his eyes full of dull anger and loathing, but the other two didn't react. She couldn't fault them for being less than pleased with how things had turned out. Still, they had no one to blame but themselves. They could've as easily rejected Ak's offer, claimed their normal pay, and preserved their reputations as honest workers.

While keeping one eye on the naked trio, Daria called over her shoulder, "Dr. Fields. Go ahead to the tunnel mouth and call for help. Have them get the winches running and at least two harnesses ready at a time." She figured it would make the most sense to get the scientists out first, followed by Gage and the treacherous laborers, with herself last. Just in case.

Footsteps moved away from them. Then the woman's shrill voice cried, "Help! Someone. Is anyone up there? Please help us! We need a winch with two harnesses. Get us out of here..."

Faintly, the sounds of commotion came down the tunnel from the dig shaft, including the garbled shouts of men. Boucher must've left some of his people near the mouth as Daria had requested.

She moved to the doorway leading out of the chamber, then backed out into the corridor beyond, motioning for the three workers to follow her. "Gage, Dr. Hurstett, bring up the rear, please. Thank you."

The laborers trudged out, sullen and shuffling, getting closer and seeming to have a better grip on themselves than they had at first. Whatever arcane methods the frigid gel in the troughs had used to put them in suspended animation, it didn't appear to have any major long-term negative effects on their health or mobility.

From somewhere in the shadows that lay closer to the faint

shafts of light from the surface, Dr. Fields' voice rang out in a loud squeal, almost a scream.

Daria's head snapped in that direction, fearing that Limbu and her supporters had sprung another trap.

"Yessss!" Dr. Fields went on. "We're free! We're going to get *out!*"

Grimacing in irritation, Daria vowed to give the scientist a talking-to later when everyone was safe. She looked back in time to see Ben charging her with a look of murder on his face.

"*Shit!*" she grunted as his shoulder slammed into her midsection. He was weak from his long period of inactivity, but he was still a big, strong man. His sheer bulk sent her sprawling back, the air knocked out of her lungs and her gorge rising from the impact against her solar plexus. Her legs kicked alternately at rock and thin air, and she barely avoided falling as her left hand reached out behind her to touch the far wall and lend her stability.

Dr. Hurstett yammered in a wordless, raspy voice, alarmed and confused as the sardonic worker shoved him back into the frieze chamber. The scientist tripped over his feet and landed on his back.

The third of the treacherous three attacked Dr. Gurung. He was the largest and tallest of them all, and a huge hand closed around Gage's right wrist a split second before the Gurkha could pivot and strike out with his kukri.

Dr. Fields' voice called, "Hey! What's going on? Is everyone—"

Daria drew her pistol while regaining her balance, but Ben had already pounced on her again, clamping a hand over her mouth before she could shout. She brought her knee up into the man's unprotected groin. He yelped in pain but grabbed her gun as he doubled over and twisted away from her. His desperate, grasping strength—the physical power of a man who cut rocks with heavy machinery for a living—was more than she could overcome.

With pain half-disabling him, Daria wasn't about to give up. She'd offered him and his friends a second chance, a fair deal. They'd responded to her overtures with a final attempt to maim or kill anyone who stood in the way of their ill-gotten payoff. There would be no *third* chance for them, no further deals.

Daria sidestepped to the man's rear in the blink of an eye, making it all but impossible for him to shoot her with her pistol. At the same instant, she drew the short knife she kept inside her belt. Ben struggled to stand, turn, and get a proper grip on the gun simultaneously.

He failed. Daria pounced on him and stabbed him in the spine. His nudity made the task easier. He squawked horribly, convulsed, and dropped the pistol. Then the Executioner pushed him back and slashed her blade across his throat. His eyes bulged as the blood spurted forth. By the time his hands went to the wound, he was already mostly dead.

Daria left him where he was to collapse to the ground and expire slowly. Instead, she dashed toward the rest of the fight.

The sardonic fellow had pushed past Gage and the third man and was running down the tunnel toward its mouth and Dr. Fields—who was a witness. A person he and his remaining comrade would need to eliminate to get away with their crimes.

No, Daria thought. He wouldn't succeed. He would *pay.*

She sprinted after him, dimly aware that Gage was struggling against the biggest of the three men. The knowledge of his wounded ankle pained her, but she had to trust him to take care of himself. The Gurkhas were renowned for their valor and skill in combat.

Daria couldn't have hoped to overtake the second man if he'd been in peak condition. He seemed slow, moving as though drunk, not yet fully recovered from the effects of the troughs. He was picking up speed, however.

Daria made the hasty decision to end the chase before it could begin. She leaped forward, throwing her feet in front of her in a kind of sliding kick, and her shins twisted around the man's left ankle.

"Fuck!" he exclaimed, hurtling headfirst toward the ground. He landed on his shoulder instead and rolled toward the wall.

Rather than give him time to recover, Daria sprang toward him on hands and knees instead of standing. The knife was still in her hand. The man looked up in time to see the blade plunging toward his face, then punching through the bone of his temple. He died instantly and crumpled into the dust.

Daria rose to her feet and allowed herself a half-second to assess the situation before she acted. Dr. Fields stood off to the right near the edge of the illuminated area at the end of the tunnel, staring in horror at what she'd witnessed.

"Wait there," Daria snapped, then plunged back toward Gage.

No sooner was she in motion than the struggle was over. The Nepali shouting in his mother tongue had somehow broken the big man's arm, shoved him away, then hacked into his chest and stomach with the fearsome blade of his distinctive knife. The last of the corrupt workers died gurgling on his own blood.

Daria slowed to a trot, then stopped. "Gage. Are you all right? How's your ankle?"

The Gurkha recovered from his battle rage and wiped off his kukri on a handkerchief from his pocket. "I am quite fine, thank you. Please check on Dr. Hurstett." The strain on his face made her suspect that he'd twisted his leg the wrong way or had to put too much pressure on his lame foot, but stoicism and adrenaline were powerful forces.

With a respectful nod, she moved past him into the crystal chamber, where Hurstett was slowly getting to his feet and dusting himself off.

"My God." The man gasped. "What a terrible turn of events. What's the matter with everyone? Why would they be so... Ugh." He seemed to be talking to himself more than to her.

Daria took him by the arm and looked him over. His fall had

done little more than perhaps give him a bruise or two, but given how weak he was from hunger and thirst, he was shaking as though far more seriously hurt. Like Fields, he probably had little or no experience with the ugliness of violence.

"Dr. Hurstett. It's over. Come, now. We're going to get you out of here." He muttered to himself but didn't protest as she led him out into the tunnel.

By now, the sound of the mechanical winch was filling the depths with its distinctive whine. Daria left Hurstett with Gage and went to fetch Fields.

The small woman was still gawking in shock. "Dr. Fields," Daria began, "I'm sorry you had to see that, but they were about to kill us to preserve their secrets. Please, come this way for a moment. I promise we'll go up as soon as the harnesses reach us."

Fields' mouth moved, but no sound came out. She followed Daria nonetheless.

With the four of them gathered in a group a short way down the tunnel—out of sight of the workers on the surface—Daria looked everyone in the eye before she spoke.

"We must not give away what's happened," she declared. "As that man said, almost half of Boucher's crew are collaborating with Dr. Limbu. We need them to suspect nothing until we're ready to spring a trap. Let us say that these three men died as a result of booby traps they encountered in the catacombs." She gestured at the slumped bodies.

Gage frowned. "I do not like this lying," he opined. With the threat neutralized, he was back to his usual kindly, mild-mannered self.

Daria gave him a sad little smile. "That's usually a good thing. In this case, we *must* lie, for now. Until Ak's greater lies can be exposed and the danger is past. Does everyone understand? Say nothing."

Heads nodded. Gage was unhappy about it, but he grasped the necessity. As for the other two scientists, they were too tired and strung out to offer much resistance, anyway. Daria only hoped that in their near-delirium they wouldn't forget and blab.

She pointed toward the steep slope of the exit shaft. "They've finished lowering the harnesses. Dr. Hurstett, Dr. Fields—you two may go first."

CHAPTER TWENTY-ONE

Daria kept blinking. The Atlanticore provided a certain degree of illumination, but it was still afternoon on the surface, and the day was clear and sunny. She would've thought her eyes would adjust more quickly. All around her, men were asking questions and offering them things. It was hard to keep up with it all.

There was no sign of Akshara Limbu.

After they'd sent up the two maddened researchers, Daria had taken an extra minute to harness up the Nepali properly to keep his ankle out of the action. She'd helped him over some of the more difficult parts herself. Soon enough, they were back aboveground.

Curious workers, not to mention Dr. Johnson and the other scientists, were barraging Hurstett and Fields with inquiries. The pair didn't have it in them to offer much more than vague gibbering about how awful it had been while demanding water and food.

Johnson said, "Very well, come back to camp, and we'll get you two nourished. Everyone else, please leave them alone for the time being. We'll have all the answers we need soon enough."

He gave Daria a knowing look. She responded with a nod.

Boucher took a step forward from the general mass. His strong body bristled with tension, and the way he folded his arms and flexed his hands suggested something close to aggression. Yet concern and even pain drew lines in his face. When he spoke, his voice was surprisingly soft.

"The three men who were down there with you. Where are they? What happened to them? Do you know?" He'd probably guessed that they wouldn't be coming out of the tunnels except for burial. But he clung to some small hope, giving Daria a chance to deliver good news if she could.

Everyone was quiet, and all eyes were on Daria. Gage looked perhaps the most uncomfortable out of them all. Daria had spent many years as a criminal by trade. She didn't go out of her way to deceive people, but lying when necessary came easily to her. Gaje Gurung, though, was an honest man.

However, he wasn't a stupid one. He kept silent.

Daria allowed her shoulders to slump a little while she drew a deep breath, giving off airs of sadness, regret, and discomfort at what she had to say. Which, in reality, was *not* a lie. She would've preferred not to have to kill the men. It would be better for everyone if they'd repented of their devil's bargain with Akshara, come to their senses, and saw the surface again.

"I'm sorry to say that they didn't make it. They fell victim to ancient booby traps within the labyrinth. Dr. Hurstett and Dr. Fields warned them to be careful and not to charge off into new areas, but they were too eager to find a way out. I cannot blame them. But their haste led to their deaths, I'm afraid."

Two other men amid the crowd hung their heads, with one covering his eyes, and a smattering of sighs and murmurs went around. The men had friends, people who wanted to see them again despite the general belief in the camp that they'd initially perished in the blinding flash of light.

The foreman shook his head and turned his eyes to the ground. "Damn. That's a shame. Doesn't surprise me; they were the sorts who would do something like that. It's part of why we put them on night shift. They weren't too bad as people go. This island has a lot to answer for when it comes to killing people off like this."

"Yes," Daria agreed. "I'm sorry that there was already nothing I could do by the time I arrived down there. What's done is done. As things stand right now, we have other serious concerns."

She paused for effect, allowing the darkness of her tone to catch the foreman's attention. Then she lowered her voice. "Where's Dr. Limbu?" She made a show of glancing around with narrowed, suspicious eyes to communicate without words that she didn't want the lead archaeologist to overhear them.

Boucher grunted and gestured vaguely toward the hills with his elbow. He took a couple of steps closer and brought his voice down several notches, too.

"She's off with one of my demolition teams. We had some, uh, interesting developments while you were gone. I overheard her— she had this idea to plan something with those guys under my nose and under the nose of her damn research crew, as well.

"They want to blast open the whole shaft, not caring if it damages the ruins down there or wrecks the artifacts and stuff. Shocked the hell out of me, to be honest. Stuff like that is the opposite of what archaeologists are supposed to do, isn't it?"

Daria grimaced. Ak was moving quickly toward her endgame. "Did she say *why* she wanted to do that?"

"Yeah." Boucher tightened the cap on his head. "They're planning to strip-mine the Atlanticore out of there. Never thought I would hear that. Of course, that's why she wanted to keep it secret from the other eggheads since they would all object and throw a fit. Is she a real scientist? She's not some company type pretending to be one, is she?"

Daria was beginning to wonder herself, though Eleanor's original briefing had said that Dr. Limbu's credentials as a researcher were well-established. "I'm not sure. Her agenda here isn't what she claimed it was, that much is sure." She moved closer to the big man and lowered her voice to a near-whisper. "She's paid for others among your crew to help her. You cannot trust all your men, I'm afraid."

Boucher's scowl deepened. "I'm afraid, too."

Then a commotion came from the edge of the crowd. Daria looked up, past the throngs of workers who'd gathered in the clearing near the tunnel's mouth. A large group approached from the valley's far side, from the general area Boucher had indicated.

At the head of the approaching gang was none other than Dr. Limbu, striding with arms bent near her chest and her chin in the air. Her dress flapped in the gentle breeze. Behind and to her sides, some of the workers held various explosives. Bundles or crates of dynamite, detonators, cords, primers, and it looked like a couple had a box of hand grenades.

Daria felt something within herself go cold. With that much destructive hardware, a lot of damage could ensue if she didn't handle things properly. Plus, she still wasn't sure who was and wasn't on Ak's side.

She scanned the faces of the men and women nearby, the ones who'd helped her and the others out of the excavation shaft. The ones who'd stuck by their foreman. Some of the compromised personnel might be among them. She suspected that the majority of those present were honest workers.

Her intuition told her that the crew now following Dr. Limbu were, for the most part, probably the ones she'd bought off. The head archaeologist needed people with her who were in on the scheme to pull off her final masterstroke.

Daria and Boucher pushed through ranks and files to stand near the edge of the group and greet Ak themselves. She frowned when she noticed them but continued her march toward the shaft as though their presence were irrelevant.

It was truly astounding, Daria thought, that the woman would ignore her and pretend that nothing was wrong after she'd personally used the metal disc to trap the Executioner within the ruins. She marveled at the fineness of the line between madness and simple arrogance.

"Stop," Daria announced in a loud, clear voice that rang throughout the clearing. She held up a hand, palm outward. "Dr. Limbu. And all the rest of you. It would seem that we need to talk."

Ak did stop, but her face contorted in indignation. The demolition crew and other lackeys flanking her did likewise, their faces confused or irritated.

Boucher commanded, "Put down those explosives. We've discovered some important stuff, okay? We're not blowing up anything. Not until a few things get cleared up here."

The workers didn't put down their gear. They did nothing, as though waiting for orders from someone else. Silence reigned. A bird chirped in the trees growing around the foothills behind them.

Dr. Limbu put her hands on her hips. "What on earth are you people doing *now*? What is this nonsense? Out of the way! We have important work to do, and once again you're obstructing us."

Daria stared into her eyes. "Akshara. Stop lying. We know what's going on here. Whatever problems you might be having with money, there are better solutions than this. Your concerns don't need to get anyone else killed."

There was an open space of about two meters between the two groups. Limbu stared across it. Her face twitched as though she couldn't decide whether to continue the charade of haughty indifference or to fly into another rage at having been found out.

Then she burst out laughing. The wild cawing sounds were loud enough that half of the assembled workers cringed.

"Executioner." Ak cackled. "You are so terribly small-minded. I'm on the cusp of something truly brilliant here. It goes far beyond mere financial success! You insult me by implying that money is all I care about. Hah!"

Whether or not she was lying, Daria realized that she'd gained an edge. Ak was once again acting crazy. By provoking her to unleash her full megalomaniacal tendencies, Daria might turn more of the workers against her. She might get even some of the corrupted ones to realize that their erstwhile employer was so unstable and untrustworthy that she risked getting them killed.

Daria smiled, deliberately trying to irk the other woman. "Oh, really? What *do* you care about, then? After all, what could be more important than a massive harvest of Atlanticore?"

"Nothing!" the archaeologist retorted. "All of you are so incredibly stupid. You think that Atlanticore's only value is monetary? Has it not sunk into each of your thick skulls how *expendable* you are unless you're helping me reach my goals?"

Her ranting wouldn't do her any favors. However, the Executioner suddenly realized she'd made a terrible mistake—she'd forgotten about the foreman's temper.

"*Damn you!*" Boucher snarled, stomping forth across the open patch of grass. "That's it! You're not getting away with this shit again, you crazy, dirty..." His words trailed off as he stormed toward her.

Akshara froze. Her eyes became wide, round orbs of darkened glassiness, shining in the late afternoon light with a kind of dumb animal fear. Daria expected for an instant that the woman was about to bolt and make a run for the road or Daria's truck—anything to get away, escape the consequences for now, and live to fight another day.

That wasn't what she did.

With truly shocking speed, Dr. Limbu pulled a compact, snub-nosed revolver from somewhere within her dress, aimed it at Boucher's head, and fired.

"No!" Daria cried, but the crackling report of the gun drowned her out.

The foreman staggered back, his neck and shoulders jerking as his head rolled backward. There was a red hole between his eyebrows, and a trickle of blood already ran down his face beside his nose to drip from the edge of his broad jaw. He made a gasping noise, and his big hands clawed in the air. Then, like a dropped sack of vegetables, he toppled over. Dead by the time he hit the ground.

Daria's pistol was out, her arm raising it toward the insane archaeologist in the familiar slow-motion hyper-focus that always accompanied the outbreak of sudden violence. Dr. Limbu was giggling wildly and dancing away from her, waving the handgun in the air as men moved in around her.

Before the first howl of rage from Boucher's supporters was complete, the brawl had begun.

CHAPTER TWENTY-TWO

Daria reholstered her pistol as fast as she could while men and the handful of women among the crew surged past her on either side. She didn't dare open fire. There were too many people in the way. Dr. Limbu had vanished, slipping away somewhere under cover of the general violence.

Shouts of anger filled the air alongside the hollow *thunking* sounds of fists and feet connecting with flesh and bone. Half of the workers in Boucher's camp had tools of some sort. Spades and shovels, hammers, coils of rope, wrenches, and knives. They swung them like warriors on a medieval battlefield, bellowing in rage as the tensions simmering under the surface since the dig had begun boiled over.

Exacerbating their wrath was the knowledge of betrayal, that some of their coworkers had plotted against them the whole time in exchange for an extra paycheck from the madwoman who nominally ran the entire operation.

The laborers whom Ak had purchased were fewer in number. As Ben had confessed, there were probably about two of them for every three who remained loyal to their original contracts and their now-deceased foreman.

Ak's cronies were better armed. They'd expected something like this to happen, sooner or later. A few of them had guns, and many had proper fighting knives or sticks specifically designed to function as clubs in a hand-to-hand combat scenario. Daria saw one man toting a police nightstick and another with what looked like a high-end slingshot.

Then there were the explosives. She hadn't been able to examine them carefully enough before the riot broke out to determine if they were primed, armed, or anything of the sort. As long as they were present, they posed a terrible danger to everyone in the valley.

The first gunshots rang out. Three of Ak's men had pulled pistols and opened fire on their fellows. Four or five of Boucher's workers fell, but amid the confusion, it was impossible to say if their wounds were mortal.

"Him!" someone shouted and pointed at the nearest of Ak's hirelings with a handgun. "He's got a gun! Get 'im!" Half a dozen men piled toward their opponent, who blasted at them again, then cried out as they engulfed him. The whole cluster of struggling bodies passed out of sight as the tangle of fighting workers surged around the grassy clearing, swirling and eddying like the water of a river.

Daria's eyes were everywhere at once. Adept though she was as a fighter, there was only so much she could do against multiple strong opponents who were determined to tear her apart. Using brute force against Ak's entire personal army at once would get her crippled or killed before she could accomplish anything useful.

Instead, she sought a path through the brawl. She had to get to her truck—she could perhaps intimidate the enemy enough to disperse them with her Uzi. Or the truck itself might serve much the same purpose.

More importantly, she had to gain control of the dynamite and the grenades.

An opening appeared in the tangle of limbs and torsos to her right. Daria ducked into it, weaving with rapid serpentine motions between them, hopping over extended legs and ducking under swinging arms as needed. Then someone bellowed, "Hey! It's that Executioner bitch!" and tripped her.

Cursing herself as she sprawled on the ground, Daria reached again for her pistol. A wiry arm held a hatchet poised in the air, and the blade descended toward her face.

Another blade flashed. The bloody stump of the ax man's elbow retracted, its owner babbling incoherently in pain and fear, while his severed forearm holding the hatchet dropped to the ground about ten centimeters away from Daria's head. She sat up and rolled into a standing position.

Gaje Gurung was briefly visible. He nodded at her, his kukri stained red. Then he waded into a trio of foes while bellowing his native war cry. The thick recurved knife hacked down into them. Despite his fractured ankle, the small man's economy of movement allowed him to get the most out of his still-formidable combat skills.

"Gage," Daria said, but he was gone. She gritted her teeth and pressed on, crawling under a clinch of two tall men and sprinting around another.

Near the edge of the battle, three men standing guard over a box of grenades suddenly confronted her. One of them saw her, recognized her, and raised a Mauser "Broomhandle" pistol. He was too slow.

Daria's gun had appeared in her hand, leaving behind its holster. She shot the guard twice in the chest. The report echoed throughout the valley as he toppled back over the box. His tumbling body momentarily tripped up the other two.

Daria targeted the one with an old Colt revolver, blasting him in the face. He spun and fell straight down, unmoving.

The last one was either unarmed or hadn't yet produced his weapon. He panicked as he shoved the body of the first guy off the box while Daria bore down on him. She kicked him under the chin, rattling his skull and sending him to the ground semi-conscious and with a nasty concussion.

She grabbed the box and heaved it up. It was heavy, but with adrenaline surging through her she lifted it to chest height and hauled it away from the battle.

Then she saw her truck. It was only about thirty yards away, where she'd left it that morning. Unburdened, she could've sprinted the distance in seconds. With the grenades, empowered though she was by the rush of battle, her progress seemed agonizingly slow.

Behind her, an unpleasant female voice barked, "Hey! Get her! *Stop her!*"

It wasn't Akshara. It was someone else. Daria ignored it and kept running. She moved in irregular patterns, twisted sideways to and fro, and ducked her head to make herself a harder target in case anyone with a gun was taking a bead on her.

No one opened fire. However, three pairs of footsteps still followed her, and they were gaining.

Trying to forget that she wasn't as young as she'd once been, Daria pushed herself into overdrive, her legs flying beneath her. At last, she came close enough to the truck to hurl the box ahead of her. It struck the ground at an angle, tipped over, and spilled its load of round green explosives into the grass, where it would be difficult to recover them except with careful searching.

The same nasty voice screeched, "You can't do that! Oh my God, she's so *stupid!*"

Daria ignored her and pulled out her keys. It took half a second—far too long, it seemed—to find the one to open the truck's door. She jostled it into place, pulled the door open, and hopped up. She spared a glance behind her.

The three pairs of advancing footsteps belonged to the trio of women Daria confronted the other day. Their ringleader, the one who'd shouted after her, still had a crude bandage over her face, the result of Daria breaking her nose after she'd threatened to drop Gage down the excavation shaft.

"Just my luck," Daria muttered and dove into the truck.

She went past the seat and steering wheel, aiming for the distinctive covered lump. Casting aside the camouflage, Daria grabbed the submachine gun beneath and rolled into a sitting position in the driver's seat.

The frizzy-haired woman with the busted nose was only three meters away. Her two cronies trailed a meter or so behind, at her flanks on either side.

"Hey!" she bawled again. "Come out and fight!" A switchblade appeared in her hand, its business end *clicking* into place. "I'm gonna take your fucking nose *off* your face."

Daria turned in her seat and charged the bolt on her Uzi, leveling it at the obnoxious worker. The woman stopped in her tracks, eyes bulging. "Watch your language." The Executioner squeezed the trigger.

The gun rattled and rocked up in her hands, spewing out empty shell casings and discharging half a dozen 9mm rounds in a roughly vertical burst. All six found their mark, perforating the woman's chest and neck, with the final one going through her opened mouth. The impacts blasted her back off her feet. She crashed into the turf, reduced to a bloody mess.

Her two cronies stood staring at the truck and Daria. Then they turned and bolted off in opposite directions.

Daria lay the gun down in her lap and plunged her key into the ignition, firing up the truck and leaving the door hanging open. A fast look out the windshield showed the brawl still raging but at a stalemate. Neither side had managed to repel the other.

She shifted gears and rumbled across the grass toward the side where Akshara's forces clustered. She maintained a low-to-moderate speed. Going too fast would make it difficult to change course or stop if a friendly worker got in the way or if she risked running over one of the crates of dynamite.

Some of the men noticed her approach and tried to flee. One of them, unable to think clearly in the heat of the moment, tried to flee more or less directly into the vehicle's front grille. He screamed as his body crashed against her hood and rolled off to the side.

Daria took her foot off the gas and leaned out the doorway to spray Uzi fire at another cluster of Ak's cronies, who were preparing to light up a stick of dynamite for use in the battle. There was a slight risk of hitting the explosive, but she aimed low. One of the men took at least one round in the legs. He screamed and fell over, wounded but alive. The others panicked and dashed off, leaving the dynamite unattended.

"Good." Daria drove over to it, stopped, and hauled the entire crate into her truck. She set it on the driver's seat and pushed it onto the passenger's side. She noted with approval that the box also contained primers and timed fuses.

When she glanced up, a guy was aiming a pistol at her, but he was shooting from the hip. She flinched when he fired, but the bullet struck the truck's frame and ricocheted away. Aggravated, she pulled her pistol and shot back. She couldn't tell if she hit him or not, but a second later another worker from Boucher's camp tackled him. Daria shrugged, hopped into the truck, and rolled forward again.

She wanted to help her friends in the melee. There was something more important she needed to do first. It would render the whole struggle moot anyway, thus ending the violence.

The engine growled as she piloted the truck across the grass, now headed for the open shaft.

Along the way, she saw another trio of Ak's men hauling another crate of explosives between them. They were jogging roughly toward the scientists' encampment on the terrace. That meant either they intended to blow up the researchers and eliminate witnesses who could incriminate Dr. Limbu, or they were simply trying to flee into the wooded hills.

Either way, Daria had no intention of allowing them to succeed. She stopped, hitched up her submachine gun, aimed, and emptied the rest of her magazine.

One of the men fell dead or dying, perforated, but the other bullets mostly destroyed the crate, blasting it apart in a shower of wooden fragments. One round found its mark within a single stick of dynamite.

"No!" the middle of the three men exclaimed. Then the stick exploded, shaking the ground for fifty meters in every direction. The man who'd cried out and his other friend blew into a cloud of red particulates that mingled with the upsurge of dust from the small crater that appeared in the scorched ground.

Daria fell back in her seat and gasped. "I didn't mean to do *that*." She set her Uzi aside, shifted gears, and barreled straight toward the shaft. It occurred to her that the explosion she intended to create might be enough to consume her truck, so she left it a safe distance away before hauling the crate of dynamite out on foot.

She was getting tired, but the adrenaline hadn't yet expired. The hand-to-hand fighting was getting closer to her position, but it looked like her side was winning. Despite being more materially prepared, Ak's forces, composed of self-serving jackals as they were, weren't as mentally and emotionally prepared as they'd thought themselves.

Plus, Boucher's people slightly outnumbered them to begin with before Daria had whittled down their numbers and broken up a couple of their formations.

She ran toward the edge of the pit and stopped next to the winch machine. The glowing face on the smooth stone disk below flashed again in her mind. She'd made it a promise and intended to keep her end of the bargain.

"Yes, all right, umm," Daria mumbled as she set down the

crate, knelt beside it, and reached in. "It wasn't too long ago, was it?"

She'd handled dynamite and explosives before, but not quite like this. She worked with haste but more awkwardly than she would've liked as she prepared primers and fuses. When the task was complete, the major bundles would be ready to blow in one minute.

Daria racked her brain, recalling things a fraction of a second before she needed to use them and barely avoiding costly delays. Someone might notice what she was doing and kill her at any moment. Plus, the group was shifting closer. If she took too long in preparing the payload, they would all be at greater risk.

Now she was almost done.

A reddish flash emerged from the melee, streaking toward Daria. As fast as her combat reflexes were, her hands were too full, and her work was too important for her to drop it. She took the risk—leaving to chance the possibility that whoever had emerged didn't mean her harm.

Her fingers finished the job. Then she heaved the crate over the edge. At the same instant, the red streak reached out and grabbed it.

"No! Not that way!" Akshara Limbu cried, her face distorted with alarm. Her bony hands grasped the edge of the now-airborne box, but she'd been half a second too late to avoid plummeting into the shaft along with it.

Daria's hands flew out. Everything happened so fast that it took her brain a moment to process it all as the sounds of shouting men and the last of the fighting rang out in the air around her.

Both of Daria's hands successfully grabbed Ak's ankles. The archaeologist dangled upside down over the artificial cliff's edge, desperately clutching the container of explosives—still primed and counting down toward detonation.

Daria had been pulled off her feet by the heavy drag of both the other woman and the crate. She lay in the grass, her left foot hooked around a spire of rock, while her shoulders, arms, and head protruded over the void.

She shouted, "Let it go, you fool!" By rights, she should've simply dropped the woman. Limbu was guilty of murdering Boucher, and her myriad plots had resulted in many other deaths. Something about the archaeologist's pathetic desperation had stayed her hand.

Akshara twisted and writhed as she dangled over certain doom. She bent her neck and looked up at Daria.

"Executioner," she wailed. "Don't you understand? I tried to explain it to you! Atlantica is a place of wonders and miracles. Things more important than the life of any one person, even mine."

The weight pulled as gravity tried to claim the crate and both women with it. Ak drifted slowly down, a centimeter at a time, as Daria's foot slipped from its rocky anchor while her joints strained with the effort.

Ak went on. "I sought to become a part of the Coven of Miracles. They're seeking full knowledge of this island's ancient secrets. They would have me—yes! I am qualified! But I need Atlanticore to test my theories. Its value to my research is incalculable. You cannot simply bury it."

"Yes, I can," Daria grunted. "And unless you *let* me, we'll both die." She wondered, in a flash of crazy curiosity, why Ak was confessing all of this to her now.

The scientist let out a wordless scream of frustrated anguish. "Then so be it! You fool... I had to earn my place while there was still time to do so—such precious little time! A new order is forming here, don't you understand that? I had to secure my place in the *future!*"

Daria suddenly felt calm. The pointlessness of trying to save the madwoman and of potentially killing herself in the process became clear at once.

"I," she stated, "am here to right the wrongs done in the past." She recalled what she'd said to the women back at the late Mateo Pastor's villa and wondered how they were faring. "The future is no concern of mine. I had promises to keep, Akshara. That is all."

Daria inhaled sharply, closed her eyes, and let go.

Dr. Limbu screamed as she fell, still clutching the crate of explosives, hurtling beyond the slanted afternoon light and into the shadows of the rocky depths.

Daria rolled over and sprang to her feet at the same instant she heard the scientist and the payload strike the nearest protrusion of stone below. They crashed and rolled deeper down the shaft. But the blast hadn't come yet.

She bolted away from the yawning hole and the expensive winch machine beside it, catching the eyes of struggling men as she ran. "Get back! Everyone get away from the shaft," she shouted as loud as she could. Pairs and trios of workers who'd been wrestling, punching one another in the face, or treating one another's wounds all recognized the alarm in her voice.

Everyone got up and ran. The last ones made it clear just in time.

The explosion was like the impact of a thunderbolt and a terrible earthquake at once. It shook the ground and nearly deafened them. The flash of light that emerged from the excavation pit wasn't as bright as the one that had transported Gage into the forgotten labyrinth, but it was bright enough, and with it came smoke, fire, and a huge cloud of dirt and debris.

Daria stumbled to her knees, then lay on her back as the earth trembled. She sat up. The blast was fading, and as the dust cleared, she could no longer see the shaft at all—only a pile of scorched earth and collapsed rock.

The entity within the underground complex, whatever it truly was, would be safe—buried within Atlantica's crust as long as Daria was around to keep her promises.

CHAPTER TWENTY-THREE

"So," Daria began. She puffed on a clove cigarette and winced as two or three of her wounds flared up in sudden pain. "How did it go?"

She reclined on a folding beach chair that Dr. Johnson had kept hidden within the scientists' encampment. He'd graciously brought it out after the violence had subsided. Across from her, sitting in a regular chair, was Tyler Katakura.

Ty blew air out from beneath his lip, so it went upward and knocked a couple of locks of his black hair away from his forehead. "Rough. Not that I expected anything less. I've seen rougher. But if I'm perfectly honest, it would've been easier with you around."

Daria laughed, then stiffened and winced again. She'd pulled a muscle in her leg when the explosion knocked her off her feet, not to mention the bruises from when Ben had tackled her in the tunnel. Plus, a stray bullet had grazed her hip during the brawl without her realizing it.

"Well, I can say the same with equally perfect honesty, Mr. Katakura. I had to invoke your name once or twice to intimidate some of these men properly. It seems I don't have quite so fearsome a reputation as you. So far. There was plenty of bloodshed at the end of it all."

Ty's face took on a brief look of grisly satisfaction.

"People are that scared of me, are they? Well, you're no slouch, Daria. I could've used you in a fight.

"I would say that you're even better during the stuff that comes *before* a fight. Knowing how to avoid violence when there are other ways of getting the job done or how to make the fight as unfair as possible in your favor. I'm a little too accustomed to bludgeoning my way through everything.

"However, those goddamn gun runners weren't the sort of people who could be reasoned with, anyway. Still, your savvy might've saved me a near-death experience or two."

Daria shrugged. "What's that thing the Americans say about risks and uniforms?" She'd lived in the United States, but not for long. She still thought of herself as more or less European.

It was odd. She lived on Atlantica, a place unknown to the world until recently. Some of her fellow Jews had finally gained their own country, half the globe away. Still, something about this strange new continent had called to her.

Ty blinked, then snapped his fingers. "Oh. 'You knew the risks when you put on the uniform.' That one?"

"Yes. That applies to both of us, does it not?"

He chuckled. "Yeah. It does. And to at least one other uniform I wore before this one. I think I like this one more, though." He fiddled with a corner of the armored plating. "It's better at stopping bullets. Anyway, tell me more about what happened here. Word always gets around on this island. Whatever happened these last few days, we might end up dealing with the repercussions of it later."

Daria took a long draw on her clove. Each moment they spent in the present, she reflected, created more potential problems that would reach out to them from the past once they left the present behind. Then, those problems became her duty. Then, she would have to swat them aside, leaving the way toward the future clear for others.

"What happened here?" Her tone was soft and dreamy. "Digging up the past, only to bury it again."

Ty glanced past her shoulder toward the rubble pile against the cliff face, which now blocked the excavation shaft. "That sounds like something out of a poem, but it's true, as near as I can tell."

"It is." She readjusted her posture, taking care not to disturb her wounded leg. "Of course, there's more to it than that. Perhaps Eleanor told you some of the details already."

He shrugged. "Not really. Only that it was an archaeological dig, there was a conflict between workers and scientists, and of course something to do with Atlanticore. Half the time, if something goes wrong, Atlanticore is involved."

Daria glanced around. The only people nearby were the scientists, who already knew as much as she did. They'd all agreed to keep a fairly tight lid on the bizarre events that had taken place here.

"Atlanticore is involved in a great many things. You don't know the half of it. If I tell you things that will sound utterly ridiculous, will you be so kind as to believe me?"

Ty had a drink in his hand, simple straight whiskey offered to him by one of the camp laborers, who was a fan of his work, but he hadn't touched it until now. Remembering that it was there, he raised it and sipped. "Probably. Let's hear it first. I trust you, of course. But people can't always trust themselves. We don't always...remember things exactly the way they truly happened."

Annoyed by the implication, Daria snapped, "Doctors Gurung, Hurstett, and Fields will confirm everything I'm about to say, since they saw it as well. Now listen closely. You might find this all fascinating. Perhaps it will even frighten you in a way that mere death does not."

Ty cocked an eyebrow. "Well, now I'm *really* curious."

Daria began her story. She left out some of the details but told him everything that had transpired. She included her unwanted trip through walls, waking up in a completely different room by means she couldn't comprehend, and her conversation with an autonomous machine that might as well have been a ghost or a guardian spirit.

And, summarizing it all, the fact that strange and terrible wonders lay beneath their feet. The island's distant history contained elements beyond the understanding of most people. The mechanical and electrical utility of Atlanticore crystal was only the tip of a massive iceberg.

When she finished, Ty stared at her in astonishment. He whistled, leaned back in his chair, and drained the rest of the whiskey from his glass.

"Well, now I understand why governments like to keep their secrets." A dark look came over his face, as though a storm cloud had parked itself above his head. "I don't like thinking of it that way. It's just how it is.

"Some of this information will come to light, and the rumors will spread. Keeping a lid on it seems like a good idea, though. I don't think Atlantica is ready to deal with the terrors of goddamn teleportation, thinking machines, gel that can put a person into cold sleep forever, and whatever else in God's name is down there.

"Maybe one day the people will be ready. We aren't there yet. This place has enough problems as it is."

Dr. Johnson appeared from around a nearby tent. "How's the beach chair working out for you, Ms. Barruk?"

"Nice," she told him. "Thank you."

He folded his hands behind his back. "It was the least I could do. Granted, you *technically* ruined our dig, but then again, Dr. Limbu was planning to do that from the beginning anyway, so after a fashion, you minimized the damage." He sighed. "If only we could have another look at that chamber, though."

Daria supposed that decent, honest scientists might glean useful things from Atlantica's buried treasures. Whatever their good intentions, there were always other people lurking in the wings and waiting to exploit their research for less-noble purposes.

That reminded her of something else as Johnson wandered off.

"Tyler," she began. "Before she died, Dr. Limbu mentioned something called the Coven of Miracles. Have you heard of it?"

He shook his head.

Daria finished her cigarette and extinguished it against a nearby rock. "I thought not. It seems to be a secretive group dedicated to uncovering the island's hidden powers, something of that nature, perhaps an offshoot of the Theosophists or what-have-you. Akshara was trying to join their ranks. Which means that whoever they are, they certainly knew about this dig."

Her partner cracked his neck. "So, we'll likely hear from them soon. Whether by in-person visit, mail, bullet, car bomb, poisoned Coke, or whatever."

"Perhaps," Daria conceded. "There's something else I wish to suggest. We need to expand our ranks. Whoever heard of an elite organization composed of *two* people? Well, there's also Eleanor and her staff, yes. But you see my meaning. I want to recommend that we recruit someone."

Ty kept silent while he turned the idea over in his mind. "Quality is more important than quantity if you ask me. But if you can have both, then great. Who is this person?"

"Dr. Gaje Gurung. Or 'Gage,' for short. He's one of the archaeologists I met here, and he also happens to be a Gurkha."

Ty raised an eyebrow. With his military background, the term undoubtedly got his attention. "Oh, I see."

"Yes. He's a capable fighter as well as a scholar, and that combination could be useful to us. Additionally, he seems to have great integrity and is a gentleman. He might be able to tread where we cannot."

She was a rogue, after all; a smuggler, an underworld figure. Tyler Katakura was almost a pure warrior. He was an honorable man but a rather unsubtle one. It might behoove their organization to have someone who could better fit in with polite society.

However, she hadn't posed the question to *Gage*. He already had a scientific career ahead of him. "So," she concluded, "I think Gage would be an excellent choice. *If* he's willing to sign up."

"Right." Ty pushed his hair away from his face again. "I think you'll convince him, though." He smiled.

Fatigued and pained though she was, Daria had to smile as well. Her experiences in convincing people to do things they might otherwise have recoiled from in horror had frequently been successful.

"If he agrees, we should have him instated soon. However, he's injured and will need time to recover from a broken ankle. I could contact my usual doctor and have him expedite the process. Going through the usual channels can take too long. Many normal people wait weeks to see a good doctor here or can only go to former Army medics and village healer types."

Ty said, "Don't underestimate Army medics." Then he perked up as though something had unexpectedly occurred to him. "Hey. This might be a chance to test out a new doc of mine. This younger guy I met. He got caught up in the business with the gun-running scheme, and, well, he isn't dead. So he owes me a favor."

Daria untied and retied her hair. She didn't like the thought of subjecting Gage to someone she didn't know, but then again, Ty could probably get the man to treat the Nepali with all due haste.

"Fine," she decided. "But if he messes up and Gage loses his foot, I'll shoot him."

Ty laughed. "Sounds fair. I don't think he has any family or friends on Atlantica, anyway."

After that, they both drifted into silence and sat together watching the sunset.

Things were changing. They felt it; they knew it without having to belabor the obvious. The shared experiences of their strange chosen profession relegated certain things to the domain of unspoken presumptions.

No longer would they simply pursue cases handed down to them by the Executives. The Pandora's Box that Dr. Limbu had opened meant digs of any sort—commercial, residential, or archaeological—were now a cause for concern, something to keep an eye on. They might have to impose patrols on certain risky areas.

That meant walking the fine line between order and tyranny.

Daria sighed. "It'll be difficult. Knowing when is far enough and when is too far. We must set our limits, of course. If we don't, someone else will. Either they'll hem us in with bureaucracy so we cannot do our jobs and evil flourishes despite us, or we'll go too far, become the evil we sought to confront, and justice will come for *us*."

"Something like that," Ty muttered.

Daria waved. "It was to be expected that other powers would rise here, with their agendas. Already there are the Executives, the criminal kingpins, ourselves of course, and now the Coven as well. It's beginning to feel crowded on the island, is it not?"

"It makes sense." Ty shrugged. "At least we have a new world here, with a chance to make a better future."

Her smile was wry, verging on bitter. He probably didn't notice.

"The future." She exhaled and reached for another cigarette. "Everyone is always talking about the future."

THE STORY CONTINUES

The story continues with book three, *High Lead and Low Deeds,* available at Amazon and Kindle Unlimited.

Claim your copy today!

AUTHOR NOTES MICHAEL ANDERLE

NOVEMBER 22, 2021

Thank you for not only reading this story but these author notes as well.

So, I was on a trip to Cabo San Lucas...via car.

On this trip, we (my wife and I) had decided to leave at 2:00 AM in the morning, hit the border in San Diego at about 8:00 AM, and get a move on down to Cabo. Everything was righty-tighty.

Until the back right tire blew out at 3:30AM in the morning outside Baker, California.

Now, I have already told this story in another set of author notes, so I'll give you the Cliff's Notes version that the tires (two—another had a screw in it) were replaced, and we made it to Cabo San Lucas a day late but safe and sound.

I only mention this story because the title of this book, Aiming Blind, made me think about how I had all of these fantastic plans on how life was going to happen and when we would hit each location as we traveled down the 1 Hwy. To share just how blind I was to the future (tire notwithstanding, I failed to figure out when the major SCORE Baja 1000 race was being held.

It just so happened it was being held WHILE WE WERE DRIVING DOWN TO CABO...

Want to guess where it ends? Right. *Cabo San Lucas.*

So, amongst all the Federal Military stops (somewhere between 6 and 8, I forget) where I would wake my Spanish-speaking wife to answer questions, I also dealt with very zealous (and very aggressive) Baja chase car/trucks.

These chase vehicles (usually massive trucks, sometimes with trailers) made for some fun times when we were all behind the big rigs, trying to pass on a two-way highway with maybe one (1) foot of space off each side in case you drove outside the lines.

I came away with a couple of observations.

The truckers who drive this route have all my respect. That road is beautiful and can be very difficult to drive with a large SUV (I have a mid-sized SUV), much less an eighteen-wheeler. Their patience with other drivers and willingness to make sure that when groups of cars got piled up behind them, they tried to help drivers pass was just amazing.

My second observation is I can't remember a bunch of the scenery because the road was so much fun to drive (lots of turns) that I couldn't look around. It was pay attention or else.

A bonus observation is that, for the most part, the people were fantastic along the route, and Ensenada (just south of the border) is a town I want to go back to and visit when I have more time. If you get a chance, check it out.

So, aiming blind or not, it was a good trip I'm glad I can say I took.

Would I do it again? That's a hard...maybe. Now, I can't stand doing long drives, so for me to say maybe is a pretty good indication of how much fun I had.

If you are into motorcycles? Well, then I highly suggest it.

Have a good week, or weekend and talk to you in the next story!

Ad Aeternitatem,
Michael Anderle

OTHER ATLANTICA BOOKS

John Chambers Books

Her Mother's Pendant (Book 1)

The Mystery Deepens (Book 2)

One Last Choice (Book 3)

Valentina Winters

The Red Countess (Book 1)

One Night to Kill (Book 2)

One Death Too Few (Book 3)

Terra Kris

She is the Law (Book 1)

Law or Justice (Book 2)

Justice Served (Book 3)

Santana Sokolov

Law of the Jungle (Book 1)

Inner City Jungle (Book 2)

Rumble in the Jungle (Book 3)

CONNECT WITH THE AUTHOR

Connect with Michael Anderle

Website: http://lmbpn.com

Email List: http://lmbpn.com/email/

Social Media:

https://www.facebook.com/LMBPNPublishing

https://twitter.com/MichaelAnderle

https://www.instagram.com/lmbpn_publishing/

https://www.bookbub.com/authors/michael-anderle